TIDEWATER INN

TIDEWATER INN

A HOPE BEACH NOVEL

By Colleen Coble

THOMAS NELSON
Since 1798

NASHVILLE   DALLAS   MEXICO CITY   RIO DE JANEIRO

For Erin Healy
Editor extraordinaire and friend

Published in Nashville, Tennessee, by Thomas Nelson. Thomas Nelson is a registered trademark of Thomas Nelson, Inc.

Scripture quotations are taken from THE NEW KING JAMES VERSION. Copyright © 1982 by Thomas Nelson, Inc. Used by permission. All rights reserved.

Publisher's Note: This novel is a work of fiction. Names, characters, places, and incidents are either products of the author's imagination or used fictitiously. All characters are fictional, and any similarity to people living or dead is purely coincidental.

ISBN 978-1-62090-387-2

Printed in the United States of America

ONE

L ibby Holladay fought her way through the brambles to the overgrown garden. She paused to wave a swarm of gnats away from her face. The house was definitely in the Federal style, as she'd been told. Palladian windows flanked a centered door, or rather the opening for a door. The structure was in serious disrepair. Moss grew on the roof, and fingers of vine pried through the brick mortar. The aroma of honeysuckle vied with that of mildew.

She stepped closer to the house and jotted a few impressions in her notebook before moving inside to the domed living room. The floorboards were missing in places and rotted in others, so she planted her tan flats carefully. She could almost see the original occupants in this place. She imagined her own furniture grouped around the gorgeous fireplace. She'd love to have this place, but something so grand that needed this much repair would never be hers. The best she could do would be to preserve it for someone else who would love it. She itched to get started.

Her cell phone rang, and she groped in her canvas bag for it. Glancing at the display, she saw her partner's name. "Hey, Nicole," she said. "You should see this place. A gorgeous Federal-style mansion. I think it was built in 1830. And the setting by the river is beautiful. Or it will be once the vegetation is tamed." Perching on the window seat, she made another note about the fireplace. "Nicole? Are you there?"

There was a long pause, then Nicole finally spoke. "I'm here."

"You sound funny. What's wrong?" Nicole was usually talkative, and Libby couldn't remember the last time she'd heard strain in her friend's voice. "Are you still in the Outer Banks? Listen, I heard there might be a hurricane heading that way." She dug into her purse for her jalapeño jellybeans and popped one in her mouth.

"I'm here," Nicole said. "The residents are sure the storm will miss Hope Island. The investor is really interested in this little town. And we have the chance to make a boatload of money on it. It's all in your hands."

"My hands? You're the one with the money smarts."

Nicole was the mover and shaker in Holladay Renovations. She convinced owners to dramatically increase the value of their historic properties by entrusting them to Libby's expertise. Libby had little to do with the money side of the business, and that was how she liked it.

"I think I'd better go back to the beginning," Nicole said. "Rooney sent me here to see about renovating some buildings in the small downtown area. He's working on getting a ferry to the island. It will bring in a lot more tourism for the hotel he's planning, but the buildings need to be restored to draw new business."

"I know that much. But what do you mean 'it's in my hands'?" Libby glanced at her notes, then around the room again. This was taking up her time, and she wanted to get back to work. "We're doing the lifesaving station for sure, right?"

"Yes, I've already seen it. We were right to buy that sweet building outright. After you get your hands on it, we'll make a bundle *and* have instant credibility here. I've started making notes of the materials and crew we'll need. But I'm not calling about the renovations. I'm talking a lot of money, Libby. Millions."

That got Libby's attention. "Millions?"

"I stopped by the local attorney's office to see about having him handle the paperwork for our purchase of the lifesaving station. Horace Whittaker. He's got both our names on the paperwork now."

"So?"

"The secretary gasped when she heard your name."

"She knew me?"

"The attorney has been looking for a Libby Holladay. Daughter of Ray Mitchell."

"That's my dad's name."

"I thought it might be. I'd heard you mention the name Ray, but I wasn't sure of the last name."

Libby rubbed her head. "Why is he looking for me? My father has been dead a long time—since I was five."

"He died a month ago, Libby. And he left you some valuable land. In fact, it's the land Rooney thought he had agreed to purchase. So we're in the driver's seat on this deal." Nicole's voice rose.

Libby gasped, then she swallowed hard. "It's a hoax. I bet the attorney asked for a fee, right?"

"No, it's real. According to the secretary, your father was living in the Outer Banks all this time. And Horace has a box of letters Ray wrote to you that were all marked *Return to Sender*. It appears your mother refused them."

Libby's midsection plunged. Throughout her childhood she'd asked her mother about her father. There were never any answers. Surely her mother wouldn't have *lied*. Libby stared out the window at two hummingbirds buzzing near the overgrown flowers.

"Do you have any idea how much money this land is worth?" Nicole's voice quivered. "It's right along the ocean. There's a charming little inn."

It sounded darling. "What's the area like?"

"Beautiful but remote." Nicole paused. "Um, listen, there's something else. I met a woman who looked like you a couple days ago."

Libby eased off the window ledge. "Who is she?"

"Your half sister, Vanessa. You also have a brother, Brent. He's twenty-two."

"My father married again?" Libby couldn't take it all in. This morning she had no family but a younger stepbrother, whom she rarely saw. Why had her mother kept all this from her? "What about my father's wife?"

"She doesn't seem to be around. But there's an aunt too."

Family. For as long as she could remember, Libby had longed for a large extended family. Her free-spirited mother was always wanting to see some new and exciting place. They had never lived at the same address for more than two years at a time.

"You need to get here right away," Nicole said. "There are a million details to take care of. This is the big deal we've been praying for, Libby. You will never want for anything again, and you'll have plenty of money to help your stepbrother. He can get out of that trailer with his family."

The thought of buying her stepbrother's love held some appeal. They weren't close, but not because she hadn't tried. "I can't get away until tomorrow, Nicole. I have to finish up here first. We have other clients."

How much of her reluctance was rooted in the thought of facing a future that was about to change radically? She never had been good with change. In her experience, change was something that generally made things worse, not better.

Her partner's sigh was heavy in Libby's ear. "Okay. Hey, want to see Vanessa? She'll be here in a few minutes. There's a beach cam out by the lifesaving station, and I'm supposed to meet her there. I'll send you a link to it. You can see her before you meet her."

Libby glanced through the window toward her car. "I have my computer in the car." She tucked her long hair behind her ear and gathered her things. "What does Vanessa think about our father leaving prime real estate to me?" She left the house and started for her vehicle.

Nicole cleared her throat. "Um, she's pretty upset."

"I would imagine. What did you tell her about me?"

"As little as possible."

"I don't know if that's good or bad."

"I wouldn't worry about them. She and her brother are fishing for info though. She mentioned lighthouse ruins and I asked for directions. She offered to show me, but I went out there by myself yesterday. I'm still meeting her today because I knew you'd want to know more about her."

It sounded like a disaster in the making. "I have so many questions."

"Then come down as soon as you can and get them answered. Wait until you see Tidewater Inn, Libby! It's really old. It's on the eastern edge of the island with tons of land along the beach. The inn was a house once, and it is a little run-down but very quaint. It's hard to get out here. Until Rooney gets the ferry approved, you'll have to hire a boat. You're going to love it though. I love this island. It's like stepping back in time. And I've even seen some caves to explore."

"No road to it from the mainland?" Libby couldn't fathom a place that remote.

"Nope. Boat access only."

Her phone still to her ear, Libby opened her car door and slid in. The computer was on the floor, and she opened it. "I'm going to have to get off a minute to tether my phone to the computer. Send me the link to the harbor cam. Don't tell Vanessa I'm watching."

"When can you get here tomorrow?"

"It's about two hours from Virginia Beach?"

"Yes."

Libby doubted she'd sleep tonight. It would be no problem to be in the shower by six. "I'll be there by nine."

She ended the call, then attached the cord that tethered the phone to the computer. She would use the cell signal to watch Nicole's video feed on the larger screen. Then she could watch and still take any calls that came in. Her skin itched from the brambles. She established the connection, then logged on to the Internet. No e-mail yet.

She owned property. The thought was mind boggling. No matter what condition it was in, it was a resource to fall back on, something she hadn't possessed yesterday. The thought lightened her heart. She stared at the grand old home beside her. What if there was enough money from the sale of the inn to allow her to buy a historic house and restore it? It would be a dream come true. She could help her stepbrother. She could buy some Allston paintings too, something she'd never dreamed she could afford.

A woman pecked on Libby's car window, and Libby turned on the key and ran down the window. "Hello. I'm not an intruder. I'm evaluating this gorgeous old place for the historic registry."

The woman smiled. "I thought maybe you were buying it. Someone should restore it."

"Someone plans to," Libby said. What if it could be her instead of her client?

The woman pointed. "I'm taking up a collection for the Warders, who live on the corner. They had a fire in the kitchen and no insurance."

Libby had only two hundred dollars in her checking account, and she had to get to the Outer Banks. "I wish I could help," she said with real regret. "I don't have anything to spare right now."

"Thanks anyway." The woman smiled and moved to the next house.

Libby ran the window back up and clicked on her in-box. An e-mail from Nicole appeared. She stared at the link. All she had to do was click and she'd catch a glimpse of a sister she had no idea even existed. Her hands shook as she maneuvered the pointer over the link and clicked. The page opened, and she was staring at a boardwalk over deep sand dunes that were heaped like snowdrifts. In the distance was a brilliant blue ocean. A pier extended into the pristine water. The scene was like something out of a magazine. She could almost feel the sea breeze.

She clicked to enlarge the video and turned up the speakers so she could hear the roar of the surf. Where was Nicole? The pier was empty, and so was the sea. A dilapidated building stood to the right of the screen, and she could just make out a sign over the door. Hope Beach Lifesaving Station.

Then there was a movement on the boardwalk. Nicole appeared. She smiled and waved. "Hi, Libby," she said. The sound quality was surprisingly good. The sound of the ocean in the background was a pleasant lull.

Libby had to resist the impulse to wave back. Her partner's blond hair was pulled back in a ponytail under a sun hat, and she wore a hot-pink cover-up over her brown bathing suit.

Nicole glanced at her watch and frowned. "Vanessa is late. Like I started to say earlier, I didn't want to wait on her to see the lighthouse ruins, so I went out there alone. I have to show it to you. Wait until you see what I found. You'll seriously freak! Hey, give me a call. This pier is one of the few places where my phone works. Isn't that crazy—an entire island without cell service. Almost, anyway."

Libby picked up her cell phone, still connected to the computer. They could talk a few minutes. Before she could call, a small boat pulled up to the shore. Two men jumped out and pulled the boat aground. Nicole turned toward them. The men walked toward her. There was no one else in sight, and Libby tensed when Nicole took a step back. Libby punched in Nicole's number. She watched her friend dig in her bag when it rang.

When Nicole answered the phone, Libby leaped to her feet and yelled, "Get out of there. Go to your car!"

Nicole was still watching the men walk toward her. "It's just a couple of tourists, Libby," she said. "You worry too much." She smiled and waved at the men.

Libby leaned closer to the laptop. "There's something wrong." She gasped at the intention in their faces. "Please, Nicole, run!"

But it was the men who broke into a run as they drew closer to the boardwalk. As they neared the cam, Libby could see them more clearly. One was in his forties with a cap pulled low over his eyes. He sported a beard. The other was in his late twenties. He had blond hair and hadn't shaved in a couple of days.

Nicole took another step back as the older man in the lead smiled at her. The man said, "Hang up." He grabbed her arm.

"Let go of her!" Libby shouted into the phone.

The man knocked the phone from Nicole's hand and the connection was broken. The other man reached the two, and he plunged a needle into Nicole's arm. Both men began dragging Nicole toward the boat. She was struggling and shouting for help, then went limp. Her hat fell to the ground.

Barely aware that she was screaming, Libby dialed 9-1-1. "Oh God, oh God, help her!"

The dispatcher answered and Libby babbled about her friend being abducted right in front of her. "It's in the Outer Banks." She couldn't take her eyes off the boat motoring away from the pier. "Wait, wait, they're taking her away! Do something!"

"Where?"

"I told you, the Outer Banks." Libby looked at the heading above the video stream. "Hope Beach. It's Hope Beach. Get someone out there."

"Another dispatcher is calling the sheriff. I have an officer on his way to you."

"I'm going to Hope Beach now."

"Stay where you are," the dispatcher said. "We've got the sheriff on the line there. He's on his way to the site. Don't hang up until an officer arrives."

She had to do something. Anything but run screaming into the street. Libby looked at the computer. She could call up the video, save it for evidence. But the stream had no rewind, no way to save it. If she could hack into the site, she could get to the file. The police could save time and get the pictures of those men circulating. With a few keystrokes, she broke through the firewall and was in the code.

Then her computer blinked and went black. And when she called up the site again, the entire code was gone. What had she done?

Two

S mog hung over the New York skyline and matched Lawrence Rooney's mood. He studied the expansive view from his penthouse office on Fifth Avenue. The senator sitting in the chair on the other side of the gleaming walnut desk had better come through with the promised plum after all Lawrence had done for him.

Lawrence kept his attention away from the senator long enough to make sure the other man knew who was in charge, then turned from his perusal of his domain and settled in his chair. "You have news for me?"

Senator Troy Bassett tugged on his tie, then pulled a handkerchief from his pocket and blotted his damp forehead. "The city is like an oven today," he muttered.

In his fifties now, he had once been handsome, but his blond good looks had been replaced by flab and gray hair. Lawrence had known him since they went to Harvard together. They knew each other's weaknesses all too well. Lawrence had funneled a fortune into getting Bassett elected. But the rewards were coming—now.

"The vote?" Lawrence prodded.

The senator nodded. "Came through. The ferry system will be added next year."

"Excellent." Lawrence sat back in his leather chair. "I will have possession of the land by the end of the summer."

"I thought the old man refused to sell it."

"Luckily for us, he died." How he wished he could have seen Ray Mitchell take his last breath.

Bassett lifted a brow. "Natural causes?"

Lawrence laughed. "Of course. We both know I like to have my own way, but I've never stooped to murder. I've found money talks well enough that it's not necessary." A smile tugged at his lips. "Though there's always a first time for everything."

"You'd met your match in Mitchell though. He was adamant."

"True enough. But his son has no such scruples. He knows when to take a good offer and run with it."

"So he's agreed to your price?"

Lawrence nodded. "He has. I was willing to go up another five million if I had to, but he didn't know that. I got a bargain."

"You always do."

The door opened and Lawrence's secretary stuck her head in. "Mr. Rooney, Mr. Poe is here to see you."

"Excellent. Send him in," Lawrence said. "Stay," he told the senator, who had started to rise. "Poe will bring us both up to date."

Kenneth Poe, in a navy suit and red tie, strolled into the office. Every dark strand of hair perfectly coiffed, he was the epitome of a gentleman. His usefulness to Lawrence had grown in the past year. If Lawrence had been blessed with a son, he would have wanted the boy to be like Poe. Smart, ruthless, and handsome. He was nearly thirty now and still unmarried. Perhaps it was time to introduce him to Katelyn. Lawrence couldn't imagine a better son-in-law.

"Sir," Poe said, extending his hand. "Senator."

The men shook hands, and Lawrence ticked another box in Poe's favor. He knew how to act around power and had made sure to show respect to Lawrence first. The boy must have taken a class on sucking up. Lawrence liked it.

"I hope you have a signed bill of sale for me," Lawrence said.

Poe settled into the other chair and casually propped one foot on the opposite knee. "Unfortunately, we've hit a snag."

Lawrence frowned at Poe's grave tone. "What kind of snag?"

"It's serious."

When Poe said something was serious, Lawrence paid attention. "How serious?"

"A young woman came to town. Very smart and nosy. She found the cave. I'm not sure if she saw the contents." He glanced at the senator.

Lawrence pursed his lips. "We just need her out of the way long enough for us to get the land signed over. Can you put her in a safe place until we accomplish that?"

"It's already done. But what if that causes even more problems?"

"If it does, we'll deal with it later. I have a great deal of money riding on this, Kenneth. I won't allow my plans to be derailed by a spelunker. Fix it."

"Yes, sir. I'll do my best."

Poe's best was usually spectacular. Lawrence dismissed his concerns and began to think about what he would do with the money that would come pouring in when he turned Hope Island into the next Myrtle Beach.

———

The sailboat was sinking fast, and so was the sun. Two people flailed about in the water below. Chief Petty Officer Alec Bourne sat on the floor of the Dolphin helicopter with his feet dangling over the edge. "Take it lower," he shouted over the roar of the rotors. His

Coast Guard team received the call for help twenty minutes ago, and he'd prayed all the way out that they'd be in time.

The hurricane had veered and was going to miss them, but its outer band stirred up fifteen-foot seas, and the small craft below had floundered in the wind and waves. It heeled to the port by about forty-five degrees. This distress call was likely to be the first of several for the day.

Aircraft Commander Josh Holman nodded, and the helicopter hovered closer to the waves pounding at the boat. Alec leaned into the wind. The stinging rain struck his face, and he smelled the salty air as he waited for the signal from Curtis Ireland, his flight mechanic and best friend.

"Stand by to deploy swimmer," Josh barked.

"Roger, checking swimmer." Curtis slapped Alec's chest.

Alec inhaled, then flipped the hinged buckle and released his gunner's belt, the last piece of gear that held him in the helicopter. He shoved off the aircraft. The wind buffeted him on the way down. The waves slapped the air from his lungs and he submerged, then popped to the surface and struck out for the first of the people in the water.

A woman in the sea struggled toward him. When she reached him, she grabbed his neck and nearly took him under the water. "Calm down!" He pushed her away, then grabbed her from behind in the traditional rescue hold. She stiffened, then relaxed in his grip. He gave Curtis a thumbs-up, and the rescue basket began to descend toward them.

"You're going to be okay," he assured the woman.

"We hit a shoal," she gasped, her lips blue. "We've been in the water for two hours."

"It's almost over." He grabbed the basket and got her inside, then signaled to Curtis to lift her to the helicopter while he went after her husband.

Five minutes later he was back aboard the Dolphin too. Mission accomplished. The health service technician, Sara Kavanagh, began to check out the woman's pulse and blood pressure. Both patients were swathed in blankets. They thanked Alec and his crew several times as the chopper veered back to the Coast Guard station, where medical personnel waited to attend the capsized sailors.

On days like this Alec knew he was right where God wanted him. There were other days when nothing went right, or when they lost someone they were trying to save.

He was smiling when he walked to the grassy picnic area of the station with his friends. Alec and Curtis had gone through training together. They were as different as two best friends could be. Curtis was the quiet, thoughtful one of the group. Though he came from money, he never flaunted it. Sara Kavanagh was the only female on their team. Her reserve kept the men at the station from making any inappropriate remarks, and she had earned their trust with her skills. He sometimes wondered if she and Josh Holman would end up a couple. Josh was a jokester and kept the rest of them laughing, but sometimes Alec thought he saw a special spark when Josh looked at Sara.

"You've got three days off, Alec," Josh said. "Gonna leave the island and head for the casino so you can win big and buy me a Jaguar?"

"I think you'll have to settle for a bicycle on what I have," Alec said. "Me and Zach will go crabbing. I hear there have been some good hauls. Maybe I'll make enough to build that back deck."

Sara was pulling food from a sack. "How is Zach?"

Alec's smile faded. He shrugged. "It's only been two weeks. You know how it is with a teenager. One minute he's got a head on his shoulders and the next he's doing something so stupid you think he was raised under a rock. He's sure glad to be back on the island though. He hated Richmond."

"There are bound to be challenges. You've never raised a kid before," Sara said.

"Darrell did most of the raising and I'll figure out the rest. He's all I have left of Darrell."

The small plane crash had been only six months ago, and Alec still missed his older brother with a painful ache. Zach was the spitting image of Darrell at that age too. The kid was a handful for his grandparents, though, and Alec had taken custody two weeks ago. He should have taken him right from the start, but Alec's mother had been adamant that the boy's place was with them. And Darrell had named his parents as guardians.

His cell phone rang and he grabbed it. The station was one of the few places on the island where his cell worked. The call was from his cousin Tom, who also happened to be the sheriff on this rock. "Hey, Tom."

"Sorry to bother you, buddy, but I've got Zach here in jail."

Alec's stomach plummeted. "What's he done?"

"He and some of his friends took it into their heads to spray-paint graffiti on the school. I caught him with the paint. I think you should leave him here overnight. Might teach him a lesson."

The thought of his nephew in jail pained Alec, but he knew his cousin was right. "Whatever you think is best."

"While I've got you on the phone, I need your help. A woman named Nicole Ingram was abducted out at Tidewater Pier."

"Abducted?"

"The Virginia Beach police called me. Her business partner saw it all on the cam."

Alec winced. "That had to have been rough."

"She was hysterical, according to the officer who called me. She's on her way here. Can I get your team to keep your eyes open on this one? The kidnappers took her in a boat."

"Sure thing. You got a description of the woman?"

Tom gave it to him. "Oops, got another call. Don't come until lunch tomorrow to spring your nephew."

Alec ended the call and put his phone away. The others were looking at him with curiosity. "Zach's in jail."

"So we gathered," Curtis said. "What'd he do?"

"Spray-painted graffiti on the school."

"I did that once," Josh said. "It's a rite of passage to adulthood."

"I never did," Alec said.

"Yeah, but you walk on water."

Alec grinned at the familiar joke. Just because he didn't drink or smoke, most of the other men thought he was some kind of saint. The truth was far different.

THREE

The trip to the Outer Banks was a blur, and Libby barely noticed the landscape, though she'd often wanted to go to the Outer Banks. She crossed the Chesapeake Bay Bridge. Route 168 turned into US 158 when she reached the Outer Banks. On her left was the Atlantic Ocean, and on the right she saw Albemarle Sound. The place felt like another world. She ran down her window to drink in the atmosphere of squawking gulls and murmuring surf.

By the time she reached Kitty Hawk, the sun had set. She parked in the Dock of the Bay lot and rushed out. Motorboats and sailboats gleamed in the moonlight where they bobbed in the dark water. There were few people on the dock at this hour, but they were tourists. She stopped everyone she met, but no one had a boat they were willing to use to get her out to Hope Island.

She found herself examining every man she saw, but none looked like either of the men who had taken Nicole. She saw a Coast Guard cutter in the distance and waved her arms, shouting for it, but it cruised on past without noticing her. How was she going to get to Hope Island tonight?

Now that she was here, her driving-induced fatigue fell away. When her stomach rumbled, she realized she hadn't eaten since lunch. She was going to be here all night, so she got a bag of chocolate-covered peanuts from a vending machine and a cup of coffee. Both left her more jittery than before. She eyed the long stretch of water. Maybe a walk along the shore would calm her down. She sat on a rock and took off her shoes, then walked along the soft sand. The salty air cleansed her head, and she prayed for God to be with Nicole wherever she was. Who could have taken Nicole and why?

A boat horn sounded out in the water and the running lights flashed. She wandered out onto the pier and sat down with her bare feet dangling over the water. A fish splashed off to her right, and the sound of the waves rolling onto shore soothed her. God saw Nicole. He was in charge here. Libby had to try to cling to that fact.

With the adrenaline draining out of her, she yawned. Maybe she could sleep for a little while, then she'd find someplace to take a shower. But she sat with her eyes open through the long night. When the sun came up, she got up again and went in search of a charter.

She reached the top of the pier and smiled at a man and woman walking their dog along the beach. The dog sniffed her leg, and Libby stooped to pet it, a cute Yorkie. "You're a sweetheart."

The woman appeared to be in her forties. Her smile lines and straw hat made her look approachable. She wore khaki walking shorts and a red top. She smiled. "It's a surprise to see you here, Vanessa."

Vanessa. Her sister's name. "I'm not Vanessa. My name is Libby Holladay."

The woman's smile faded. "Oh my dear, I'm so sorry. You look so much like a young woman I know on Hope Beach. Pardon me."

"Someone else told me that. Are you from Hope Beach?"

The woman brushed a strand of hair from her eyes. "I used

to be. I taught school there for four years. Vanessa was one of my students. It's amazing how much you two look alike."

"I'm trying to find a charter out to Hope Island. Do you know where I might ask?"

"My husband and I are going there in a few minutes. We'd be happy to give you a ride." She put out her hand. "I'm Naomi Franklin, and this is my husband, Earl."

Libby shook hands with them. "That would be wonderful!" She'd been afraid of how much the charter might cost. "What time?"

"Right now," Earl said around a toothpick in his mouth. "Our boat is the *Blue Mermaid*. It's there." He pointed to a big sailboat. I just have to fill the tank and pack the supplies we brought for our summer house."

"She's beautiful," Libby said.

He beamed. "We've only had her a month." He took his wife's hand. "You can take her aboard, honey, and I'll get the supplies."

"What about my car?"

"It's safe here. Just leave it in the lot. You can rent a car on the island. Pricey, but maybe you won't need it for long," he said.

Libby rushed back to her car and grabbed her suitcase, then locked the vehicle and joined them at the dock. Earl helped the women aboard, and moments later the sea spray struck her arms and was dried off by the hot sun.

She stared at the horizon. "How far to the island?"

"About half an hour. You have business in Hope Beach?" Naomi asked.

Libby hesitated. "My partner and I restore historical buildings and sell them. She's been on the island investigating the idea of helping to restore the downtown area."

"There are some beautiful old properties on the island. Many of them have fallen into disrepair, so you'll have your work cut out for you." Naomi tipped her head to the side. "You really do look like Vanessa Mitchell in a most astonishing way."

Libby managed a smile. "They say everyone has a twin somewhere in the world. Have the Mitchells been there a long time?"

"Oh yes. The old Tidewater Inn is the matriarch of the place. Make sure you see it. Since you are into historical buildings, I'm sure you'll be fascinated. It's lovely. Ray Mitchell's dad bought it in the thirties and raised a big family there. Ray bought out his siblings after their father died and turned it into an inn. Not that there are many tourists on the island, but he hoped he could entice families who wanted a quiet getaway."

"Are his siblings still around?" Aunts, uncles, cousins. The idea tightened Libby's chest.

"Just his sister. The rest moved to the mainland." Naomi opened the ice chest. "Water?"

"Sure." Libby accepted the cold, wet bottle and uncapped it. "Is that Hope Island?" she asked when she saw a speck of land in the distance.

"That's it," Earl said.

Libby almost forgot to breathe as the island neared. Why did the island appeal to her so much? She'd never been here, had she? Charming houses lined a small bay with a well-maintained dock. Most of the houses could use a coat of paint and some repair to the gutters, but the village was like something out of a painting from the eighteen hundreds.

"Where can I rent a car?" she asked.

"No need for one, really," Earl said. "Not if you're staying in town. You have a room?"

"Not yet." She ignored the lift of his brow. "Can you recommend a hotel?"

"Tidewater Inn would be your best bet. If you call them, they'll fetch you," Naomi said. "Stop at the general store. They'll give you the number. We don't have a car on the island or we'd run you out there ourselves."

"There's a small lot by the harbor where you can rent a car though," Earl said. "Some people like to explore."

Home. The place felt like home. That was the sensation in her chest.

———

The sheriff's office felt deserted when Libby stepped onto the worn wooden floor. "Hello?" she called.

A man in a uniform came down the hallway. He was in his late thirties with dark hair just beginning to get salty. His tanned face was good-natured. "Can I help you?"

"I'd like to see the sheriff."

"That would be me. Sheriff Tom Bourne. Come on back." He led the way to a small office that held a battered desk and a metal filing cabinet, both overflowing with stacks of paper. He lifted a batch of files from the chair opposite the desk. "Have a seat and tell me what I can do for you."

She settled onto the hard chair. "My business partner was kidnapped yesterday."

His gaze sharpened. "You're Libby Holladay, the one who witnessed the kidnapping?"

"Yes. Is there any news?" Surely they had found Nicole by now. Alive, she prayed.

He shook his head. "Nothing. All I found when I got to the lifesaving station was her car. No sign of her. I've called in the Coasties, but they've seen nothing."

"Coasties?"

"Coast Guard. What can you tell me about your conversation?

You rushed off before the Virginia Beach police arrived to take your statement."

"I wanted to get here and find her." She described the men she saw, and he took notes. "One man gave her an injection."

"It would help if we could call up the video, but it seems to have been erased from the server."

She bit her lip. Should she admit what she'd done? How much trouble could she get into for that? It was an accident, after all. But didn't the police tend to blame the person closest to the victim?

The phone on his desk rang, and she sat back in the chair while he talked. He rose when he hung up. "I have to go. There's a problem at the jail. Where are you staying? Tidewater?"

She nodded. "I hope to. I haven't called yet."

He reached for some keys and tossed them to her. "I've got an old car I loan out sometimes. Go ahead and take it out to Tidewater. I'll catch up with you there and get it back. Just follow Oyster Road to the end. You can't miss it."

She took the keys and followed him out the door. There would be time to tell him about the video later. Maybe she could find the file and restore it. Then she wouldn't be in trouble.

———

The old truck reeked of fish, but it was the smell of money to Alec. The morning's excellent haul would fetch a premium price at the restaurants. But he needed to get to the jail and pick up his nephew. As he maneuvered the truck along Oyster Road just outside of town, he noticed Tom's red Honda along the shoulder. A woman crouched beside a flat tire. Tourist, from the looks of her.

He parked his truck behind the car and got out. "Need some help?"

Her sun-streaked light-brown hair framed a striking face with bold brows and large brown eyes. In her early thirties, he guessed. There was an air of tension around her as if she were about to explode.

She held up the tire iron. "I'm not quite sure how to use this."

"Let me see if I can help." Alec took the tool from her. "Everything okay?" He knelt by the tire and began to remove the lug bolts. "You're driving the sheriff's spare car."

"My business partner is missing." Her voice trembled. "I was watching on a beach cam, and two men kidnapped her right in front of me."

His hands stilled, and he looked up at her. "Nicole Ingram?" He'd gone out last night on the search for the missing woman. All they'd found was her cell phone on the sand, a chilling sight.

She nodded. "She'd told me when she would be at the cam, so I got on the computer. Two guys came ashore in a small boat and took her away. I called 9-1-1, but by the time the sheriff got there, all he found was her car parked along the side of the road. No sign of Nicole."

"No sign of her in any boats that were stopped yesterday either."

She studied him as she fidgeted with her large leather bag. "How do you know that?"

He rose and stuck out his hand. "Alec Bourne. Part-time fisherman and full-time captain in the Coast Guard. The sheriff is my cousin, and he told me about your friend. My crew did a run through the area on one of the boats, but we didn't see anything suspicious."

She grasped his hand in a tight grip. "I'm Libby Holladay. You have to find her."

He checked the spare. "This spare tire is flat too. Tom needs to take better care of this vehicle. Hop in. I'll take you anywhere you need to go. Tom can collect the car later."

She studied his face. "I'm sorry, but I don't know you."

He couldn't blame her for being cautious, especially considering what had happened to her friend. He dug out his Coast Guard ID and held it out. Her fingers grazed his when she took it, and the bolt of adrenaline he experienced nearly made him snatch his hand back. She was beautiful, but he'd seen beautiful women before.

She returned his ID. "Thank you. I'm sorry if I offended you."

"No offense taken," he said while he fetched her belongings from Tom's car. "It's always wise to be cautious." He jerked his head toward the passenger side of the truck. "The door sticks. Give it a jerk." He put her suitcase in the truck bed, then slid behind the wheel of his truck and quickly moved some nets and tackle off the seat.

She yanked on the door, then climbed in. She wrinkled her nose as she shut the door. "I guess you *have* been fishing. The truck reeks of it." She smiled. "Sorry, I don't like fish much."

"You just haven't had the right fish. I went crabbing this morning. Nice haul." He started the engine. "The smell grows on you. Where you headed?"

She hesitated. "I was going to go to the Tidewater Inn, but you can just take me back to town and I'll call them."

"You live in the Outer Banks?"

She shook her head. "Near Virginia Beach."

"Your friend was here on vacation or something?"

She stared out the window. "Or something."

He didn't like the way she didn't look at him. Like she was hiding something. "By herself? She didn't say anything about being worried about someone? No one was following her?"

She shook her head and rested her cheek on the window.

"I get the feeling you're not telling me everything," he said. "I have a nose for deception. Comes with the job."

She finally lifted her head and turned to face him. Her dark eyes were anxious and strained. "It's personal."

He turned the truck into Dead Man's Curve and headed for downtown. "Might have something to do with your friend's disappearance though."

Her face was pale. "Do you know Horace Whittaker?"

Was she in some kind of trouble? "Sure. He was born and raised here on the island. Good man, good attorney."

"His secretary gave Nicole some interesting news. She said my father has left me some property out here."

He tried to think who had died lately. "Who's your father?"

"Ray Mitchell."

Alec raised his brows. "You're Ray's daughter? I never knew he had any other kids except for Brent and Vanessa. You never visited him here. I would have seen you."

"I *thought* he died when I was five." She pressed her lips together and looked down at her hands.

He absorbed the news. So the information that Ray had only died a month ago would have come as a shock. "Who told you that?"

"My mother."

"Your mom lied to you?"

She gave a barely perceptible nod.

He made a quick decision as he parked in front of the jail. "Give me Tom's keys. I'll have a couple of deputies handle the car situation, and we'll go see Horace."

She handed him the keys. "You think he knows what happened to Nicole?"

"He can tell us what he knows of her visit here. Maybe something will point to whatever happened. Though I doubt it's related to your inheritance, I could be wrong. Do your brother and sister know you're here?"

She shook her head. "Seems crazy that I have a brother and

sister I didn't know about until yesterday." She stared at him. "Did you see any boats out yesterday at all?"

He shrugged. "Fishing boats. Like I said, we stopped a couple but found nothing suspicious." He got out of the truck. "I'll be right back," he told her through the open window. He'd spring Zach while he was at it and tell the kid to go home and stay there.

FOUR

L ibby craned her neck to take in the village of Hope Beach. The main street, Oyster Road, ran straight through to the harbor. Small shops lined the road and displayed wares ranging from beads to beach gear to driftwood furniture. Alec drove the truck past a restaurant with tables on a terrace. There was an ice-cream shop and a coffee shop across the street.

It was a town unlike anything she'd ever seen. She almost felt like she had stepped into a movie about a beach town in the fifties. There were very few cars but a lot of bicycles. So quaint and charming. What a wonderful place to grow up. Live oaks lined the sidewalks, and the street itself was cobblestone. The shop fronts were mostly clapboard. Libby loved it already.

She eyed a Victorian home with decorative siding in the gables. "Why isn't this place on the historic registry? It's like stepping back in time."

"You sound like an expert or something," Alec said.

She stared up at the fretwork on the next house. "I'm an archaeological historian. I work in historic preservation. Some of these places are real treasures."

She glanced back at the man beside her. Alec was a handsome guy, about six-two with sun-streaked brown hair. His blue eyes were startling in his tanned face, and his muscular frame was from either hauling in nets or working out.

He parked in front of a clapboard house that appeared to be freshly painted. "It's expensive to renovate out here. Material has to be ferried over, and workmen are at a premium. So most make do with what they have or what they can accomplish by themselves."

She continued to stare at the buildings. "That's why they're still intact, then. In college I did my thesis on historic homes in Charleston. I compared contemporary photos that I'd taken to historic pictures I found in the archives. I wanted to show the progress over the years. What I set out to prove was that, historically, homes in Charleston were owned by folks who were too poor to paint but too proud to whitewash. So those places stayed the same."

He nodded. "You might be right about that. Happened here for sure."

She got out of the truck and shut the door behind her. "Why hasn't the charm been destroyed by tourism?"

"Your father gets the credit for that. He owned most of the town, and he refused to sell to outsiders. Some called him a genius and others said he blocked progress."

A rustic sign proclaimed the building to be that of Horace Whittaker, Attorney-at-Law. The place had so much gingerbread in the gables and on the porch that it looked like a fairytale cottage. She followed Alec through the entry and into the foyer, which was surprisingly dim. A young woman in jeans sat behind the counter.

Alec glanced around. "Hi, Mindy. Why are you sitting in here with no lights?"

She rolled her eyes. "Horace forgot to pay the electric bill again. And his bill at the dive shop. That man is so forgetful."

Or so irresponsible. Libby was quite familiar with irresponsibility. Her mother always wanted to play and let the bills take care of themselves. Except they never did.

"They're supposed to turn it on any minute. I don't mind." Mindy held up a romance novel. "I get to read instead of work. At least I have a window." The woman's eyes were sparkling. "You hear about the hurricane? The first one missed us but there's another heading this way."

Alec shrugged. "It's only a category 1. We'll be fine. Listen, is Horace busy?"

The secretary shook her head and picked up the phone. "Horace, Alec is here with a lady to see you." She listened a moment, then replaced the receiver. "You can go on back."

Libby saw the speculation in the woman's eyes. "I'm Libby Holladay."

The woman's eyes widened. "I'm Mindy Jackson. I met your business partner." She put down her book. "I got into so much trouble for telling her Horace was looking for you. He hates to appear incompetent. I was just trying to help though." She tipped her head and stared. "You look a lot like Vanessa."

"So Nicole said."

Mindy winced. "I heard on the radio this morning about her kidnapping. You're the friend who saw the men take her via the cam?"

"Yes."

"I see. Well, welcome to Hope Island, Ms. Holladay. I'm sorry about your friend. Hopefully the sheriff will find her soon."

Libby tensed at the doubt in the secretary's voice. "I'm sure they will," she said. "Did Nicole mention what she'd been doing? Did she seem afraid of anyone?"

Mindy shook her head. "She came in to have Horace help her with some paperwork. But she seemed more interested in the inheritance when she heard about it." She pointed down the hall. "You know the way to his office, Alec." Her tone dismissed them, and she stuck her nose back in her book.

Libby followed Alec down the wide hall. The woodwork was

quarter-sawn oak and appeared to be original. The plaster walls were painted an accurate period gray-green. She was sure there were original hardwood floors under the carpet. Alec pushed open a door at the end of the hall, and she glimpsed a man in his fifties behind a massive cherry desk. He looked like Burl Ives with his round face and belly and his pointed beard.

When he spoke, even his voice had that rich Ives timbre. "Alec, can't say I was expecting to see you in need of an attorney." His gaze went to Libby. "Or is it your friend in need of my help?" He rose and extended his hand. "Horace Whittaker."

She put her hand in his. It was warm. "Libby Holladay."

His fingers tightened on hers. His white brows rose. He pointed to the overstuffed leather chairs. "Have a seat. Let me save my work. I'm updating my website and I don't want to lose it."

Libby sat. "You saw my friend two days ago, Mr. Whittaker?"

He nodded. "Call me Horace. It was rather embarrassing that my secretary was so unprofessional." He smiled. "Still, it allowed me to finally track you down."

"You'd had trouble?"

He nodded. "The last address Ray had for you was in Indiana. Your friend said you're in Virginia Beach now?"

"Yes. For the past year." Libby leaned forward. "About my father . . ."

Horace's round head bobbed. "Ray. The town misses him already. He was a great philanthropist, always contributing to those in need. You would have passed the school on the way in. The playground equipment was bought by your father. He's been a driving force in the village for the past twenty-five years."

A lump formed in Libby's throat and she blinked rapidly, determined not to let these men see the emotion that threatened to overwhelm her. If he was so generous to everyone else, why had he ignored her all these years?

Horace wheeled his chair around. "In addition to the old letters, Ray gave me a package for you. It's in my safe." He leaned over a safe behind him, twirled the dial a few times, then popped it open. He reached inside, then shut and locked it again. "Here we are." He held out an irregularly shaped envelope. When she took it, he reached into a drawer and pulled out a shoe box. "Here are the letters."

"What's in this?" She felt the package and couldn't tell what it contained.

"I have no idea. He gave it to me shortly before he died and asked me to put it away."

Libby tucked the envelope into her large bag and put the box of letters on the floor beside it. She wasn't ready to read anything from her father in front of spectators. "Thank you." She leaned forward. "What about my father's second family? They all live here?"

The attorney nodded. "His sister, Pearl, too. She's the town postmistress. She moved into the big house to take care of him before he died."

"What did he die from?" she asked.

"He had a heart attack a year ago and went downhill afterward. He knew his time was short, so he transferred all of his cash to a trust fund for Brent and Vanessa."

"Do my siblings know that I've inherited something?"

"I just informed them last week. Brent was on a trip to England, so I delayed the reading of Ray's will until he got back." Horace nodded. "He's a young hothead, and he demanded that we break the bequest. I told him he didn't have any legal grounds."

She didn't want to admit to herself that her brother's objection hurt. "Is the inheritance so valuable?"

The attorney retrieved a file from his drawer and slid it across the desk to her. "The entire west side of the island as well as an old inn is all yours. Now, it's not as valuable as if it were on the mainland, because progress has passed us by for now. But if tourists ever start flocking here, it could be worth a lot of money. Even in its current state, it's valuable."

She flipped open the folder. The first page was a photograph of a lovely Georgian hotel with porches and balconies. The second was of sand dunes and rolling whitecaps. "My siblings also have an inheritance? A trust fund, you said?"

"Oh yes, they're well taken care of. They each have more than a million dollars in the bank." He steepled his fingers together. "You really should draw up a will. The property is worth well over a million dollars," Horace said. "More if progress ever finds us."

No more money worries for her stepbrother. And that lovely old house she was in yesterday could be hers. She could create a foundation to help preserve the neighborhood. "I think I'd like to set up a foundation after it's sold," she said slowly. "For historic preservation." She sat back in her chair and exhaled. "I suppose I'll need a will too."

"I can draft something simple for you," Horace offered. "So you have something in place for starters."

"That would be nice. Thank you. I can't even think straight right now. I just want to find Nicole. The rest can wait."

Wind-tossed sand stung Libby's cheeks and arms as she stood on the boardwalk staring out to sea. Gulls swooped low over the water, and a crab scuttled across the wet sand. A few clouds floated on an impossibly blue sky. It should have been paradise.

"It's so beautiful," she said, then shivered. "And so deserted. This is the spot. I recognize the lifesaving station." She pointed to the lone building, a low-slung clapboard structure with a hole in the roof. "You say this belongs to me?"

Alec gestured to the west. "Not the station. That belongs to the town. Just over the hill is Tidewater Inn. You own this stretch clear to the inlet."

"Nicole was here to finalize the purchase of the station. We're going to restore it as a museum for the island." She scanned the area and saw what she was looking for. "There's the cam." It was mounted on one of the posts. She walked directly to it and stopped a few feet away. "Whoever you are, if you have my friend, please don't hurt her," she said. "Her name is Nicole."

Alec's eyes were warm with sympathy when she turned toward him and brushed moisture from her cheeks. "I thought they might be watching. They say an attacker usually goes back to the scene of the crime. And professionals say friends and investigators should try to personalize the victim."

Alec stood with his hands in the pockets of his denim shorts. "It's possible someone's watching. A plea doesn't hurt." He pointed to the final landing before the sand. "Her cell phone was found there. Her rental car was parked along the road with the keys in the ignition."

She winced. "I saw one of the men toss the phone. Would his prints be on it? And what about her hat? I saw it fall off."

"I'm sure Tom is checking that out. I'll do what I can to find her," he promised. "The first thing we have to figure out is where she was staying. My cousin may know." He pulled out his phone and placed a call. "Hey, Tom, I'm with Libby Holladay. Have you found out where Nicole Ingram was staying?"

His voice faded to a drone as she stepped away and stared down the deserted beach. Not a house was in sight of where she stood. No wonder the men had taken Nicole from this location. Gooseflesh pebbled her arms at the thought of what they might be doing to her friend. She swallowed down the wave of nausea that rose in her throat. She had to find Nicole. The most likely reason she was taken was too horrible to contemplate, so she considered whether there might be another reason. Nicole had been poking around about Libby's inheritance. Could there be any connection?

Libby took off her sandals and dug her toes into the warm sand. The sound of the surf washed over her in a rhythm that would have been soothing in other circumstances. Carrying her shoes, she stepped back to find out what Alec had learned. He was just finishing his call.

"Uh-huh. Okay. I'll tell her, thanks." He dropped the phone back into his pocket. "She was staying at the small inn you own. Tom was just about to head out there. We can meet him there and see what is in her room."

Libby glanced around one final time, but there was still nothing pointing her to Nicole's whereabouts. This search was already beginning to feel hopeless.

FIVE

iltered light struck her eyelids. Nicole groaned and threw her hand over her eyes. The brightness pierced her skull like a knife. She licked dry lips, then pried one lid open, wincing when the brilliance intensified. She rolled to her back, then sat up.

Where was she? The sound of the surf rolled through the small window covered by a grimy curtain. Her head pounded, and she staggered to her feet. Her eyes were beginning to adjust to the light, and she glanced around. She seemed to be in a small building. Overhead were wooden planks, and she could see thatching through the boards. Her sandals and hat were missing, and so was her pink cover-up. She wore only her swimsuit. The dirt floor under her bare feet was cool and damp.

When she put her hand on the door, a rough wooden one, it moved. Surprised it wasn't locked, she stepped out of the shack and onto a mixture of sand and grass. A small beach began twenty feet away. She glanced around and realized she was on a tiny island, barely as big as her yard at home. No other land in the distance as far as she could see. Trying not to panic, she walked along the shore, straining to see something—anything—in the distance. There was nothing but seagulls and waves.

She was incredibly thirsty. Maybe there were provisions in the shack. And what was she doing here? The last thing she could remember was talking to Libby about the inheritance she'd discovered.

She fingered the soreness on her jaw. Ducking into the shack, she circled the perimeter of the space, about sixteen feet square. There was no kitchen, just the small cot and a camp chair. No food or water. Maybe there was a stream on the little island that she'd missed.

She went back into the sunshine and cut behind the shack. No cistern, no stream. Her head spun, and she fought back the rising panic. She'd better get out of the heat and inside. As she skirted the side of the shack, she heard a boat's motor *putt-putt*ing along. Maybe she could get help! She ran to the beach and shaded her eyes with her hand. A small craft rode the waves. Maybe a fisherman?

She shouted and waved. "Help! I need help!"

The bow of the boat headed for the beach where she stood. As it neared, she saw that it held a young man about seventeen or eighteen. The wind whipped his dark hair, and he waved back. When the boat was just offshore, he shut off the motor and threw an anchor overboard. He jumped into the water, and the waves came to midthigh, barely dampening the hem of his black shorts. He reached back into the boat and extracted a box.

She waded out to meet him. When he reached her, she grabbed his arm. "I'm so glad you came this way. I need help. I don't remember how I got here, but I'll pay you to take me back to Hope Island."

Frowning, he shook off her grip. "I brought you some food and water."

She took a step back. "You knew I was here?" She struggled to make sense of it.

He brushed past her and walked toward the shack. "The water should last a couple days and the food is stuff like bread and peanut butter. Your brother will come get you when the room at the mental facility is ready."

She followed him inside. "I don't understand. I don't have a brother. You're not making any sense."

He set the box on the dirt floor by the cot and opened it. "Like I said, this should last you a few days. I'll be back then with more."

He was going to leave her. She grabbed his forearm and squeezed. "Listen to me! I don't have a brother. You can't leave me here."

He glanced at her, then backed away as if she frightened him. "He said you'd say that. It's only for a little while, until he can get you in. You tried to stick him with a knife, and he can't trust you around people. The mental hospital will have an opening in a couple of weeks. It's for your own good."

His expression was closed. She bolted for the door, slamming it shut behind her to slow him down. If she could get to the boat first, she could get away. She ran to the water and struggled through the waves to the craft, where she threw herself into the bottom of it. Sitting up, she saw him running toward her. She grabbed the rope with the anchor and yanked it up, then scrambled back to try to start the motor.

He reached the water and plunged toward her. She tugged on the rope to start the engine, but she didn't pull it hard enough. Before she could try again, he was at the side of the vessel. She kicked at his hands with her bare feet, but he hauled himself aboard. He grabbed her arm, and she bit his hand. Tasting blood, she bit harder and clawed at him with her nails. He grabbed her hair, tearing the dangling ponytail holder free before he finally seized her.

He shoved her overboard, and she came up spitting salt water. "Please, you have to help me," she panted.

"You are one crazy chick," he said. Using an oar, he pushed the boat away, then turned and started the engine.

She screamed and shouted for him to come back, but he didn't even look at her. Sobbing, she collapsed onto the beach.

Alec cruised by his house on the way to the hotel. Zach's bike was parked in front of the house, but Alec's gut clenched when he saw Zach tying off to the piling. He'd obviously been out in the old boat in spite of having been grounded. What was he going to do with that kid? Alec couldn't be here 24/7 when he had to work. And Zach was old enough to start taking responsibility for himself.

"I need to stop here at the house for a minute if you don't mind," Alec said.

"Of course. Is that your son?"

Alec parked the truck by the garage just off the street. "My nephew. My brother and his wife are dead, and I've got custody. As of two weeks ago." He shoved open his door.

"I'm so sorry," she said.

"I am too." He led the way to the house.

"Do you mind if I use your restroom?"

"Help yourself." He should have thought to offer. He got out of the truck and led the way to the house.

"Cute," she said, pausing on the stoop. "Built in the fifties?"

He nodded and took a glance at the all-too-familiar two-story. It was white clapboard with gray shutters and a red door. "You're good. I bought it from my parents when they moved to Richmond." He held the door open for her and pointed down the hall to the bathroom. The place was fairly clean. "I'm going to go down to talk to Zach."

His house was right on the harbor, and his fishing boats were docked just offshore. He stepped around to the back by the upper deck, which was anchored into the sand with pilings. Zach climbed down into the rubber boat and rowed to the small dock by the house. The boy had to have seen him standing on the pier, but Zach didn't wave. He probably knew he was in trouble. Alec waited until the raft reached the dock. Tight-lipped, he tied up the rope Zach tossed to him.

Zach stepped over the side of the boat and onto the pier. He tossed a cheeky grin Alec's way. "I got a job, Uncle Alec!"

Alec's lecture died on his lips. "What kind of job?"

"I'm delivering some supplies." Zach glanced at him from under a lock of dark hair. "I know I was grounded, but Grandpa has been on me to get a job, and this was too good to pass up."

He wanted to ask how the job had come Zach's way while he was supposed to be staying home, but Alec bit back the words. "School is starting again soon. Will the hours be okay?"

Zach shook his head. "It will be over before school starts. It's supposed to last from two to four weeks."

"You should have called me."

"I tried. You didn't answer your phone."

Alec lifted a brow and pulled out his phone. Sure enough, it showed a missed call. Maybe when he and Libby had been in transit to the beach. It hardly paid to have a phone on the island. "Okay, but when you're not working, you still need to be at the house."

Zach brushed past him. "I know, I know. Sheesh, give me a break. I'm doing the best I can."

Maybe he was. The boy was so much like Alec was at that age. Always pushing the boundaries, impatient to be his own man, looking at anyone in authority with derision. At least Zach had a job. That was progress.

"Okay," Alec called after him. "I'm proud of you for getting a job."

Zach just hunched his shoulders and bounded up the stairs to the deck overlooking the water. He plopped down in a chair and pulled an electronic game out of his pocket. The back door opened, and Libby stepped out onto the deck. Alec jogged to intercept her. She'd take one look at Zach and think the kid was a hoodlum. Alec reached the top of the deck as she stepped to where Zach sat.

"You must be Zach," Libby said.

Zach didn't look up from his game. "Yeah."

"Ready?" Alec said. "Your place is about two miles out of town."

Zach looked up then. "The old Mitchell place?"

Libby nodded.

"You're staying there?"

"I own it," Libby said. "I'm Ray Mitchell's oldest daughter."

Zach looked her up and down. "Boy, is Brent ticked. He had plans for that place."

"He's twenty-two," Alec pointed out. "What kind of plans could he have?"

Zach slouched into his chair. "Forget it."

Suppressing a sigh, Alec touched Libby's elbow. "Tom should be there any minute."

She resisted the pull on her arm. "I'd really like to hear what Zach has to say," she said. "You probably already know this, Zach, but I didn't even know I had a brother and sister until yesterday."

His head came up and his eyes widened. "No kidding? Brent didn't say anything about that in the ice-cream shop. Just that some woman he'd never met was going to have the property. Said it was his sister."

"Did he know about me before our father died?"

Zach shrugged. "I don't know."

"I'd like to meet him. And Vanessa. Do they know I'm here?"

"I don't think so. He figures you'll sell the place. There's an investor after it hot and heavy."

"Oh?" There was interest in her voice.

Alec had heard the rumors. Now that the land was out of Ray's hands, everything was liable to change. He didn't know if that was good or bad.

SIX

Sand drifted across the pavement in places. The island was
unlike any place Libby had ever seen. Wild, remote, and
unbelievably beautiful with whitecaps rolling to dunes on
one side and tangled maritime forest on the other.

She leaned forward as Alec's truck crested the hill. She caught
her breath when she saw the inn standing guard over the empty
beach that stretched in both directions. A small but inviting dock
jutted over the water. Her chest was so tight she couldn't breathe,
couldn't do more than take in the lovely Georgian mansion overlooking the Atlantic. Large trees sheltered it, and it looked as if it
had been in that place forever. In a moment, she felt she knew the
spot as if it had always been a part of her.

She could almost hear the voices of previous owners in her
head. Pioneers, business owners, statesmen. The inn was alive
with the history of its past. She couldn't wait to explore, to touch
the woodwork and plaster walls.

"Th-This is mine?" she asked, getting out the truck when it
rolled to a stop.

"So I hear."

The place clearly needed work, but she didn't care. She stared
at the front of the building. "You said it was an inn." She eyed its

elegant lines. "It looks like a mansion. It's Georgian. Built in the late seventeen hundreds or early eighteen hundreds."

"It's an inn now. Small, I know. About fifteen suites, I think."

There were two curving staircases up to the porch, one on each side. There had to be two thousand square feet of balconies and porches. Great arched windows looked out on the waves. The place was in serious need of paint, but her mind's eye could see it restored to its earlier glory. How could she bear to sell it? But she had to. For her stepbrother. For Holladay Renovations.

He took her elbow and guided her up the nearest steps. "It used to be a single-family home. There should be some stuff about it in the attic."

No wonder Nicole had said she would love it. Libby took in every angle, every graceful line. "It's so large. Who would build such a magnificent place clear out here?"

"I don't remember all the history, but the builder had some kind of role in early government, and I guess he wanted to impress everyone. Though there weren't many to impress out here but Hatteras Indians. This place is really the beginning of our history as we know it, so it's in the school book about our island."

The porch was expansive, but the floor needed paint. Now that she was closer, Libby saw the signs of decay in the peeling shutters and rotting fretwork. It would take a lot of money to restore this place. Money she didn't have. But oh, how she wanted to keep it.

Alec opened the oversized front entrance. "The lobby is the room to the right."

Sand and salt had scoured the wood floors. Libby ran her fingertips along blistered paint on the plaster walls. She could repair it. She went down through the foyer to what would have been a parlor on the right. Ceilings soared to twelve feet. She glanced up and saw that the plaster drooped in places. It needed to be put back in place with plaster washers and screws. Or replastered altogether.

The reception counter was made of driftwood and marble. The woman behind the counter was in her early thirties. Her dark hair was up in a ponytail that curled down her back. She wore no makeup, and her strikingly beautiful skin didn't need any help. She smiled when Alec introduced Libby.

"I'm Delilah Carter, Ms. Holladay," she said. "I'm so sorry about your trouble. If there's anything I can do to help, just let me know." She rose with a key in her hand. "Let me show you to your friend's room."

"I see Tom outside," Alec said. "I'll join you upstairs in a minute." He walked back the way they'd come.

Libby fell into step beside Delilah. "Did you get a chance to talk to Nicole?"

The woman stepped into the foyer and started up the steps, easily six feet wide. "Oh yes. Lovely girl."

Libby mounted the steps with her. "Did she tell you why she was here?"

"For business, so she said." Delilah inserted the key into the lock and turned it. She opened the door and stepped aside for Libby to enter. At the first sight of her friend's familiar pink suitcase, Libby's eyes burned. Nicole's pajamas were in a heap on the floor. Her clothes spilled from the top of the suitcase. In the bathroom, her makeup littered the sink counter. Libby picked up her friend's hairbrush and caught a scent of the shampoo Nicole used.

She swiped fiercely at the moisture on her face. Crying wouldn't find Nicole.

———

Alec intercepted Tom on the porch. "Any news?"

Tom's lips flattened. "Not about Nicole."

"What's that mean?"

"Ms. Holladay hasn't been truthful with us." Tom took off his hat and wiped his brow with the back of his sleeve. "The reason I can't view the video of the abduction is because it was wiped off the server. The computer's IP address was traced. Libby did it."

Alec's gut clenched. Though he'd known her only a few hours, he would have sworn her innocence and concern were genuine. "So there is no proof her story is even true. The cell phone could have been planted. The car could have been left out there by anyone. We know she only came to town today though, right?"

Tom nodded. "I talked to Earl Franklin and his wife. They met her this morning. But I'm questioning all the charters I know of to make sure she didn't get here a few days ago to lay out her plan."

Alec marshaled all his objectivity. Since when had a pretty face blinded him? "When was Nicole last seen?"

"I was about to question Delilah. No one in town saw her yesterday."

"What about Vanessa? Libby claims she was meeting Nicole."

Tom returned his hat to his head. "I haven't spoken to her yet, but I will. Right now I want to look through Nicole's room and talk to Delilah."

"You haven't gone through her belongings yet?"

Tom shook his head. "My first priority was to find her."

"Delilah just let Libby into the suite."

"Great, just great." Tom jerked open the door and rushed into the house.

Alec followed. He'd sure botched that one.

———

"Libby?"

Libby put the hairbrush back onto the sink when Alec called to her from the bedroom. "In here."

44

When she stepped into the bedroom, she found identical expressions on the faces of the two men in the doorway. Alec was making an obvious attempt to mask his suspicion, but the sheriff's gaze bored through her. She took a step back.

"What have you touched?" the sheriff demanded.

"Nothing but the things in the bathroom." She stepped out of the doorway so he could brush past her. "What are you looking for?"

He glanced around the small bathroom. "You had no business coming in here until I had a chance to clear the scene."

"It's not a crime scene," she said.

"There may still be clues to what happened to her."

He hadn't been nearly so unfriendly at his office. And even Alec was tense. "H-Have you found her?"

The sheriff whirled and glared at her. "You mean her body? Is there something you want to tell us?"

The kidnapping had changed into a murder, and she was a suspect. That was the only possible reason for his change of demeanor. "You found her body, didn't you?"

"What was on that video that you were so eager to make sure no one saw?" the sheriff asked.

His accusing tone made her swallow hard. He knew she'd erased the video. "It was an accident. I was trying to save it so I could show it to the police. The screen went blank and it was gone."

"I might have believed you if you'd admitted it from the first. But you said nothing about it when you were in my office."

"I was going to, but—"

"Right." He turned around and stared at the room. "Delilah, did she touch anything in here?"

"No, sir," Delilah said. "I could see her when she was in the bathroom too. She didn't do anything." The phone rang in the distance. "I'll be right back." She dashed out of the room.

"Alec, take a look in the suitcase. I'll go through the drawers."

Libby curled her fingers into her palms and prayed that he would find something that would lead them to Nicole and those two men. "Just so you know, I did touch the hairbrush."

Tom looked her over. "Thanks."

Alec pulled shorts and tops out, then dumped out a bag with suntan lotion, sunglasses, and other sundries in it. The sheriff was opening the furniture's drawers and looking through them.

Libby spied Nicole's laptop on the desk and picked it up. "Maybe there's something on this."

The men glanced up. Tom scowled. "I told you not to touch anything. Alec, you know more about computers than I do. Have a look."

Alec lifted a brow and reached out his hand. "May I?"

Surprised he was gentlemanly enough to ask in spite of the suspicion in his expression, she handed it over. "You know anything about Macs?"

"I have one myself." He set the laptop on the desk and opened the lid. Pulling out the chair, he sat down and began to peruse the files. "She has a lot of files on this."

Libby stood behind him and watched over his shoulder. "Sort by date," she said.

He did as she suggested, then leaned forward and read through the sorted files. "What's this one?" He clicked on a file titled "Hope Beach."

The file opened with the picture of a woman. "Who is that?" Libby asked.

"Your sister, Vanessa. Definitely a family resemblance," Alec said, his voice distracted.

Libby drank in the woman's photo before the sheriff blocked her view.

He bent down to read the document. "It's kind of a diary.

Ms. Ingram is talking about everything she saw and did since she came. Scroll to the bottom first. Maybe there's an entry for yesterday."

Libby peered over his shoulder and read the entry.

Someone was outside my door last night. He whispered my name. I think it was Brent trying to scare me into doing what he wants. I'll have a talk with him tomorrow.

Libby drew in a breath. "Would Brent have hurt her?"

Tom straightened and stared at her. "Let me handle the investigation."

She clasped her hands together. "Look, Sheriff, I know it looks bad that I didn't tell you about the file, but you're wasting precious time by investigating me. I didn't have anything to do with her disappearance. I can prove where I was when she went missing."

He said nothing at first and continued to stare at her with those accusing eyes. "What kind of proof?"

"For one thing, you can track the time on my cell phone when I called in the abduction."

"You could have disposed of her and gone back to Virginia Beach before you made the call. It's not that far."

Delilah poked her head into the room. "Hurricane warning just came through. That smaller one has veered this way. We need to get the hurricane shutters in place."

"Is the Tidewater in danger?" Libby asked.

"We're on higher ground here so we're safe from the surge," Delilah said, "but we don't know how much wind we're going to get."

"I'd better check in at the station," Alec said. "I'm off duty, but they may need me to begin evacuations. How long do we have?"

"Twenty-four hours or so," Delilah said.

This was her place now. Libby roused herself. "I'll help with the shutters."

The wind had freshened, but it was far from gale strength yet. The hurricane wouldn't be here for hours, if it even hit. Storms were notoriously capricious. Alec strained to see any sign of movement on the tiny strip of land below as the helicopter powered toward it. He'd already helped evacuate several families to the mainland.

"What's wrong with McEwan?" he asked Curtis.

"Said he thought he might be having a heart attack. The boat is too far away, so they called us."

Alec winced. "We're nearly there. We'll have Sara check him out." She had a manner that generally soothed patients.

The chopper reached an open field just past the pier on the small island below. Though the island had no official name, those in the Banks referred to it as Oyster Island, because some of the best oyster beds were found a few hundred feet offshore. Five families lived on it, all related in some way. McEwan lived in a shanty on the north side. He'd built the place when he was forty and hadn't left the island since. He had to be in his eighties now. He relied on his son to go for supplies. Alec had always liked the old fellow's stories about life in the old days. Alec suspected McEwan had been a rumrunner back in the day.

The rotors were still whirring when he ducked out of the helicopter with Curtis and Sara. They ran through the pelting rain toward the small cabin. The three of them rushed with the stretcher into the building, where they found McEwan moaning on his cot.

"Took you long enough," he gasped. "Ticker's acting up." He hadn't shaved in several days, and the gray stubble added to his pallor. He wore a dirty T-shirt and cotton pajama bottoms that looked like they hadn't been washed in a month.

Sara brushed past the men and knelt by the bed. "Let me take a peek." She pulled out her stethoscope and listened to his heart.

"I'm going to give you a shot to relax your arteries," she said. "We'll get you to the mainland where the doctor can look at you, but I don't think it's a heart attack. Might be indigestion or gall bladder."

"I knew I shouldn't have had those raw oysters," the old man said. "They smelled a little nasty."

Alec grimaced. Oysters could contain dangerous bacteria when eaten raw, though oysters found offshore here were generally safe. It was hard to say what the old man had consumed. "We'll get you taken care of."

Once Sara administered the shot, the pain lines around the old man's face eased. Curtis and Sara got him onto the stretcher while Alec gathered a few items from the battered dresser by the bed. "Anything else you need?" Alec asked.

"My gun." McEwan pointed to a shotgun leaning by the door. "And the old suitcase under my bed."

Alec grabbed the gun, then reached under the bed for the battered old metal case. "Here, Sara, you take this stuff and I'll help Curtis carry the stretcher."

"I'm perfectly capable of doing my job." Sara grabbed the bottom of the stretcher.

Touchy. Alec raised his hands. "Suit yourself." Sara leaned in to whisper in his ear. "We'd better take him to the doctor at Hope Island first. I don't think there's time to get him clear to the mainland. I don't like the sound of his chest." Carrying the old man's belongings, Alec led the way back to the helicopter.

"Did that boat get back okay?" McEwan's voice was slurred and his lids droopy.

"What boat?"

McEwan waved his hand to the east. "Saw two men motor by yesterday. They didn't look like no watermen to me. One was yelling at the other one about how to steer. Didn't seem to bother the woman who was sleeping though."

Alec exchanged a glance with Curtis. Two men and a woman? Could it possibly be Nicole Ingram? Or was the old man out of his head? "Where were they headed?"

McEwan's eyes fluttered, then closed. "Out to sea. East."

Alec wanted to ignore the information, but what if the men were heading out to dump Nicole?

———

The inn was dark and gloomy with the hurricane shutters closed. Libby had never been in a hurricane before, and the breathless quality of the air added to her unease. "I think I'll sit on the porch and give my stepbrother a call," she told Delilah, who was instructing the housekeeping staff to ready some extra rooms.

Delilah nodded and Libby stepped out into the twilight air with the inn's portable phone in her hand. The sun was almost down and the sound of the cicadas enveloped her as she settled on the swing at the end of the porch. Could the police seriously think she might have hurt Nicole?

Libby put down the phone and clasped her knees to her chest. She had to figure out a way to prove her innocence. As long as the sheriff was investigating her, his attention wasn't on the right person. She should have told him about her mess-up with the computer. Everything was spiraling out of control because of her lapse of judgment. She could kick herself.

She still hadn't opened the items from her father. There hadn't been time, and she wanted no interruptions when she took a peek at the letters and the contents of the envelope.

The sand glimmered in the moonlight. The scene reminded her of when she was a little girl. She and her mom usually spent two weeks along a beach. One year it was California, another year the Texas Gulf, and yet another the cold water of the Pacific

Northwest. The various vacations were a kaleidoscope of memories, all slightly hazy with an aura of warmth and love.

That zany woman with the long braid and beads who had been her mother was hard to reconcile with a parent who would lie and deprive her daughter of all contact with her father. Yet that was the situation, if everything she'd learned today was true. But was it?

Libby stood and walked restlessly to the other side of the large porch. No matter what, she knew her mother had loved her. In spite of their constant travels and the many men in her mother's life, Libby's well-being had always been primary. She would cling to that fact for now.

Headlamps pierced the gloom and tires crunched on gravel. Her pulse jumped when she recognized Alec's truck in the glow of the security light. His door slammed, and he went around to the passenger side and helped an old man out.

Libby met them at the foot of the steps. Alec was assisting the man to the inn. "Is he all right?"

"This is Mr. McEwan. He lives on one of the unnamed islands. He had a little bit of angina, but the doctor says he's going to be okay. We generally bring people to the inn during a big blow. I assume that's still okay?"

Libby swallowed her disappointment at his distant tone. "Of course. Let me get the door." She jogged up the steps and held open the front door. "Delilah, we have a guest."

Delilah appeared in the entry. "I'll put him in one of our three downstairs rooms. This way." She led Alec and Mr. McEwan down the hall.

Libby wanted to rush to her room and eat a whole bag of jalapeño jelly beans, but she forced herself to walk back to the swing. Hiding away would make her look guilty.

SEVEN

The windows in Alec's house were boarded, and all they could do was wait. Few of the Hope Beach residents had left for the mainland. Too many times they'd evacuated and then been refused entry to their homes for weeks.

He paced the wood floor in his living room and listened to the wind beginning to pick up outside. The house was on stilts to deal with storm surges, so he and Zach should be okay. It still stood after Hurricane Helene's visit in 1958, a category 3. This was only a 1. Other 3s over the years, Gloria and Emily, had left the house fairly unscathed as well, so he wasn't worried, but he couldn't say the same for Zach.

Zach put down his game, then picked it up again and glanced toward the boarded windows. "You think we'll take a direct hit? And what about the smaller islands offshore? Will they flood?"

The boy's eyes were wide. Alec still remembered the first hurricane he'd gone through. He was just as nervous as Zach.

"We'll be all right," he assured his nephew. "It's supposed to give a glancing blow to this side of the island. That's all. And God is here with us."

The boy blinked. He got up and paced to the other side of the living room. "That's the thing, Uncle Alec. I've heard that my whole life, but where was God when my parents went down in that plane? If God loves me, then how could he let them die like that?"

At least Zach was talking. "He was with your dad in the cockpit. They are with him now. Being a Christian doesn't mean trouble never comes our way, Zach. It just means God is here, and he gives us the grace to get through the heartache."

Zach hunched his shoulders. Alec could feel the boy's pain. He was an adult, but he'd wrestled with his brother's death too. Why do bad things happen to good people? It was an age-old question, and every Christian dealt with it sooner or later. Poor Zach had been faced with it much too soon.

The phone on the end table rang. Alec glanced at the screen. It was Frank Bowden, Zach's maternal grandfather. Alec's gut tightened the way it always did when he had to speak with the man.

"Hey, Frank," he said. Zach's head came up when he heard his grandfather's first name. Alec shot the boy a reassuring smile.

"Alec." Frank's voice boomed in his ear. "I hear there's a hurricane headed your way. Why haven't you evacuated?"

"I'm needed here to help. We're riding it out."

"We?" Frank demanded. "My grandson is there too?"

"He's fine."

"You have a boat. You could have taken it to the mainland! Or that fancy helicopter you're so fond of hotdogging in."

Alec pulled the phone away from his ear a bit. Frank's voice had nearly deafened him. "Yes, I could have, but it's only a category 1. We'll be fine."

"That's the problem with your family, Alec. None of you ever gives any thought to what's best for everyone. You think things will automatically be all right."

Alec clutched the phone almost tight enough to break it. He couldn't lose his temper. Frank had his own view of the world. It was varnished tightly in place, and no one was going to change it.

When Alec made no comment, Frank huffed. "I want to talk to my grandson."

Without another word, Alec took the phone from his ear and handed it to Zach. His nephew took it hesitantly. He had an uneasy relationship with his mother's dad. No one could live up to Frank's high standards, and Zach had given up trying by the time he was five.

"Hi, Grandpa," Zach said. "No, we're fine. I'm not scared. I want to see what a hurricane is like. It's only a category 1. We'll be fine."

Alec hid a grin and went out to the back deck. The gray waves crashed over the pier and rolled dirty white foam onto the sand. The tide left flotsam behind as it receded for another attack. A dark sheet of rain that was the first outer band of the hurricane was just offshore and would be on him in a few minutes, but he lifted his face to the wind and exulted in God's power.

Such an awesome display. God could choose to spare this little spot or wipe it out. It was all in his control. Alec stared another minute, then the first drops of cold rain struck his face. He returned to the house and got inside just as the deluge hit. The rain thundered on the metal roof. It sounded as though the house was coming in on them, and he began to wonder if he'd made the right decision to ride out the storm. Even a storm this weak could kill.

Zach's eyes were wide and fearful. "Uncle Alec!" His nephew swallowed hard and handed the phone back to Alec. "It's Tom."

Alec took the phone. "Trouble?" he asked his cousin.

"We just got word that high tide is going to hit at the same time in the morning as the storm surge." Tom's voice was tense and clipped. "And Mr. Carter called. Can you evacuate him to the Tidewater Inn?"

It was going to be a long night.

"On my way." Alec hung up the phone. "I need to help some of the shut-ins. You can wait upstairs in case there's a storm surge."

Zach shook his head. "No way! I'm a man now, Uncle Alec. Let me come along and help."

Alec grabbed a yellow slicker and boots. "Get dressed, then." He tossed Zach's gear at him. "Hurry."

He prayed for those caught in this storm. That no lives would be lost. Property could be replaced, but lives were much more precious.

———

The storm would be on them soon. Libby sat in a swing on the expansive porch with her father's package in her hands. Bob Marley was crooning to her through her iPod earbuds, and the reggae soothed her ragged nerves as she waited for the rain to hit. The windows were shuttered and ready. The generator was gassed up, and the house hunkered down before the coming storm.

She stared out at the sea. The waves were high, and a few surfers were out braving the massive rollers. Crazy. She watched them for a few minutes, but her task couldn't be delayed forever. Libby pressed the envelope between her hands and felt something hard inside. A small locket with a photo? A bracelet? She couldn't tell. She flipped the envelope over and slipped her finger under the flap. It opened easily. She inhaled, then upended the envelope so the contents slipped out onto her lap. A necklace, a notebook, and a letter fell out.

She picked up the necklace first. There were beads strung on jute. It was quite worn. She rolled one bead over to see an engraved letter on the other side. She could barely make out a J. The letters on the other beads had worn off, and she had no idea what it was supposed to spell. The paper might explain, but she found herself a little reluctant to unfold it and read it—almost frightened, though there was no reason for the pounding in her chest. Who was this man Ray? And why had he deserted her?

She laid the necklace on her lap, unfolded the letter, and glanced at the greeting. *Elizabeth*. No one called her Elizabeth. That made the letter even more special in a strange way. Had he called her by her full name when she was a baby? No matter how hard she tried, she couldn't dredge up a memory of the man who had fathered her. Her gut tightened again, and she pressed her lips together. He was dead and gone, unable to hurt her any longer. These were just words on a page. She moved so the porch light shone on the letter and she forced herself to read.

My dear Elizabeth,

So here you are in my home. Finally, you are where I've longed for you to be these past twenty-five years. My biggest regret in life is that I was not part of your formation, but God assures me he has kept you safe under his wings. I have prayed for you every day of your life, and even now as I face my final days, I desperately pray that you will walk with the Lord. I want to fold you in my arms when you step onto heaven's golden streets.

I know there is so much you don't understand. I trust my sister, Pearl, will fill you in on many of the circumstances that forced me to abdicate my responsibilities. Just know that I have loved you so much even when I've been unable to contact you. I hope the inheritance can make up in some small way for my neglect. I know Brent and Vanessa have never really cared for the inn. Somehow, I believe you will love it as I have loved it. Do with it as you will though. It's yours.

Perhaps you are wondering what this old necklace means. My wife made it for me in 1992, and it never left my neck until

I took it off to give to Horace for you. "What Would Jesus Do?" has been the guiding mantra of my life. As you try to acclimatize yourself to the island and to your siblings, I want you to think about those words in all the challenges you face. Every day, I'd like you to jot down when you succeeded in the right responses and when you didn't.

I realize I have no right to ask anything of you. Any rights I might have had were destroyed when I walked away. I make no excuses for my failures. But if you'll wear this necklace and heed its reminder, it would be the greatest of all the possible legacies I might leave you. Much more valuable than the inn and the land.

I pray my God keeps and protects you all the days of your life. That you will walk humbly before him and serve him always. Your siblings will take this very hard, so I ask you to be generous in grace toward them. Extend them as much mercy as you can. The transition into the family will be challenging, and I wish I could be here to help with that. But even though I am absent in the body, I'm rooting for you from heaven. I love you, my dear girl, and always have.

Dad

Libby's face was wet, and she choked back the sobs building in her chest. He'd loved her. All these years when she thought he didn't care, he'd loved her and prayed for her. And had God *really* assured him that he'd kept her safe? She didn't understand any of it. Her father said to talk to her aunt, and tomorrow she would ask Alec to introduce them. Pearl. She liked the name and only hoped she could learn to love this unknown aunt—and even more importantly, that her aunt Pearl would love her.

The jute was rough in her hands. The necklace took on special meaning. Her father had worn it for twenty years. The worn beads had been smoothed by his skin. It was so loved that his fingers had worn off all but one of the letters. But now she knew what they were. *WWJD.*

She lifted it to her neck and fastened it. The beads felt warm, almost alive. She'd become a Christian two years ago, but there was so much about faith that she didn't understand. And she didn't know if she'd ever stopped to consider what a godly response to any tough situation might be. Too often she reacted without thinking. She fingered the beads. What would Jesus do about this place? How was she supposed to know?

EIGHT

Nicole waited in vain for rescue as the wind rose through the afternoon. When the wind had first started to freshen, she was sure someone would be along any minute. But the hurricane was upon her. And she had nowhere to go for safety.

She peered through the single window of the shack. The sea was much too rough for anyone to come now. She was on her own. She opened the door. The sky was downright scary with black clouds blocking the sun. Tossing waves that left her breathless with fear crowded the shack. The flashes of lightning and rolls of thunder were terrifying, but not as frightening as the thought of drowning. If she didn't get higher, she was going to die. The surge was already swirling around her feet. The best she could do with her food and water was put it on the cot, but she feared it would soon be underwater.

She swiped the rivulets of water from her eyes and clung to the door as she stared at the small island. Through the driving storm, she could see a lone palm tree, but the wind had nearly bent it double. No sense in climbing that. More surges of water would be coming through. She had to get on top of the shack. It was her only hope. The sides of the building were rough-sawn boards, but there was a small window ledge that might help her climb. She grabbed hold of the top window frame and hoisted herself up, planting one bare foot on the window ledge. The wind buffeted her back to the ground, and she splashed face-first into the seawater. She came up spitting salt and sand.

Maybe around back she would be protected from the wind enough to climb. Sloshing through the flood, she hurried to the rear. A plastic five-gallon bucket floated in the water. She upended it, then stepped on its bottom and managed to grasp the low roof. As she hauled herself up, the wind hit her again, driving stinging water into her face.

She wasn't going to survive this. Pushing the thought away, she swung one leg onto the roof. She got the other leg up too and lay gasping on the splintered surface with the wind trying to dislodge her. She forced her fingers and toes into every crevice she could find, but it took every bit of strength she possessed to stay atop the shack.

She pressed her face into the shingles and held on. If she fell again, she didn't think she would have the strength to climb, or to survive the night in the water.

———

Tidewater Inn seemed to shrug off the effects of the wind, though the storm howled mightily in rage at the way the inn withstood its power. Libby huddled under an afghan on the armchair in the parlor. Mr. McEwan seemed oblivious to the danger as he sat drinking his coffee and eating Delilah's fresh-baked cookies. The roar outside made her shudder. Where was Nicole in all this? Libby could only hope and pray she was all right.

Delilah flipped off the television. "The rain has messed up the satellite signal," she said. "Would you like some cookies, Libby?"

"No thanks."

"I'm always hungry when I'm nervous." Delilah headed toward the kitchen.

Libby rose and paced the Oriental rug that covered the oak

floor. *Please, God, don't let Nicole be in any danger from this storm. Let us find her alive and unharmed.*

A thunderous pounding came on the front door. She rushed to answer it. Alec stumbled in with a deluge of rain and wet, salty wind. Libby caught a glimpse over his shoulder of the stormy sky and ocean. Scary. Alec was supporting a wizened old man. Zach was behind him with an older lady almost as round as she was tall.

Alec slammed the door behind them. "I have two more guests for you. I hope that's still all right."

"Of course. We have plenty of empty rooms. Let me fetch some towels." She raced to the laundry room and grabbed a stack of fluffy towels, then hurried back to the parlor where she helped the elderly couple dry off. A thought flickered through her head. What would taking in people cost her? Could these people afford to pay for the room?

"Alec arrived just in time," the lady said. "But I'm worried about my angels."

Alec put his hand on her shoulder. "I had Zach load them in the back of the SUV."

She patted his hand. "Oh, Alec, did you really? You're a darling young man. Could you bring them in?"

"I'll get them." He glanced at Libby and motioned for her to follow him. At the entry, he stopped and folded his arms across his chest. "The lady is Pearl Chilton. Your aunt."

Her pulse kicked. "My father's sister?"

He nodded. "She's a sweetheart. I think you'll love her."

He was still staring at her with a wary expression. "Did you tell her I was here?" she asked.

He shook his head. "I thought I'd leave that up to you."

"Who's the older gentleman? I thought they were married."

"Her neighbor, Thomas Carter. Their houses were both flooded. He was at her house when I got there. Pearl still works as the town postmistress. She's done that for thirty years."

"She's been looking in on my brother and sister since my father died, correct?"

He nodded. "She should have been at your dad's house in town, but she was at her cottage trying to get her angels."

"Angels?"

"Collectible angels. The living room is stuffed with them."

"I can help you bring them in."

"I can handle it. I'll be back in a few minutes." He opened the door and stepped into the driving rain.

Thunder boomed overhead, and Libby shut her eyes against the brilliant flash of lightning. She slammed the door, then took a deep breath and went back to the parlor. Pearl had taken her long hair out of its bun, and the salt-and-pepper tresses lay drying on her shoulders and down onto her huge bosom. Barely five feet tall, she was round as an egg except for the shapely legs revealed by her skirt.

Pearl seemed to realize Libby was staring at her. "Is something wrong, young lady? I have a smudge on my nose?"

Family. She had an aunt, siblings, probably cousins here. Libby couldn't take it all in. If only she knew Nicole was all right, the moment would be perfect.

She shook her head. "I . . . I'm sorry for staring." She walked nearer to the fireplace where Pearl sat combing out her hair. "I'm Libby. Libby Holladay."

Pearl put the comb down. Her gaze searched Libby's face as she heaved herself out of the chair. "Ray's Libby?"

Libby's throat locked, and she nodded.

"Oh, my dear," Pearl said softly. She held out her arms.

Libby leaned forward and was enfolded in soft arms and an immense hug that smelled of lavender and mint. It was all she could do not to break down. Had her father ever held her like this? Once the fervency of Pearl's embrace lessened, Libby pulled away and swiped the back of her hand across her damp eyes.

Pearl's faded green eyes studied Libby's face. "I see your father in you," she said. "You have his dark eyes. I wish he were still alive to see you. Not raising you was his greatest sorrow in life."

Libby couldn't stop the tears that welled then. "I never knew he cared," she choked out. "My mother said he didn't."

Pearl pressed her lips together. "I don't like to speak ill of anyone, but your mother was determined to be free."

Libby sank onto the rug by Pearl's feet and struggled to keep her expression neutral. Just listening didn't mean she was betraying her mother's memory. There were two sides to every story.

Pearl settled back on the chair. Clasping her knees to her chest, Libby watched her aunt's face in the firelight. "What was he like, my father?"

Pearl smiled. "Generous as the day is long. He was always helping other people. I think that's why God blessed him so with material things. He knew Ray would let them run through his hands to other people."

"I—I hear my siblings are not too pleased to learn about me."

Pearl's lips flattened. "Oh, they always knew about you. Ray never made a secret of it. He spoiled them too much though, and they think the world owes them a living. This will be good for them."

Libby's growing impression of her siblings wasn't flattering. How long before she met them? The wind rattled the door. Did her aunt realize that Nicole was her friend? "I'm here to find my business partner, Nicole."

Pearl gasped. "The girl who was taken—she's your friend?"

The compassion in her aunt's voice nearly broke Libby's composure. She nodded and swallowed hard. "I saw them take her on the beach cam."

"Oh, my dear girl." Her aunt leaned over and hugged her again. "I've been praying for that young woman. Somehow, I think she's all right."

"You do?"

Pearl nodded. "When I pray, I have a sense of peace. You're going to find her."

"I hope so. It's so scary."

Pearl pursed her lips. "What about your mother? Where is she now?"

Libby shook her head. "She's gone. She died a year ago."

Pearl's lips flattened. "She was always a bit of a hippie. I imagine you took care of her—made sure she ate and took care of the house. You have that competent air about you."

Her aunt was perceptive. Libby nodded. "Mom always had a childlike way about her, but she was a good mother. Our house was always fun." *Until it was time to move on to the next town.* "I got a job in a museum when I was sixteen. That's where I learned to love history. I got a scholarship to college and got to follow my dream."

"What are you doing these days?"

"Nicole and I restore historic houses, then sell them. I love preserving part of the past."

Pearl stared at her. "Your father would have been proud of you. I wish he'd gotten to meet you."

Libby was forming a picture of her father that was very different from all she'd been told. But which was right?

NINE

The wind howled and Libby paced through the night. With every rattle of the storm against the windowpane in her bedroom, she prayed for Nicole, then for herself and the siblings she had yet to meet. Where was Nicole riding out the storm? Was she hurt? Would her siblings like her when they got to know her? The questions battered her.

The clock said it should be daybreak, but the black clouds outside blocked the sunrise. She might as well get up. The bedroom door creaked when she opened it, but she doubted the sound would carry above the pounding of the rain against the house. She slipped down the hall to the back stairway that led down to the kitchen. The house shuddered, and she grabbed the doorjamb, then felt along the wall for the switch. The bulb in the stairwell was dim, but its comforting glow lit the rubber-covered stairs.

In the kitchen she fixed some tea, then carried the hot mug to the parlor, where she curled on the sofa with just one light on to push back the dark. The storm still raged outside, but she felt safe and snug surrounded by the possessions of her father.

A shadow loomed in the hall, then Alec spoke her name. "You okay?"

She set her tea on the coffee table. "Did I wake you?"

He shook his head and stepped into the room. "I wasn't sleeping. You had the same idea as me." He held up a Pepsi. "Only mine was easier."

Once he was settled into the armchair, she leaned her head back against the sofa. "I know you're wondering if I did something to Nicole," she said. "I didn't."

"I didn't say you did."

"Your cousin thinks I did. And you're acting differently now. Wary."

He took a gulp of his soda. "You have to admit it looks bad."

"I agree." She held his gaze. At least he wasn't afraid to look at her. "I care about Nicole. That's why I'm here. Will you give me the benefit of the doubt?"

"Okay, I can do that much."

She exhaled when his expression went from cold to lukewarm. "Good." Better to move on to another topic. "I like Pearl."

He wiped the moisture from the soda can. "I knew you would. She's an institution in town. Everyone loves her, even though she knows everyone else's business."

"I noticed that. She already knew my life story."

"She won't repeat it either."

"I didn't think she would." Libby paused, uncertain how much he knew. "She said my mother was adamant about no contact. My father didn't want it that way."

"I'm sure that's true. Ray loved his kids. Sometimes to a fault."

"Did he ever speak of me?" She held her breath, hoping to hear some small snippet of her father's love for her.

He shook his head. "Not to me."

Libby picked up an enameled egg from the table and rolled it in her palms. "According to Pearl, my siblings knew about me. She said my father made no secret of my existence."

"Pearl would know."

She put down the egg and pressed her hand against her forehead. "So much coming at me so fast. I just want to find Nicole, but there's all this other information clamoring to be absorbed. I can't even think."

"You saw the cam late in the afternoon?"

She nodded. "I came right away, but I couldn't find a boat to bring me across the sound until yesterday morning."

"What did you do all night?"

"I sat on the pier. I paced the dock and prayed."

He smiled. "So you're a believer too."

She glanced at him, surprised at the approval in his voice. "Not a very good one. I make it to church about once a month. Maybe that's why this has happened. God is punishing me."

"Forget that idea. Bad things happen even to good people. Life is hard. God never said it wouldn't be. And he's with us in the hard times."

"I feel very alone," she admitted.

"I know Tom will do all he can to find her."

"I might believe that if he will look somewhere other than at me." She finally spoke her greatest fear. "What if they dumped her at sea and she's fighting the waves out there?" He didn't have to answer that. If that was Nicole's fate, she'd be dead by now.

"There's no reason to think that."

She stared at him, caught by a certain tone in his voice. Almost a hesitancy. "Do you know something you're not telling me?"

There was a long silence before he spoke. "Mr. McEwan said he saw two men go past his little island in a boat. He mentioned a sleeping woman."

She sprang to her feet. "Nicole! Did he see Nicole?"

He held up his hand. "We don't know that. I'm going to take a run out there in my boat though. Once the storm subsides."

"Can I come?"

"If you like."

She bit her lip. "Everyone thinks she's dead. I can sense it. I just can't believe that. We have to find her." She willed him to agree with her, but he looked down at his hands.

He rose from the armchair. "I think I'll call into the office and see if I'm needed."

It was clear that he thought Nicole was dead.

———

The storm had finally died. Though it was still early, Libby took her mug of tea to the porch. The jute necklace was warm at her neck. She touched it, then opened the notebook her father left. What would Jesus have done yesterday? She grimaced when she realized money had been her first thought when Alec brought in people escaping the storm. Jesus would have been concerned about people, not money. She wrote down yesterday's date and jotted down how she'd failed. Today she would try to do better. She closed the notebook and tucked it into the cloth bag at her feet, then went down the steps to the beach.

Debris littered the lawn, but the old house had withstood the blow like the proud matriarch she was. Libby studied the stately lines of the house. It was so beautiful. Someone would pay handsomely to own this. She walked down the sloping sand. The boardwalk and cam where Nicole had been taken were about a mile down the beach. This stretch of sand seemed to go on forever. Did she dare walk along the shore alone?

Then a figure caught her eye. A man strode along the beach with a clipboard in his hand. Strikingly handsome, he had almost-black hair and broad shoulders. Muscular legs extended from walking shorts. As he neared, she realized his eyes were a vivid blue. He put her in mind of a young Elvis Presley. The breeze lifted his dark hair from his forehead.

She lifted a smile in the man's direction when she saw him looking at the inn and writing in his notebook. "Can I help you?"

He smiled and stopped about four feet from her. "I'm looking over the property for a client who is going to buy it."

Her hackles went up. "Oh? I think you should make sure the owner wants to sell it."

"Oh, it's a done deal," he assured her. "Are you a guest?"

"No, I'm Libby Holladay. The owner."

His smile vanished. "That's not possible. Mr. Brent Mitchell agreed to sell it to me." His eyes narrowed. "What kind of scam is this?"

The proprietary way she felt about the house already was a shock. This was *her* house. "He was unaware until recently that I inherited the house, not him."

He smiled, an obvious attempt to regain his composure. "Then I will direct my client's interest to you." He held out a card. "I'm Kenneth Poe. I have a client who would like to purchase this property."

She couldn't afford to reject his offer. "Why does your client want the property? It's not really a moneymaking venture at the moment. Tourists have to rent a boat to get here. I had a hard time getting here myself." She decided not to tell him about Nicole's disappearance. It was none of his business.

He shifted his clipboard to the other hand. "I'm sure you see that the place is a monstrosity. It's going to take a lot of money to fix it up. Better just to tear it down."

She gasped. "Tear it down? You have to be joking."

He held up his hand. "Look at the place. Rotting wood, peeling paint, outdated rooms and baths. It would be cheaper to bulldoze it and start over."

"The mansion should be on the historic registry. It will be if I have my way. I've spent my life protecting historic property. I'd die before I saw this place bulldozed."

His smile was entirely too smug. "Come now, Ms. Holladay. I think we can persuade you. My client is willing to pay you ten million dollars for this property."

The blood drained from her head, and she felt dizzy. *Ten million dollars.* The amount was outside her comprehension. She could buy a house outright, two houses, one for her and one for her stepbrother, here in town if she wanted. She could get a new car before her old clunker died for good. The future stretched out in an enticing way. But to follow that path, she would have to sacrifice an important piece of history. Could she turn her back on her convictions?

She wetted her lips. "I'll think about it."

"You do that. I think you'll see it our way. And my client might be persuaded to give you other incentives, such as a parcel elsewhere to build your own place. I'm sure we can come to an agreement. He's very eager to have this property."

Hope Beach would be just like the rest of the beach towns. There wouldn't be anything unique about this little bit of paradise any longer. Libby couldn't bear the thought, but she couldn't afford to reject it out of hand either. Any other investor would have the same idea, and this one seemed eager to move now.

"Like I said, I'll think about it."

"The offer won't be extended for long. If you don't wish to sell, he'll go after something else. I'd advise you to accept his offer before he loses interest. There are other properties he can purchase."

She bit her lip. "Could I meet with him? See what his plans are?"

Poe shook his head. "I doubt he'd have the time. He would tell me to say take it or leave it."

"I'll let you know next week," she said.

She watched him walk away and chewed her lip. What should she do? That was a lot of money.

What would Jesus do?

TEN

The expansive lawn had been meticulously groomed. The flower beds were in perfect condition for the garden party, and Lawrence smiled with satisfaction. His wife wouldn't be able to complain that he hadn't taken care of his duties as a host.

"How do I look, Daddy?" Katelyn twirled in a gauzy white dress.

His daughter might not be the most beautiful young woman he'd ever seen, but she was elegant and well bred. With her by his side, Poe could go far. Someone needed to be groomed to take over the Rooney businesses. Poe was the first man to come along who Lawrence felt might fill the ticket.

"Like a princess," Lawrence said, kissing her cheek. "There's someone I want you to meet today."

A dimple appeared in her cheek. "Your amazing Kenneth Poe?" she said. "I saw a picture. He's quite handsome."

When she blushed, Katelyn was downright pretty. Lawrence hoped Poe could see her attractions. "There he is now," Lawrence said, waving to Poe, who stood at the edge of the lawn looking around.

"Oh my," Katelyn said. "H-He's like Elvis."

Like Elvis. Lawrence hid his amusement. The girl was already halfway in love. Poe acknowledged the wave with an answering smile and strode across the green carpet of grass with a confident air. Lawrence liked arrogance in a man. Poe had the strength to tame Katelyn. And he'd dressed nicely for the occasion. The suit he wore was an Armani, if Lawrence was any judge—and he was. Poe's tie was silk, and he'd had a fresh haircut.

Lawrence put his arm around his daughter as Poe reached them. "You just flew in, Kenneth?"

He nodded. "My chopper landed an hour ago."

Lawrence put his arm around Katelyn. "Kenneth, my boy, I'd like to introduce you to Katelyn. My one and only heir." He put the emphasis on the last word.

Poe took her hand. "I'm honored to meet you, Ms. Rooney."

"Call her Katelyn," Lawrence ordered.

He noted the way Poe kept control of her hand for a little longer than necessary. The boy wouldn't let any grass grow under his feet. Poe kept his attention on Katelyn too. Smart. They chatted for several minutes, and Lawrence saw how Katelyn flirted. She liked him. And why not? Poe was certainly handsome enough. Their children would be good-looking too. And with any kind of luck, they would possess Lawrence's business acumen.

His wife called to Katelyn over by the food table. "I'll be right back," Katelyn said with a lingering glance at Poe.

Poe watched her leave. "Your daughter is lovely."

Lawrence put his hand on Poe's shoulder. "Feel free to call on her. I'd like nothing more than to have you for a son, my boy."

Poe's eyes widened and he smiled. "I'm honored, sir. Do you think your daughter would be agreeable?"

"I'm sure you could persuade her."

Poe's smile widened and his blue eyes were bright. "I'd like nothing better." He glanced toward where Katelyn stood talking to guests. "Before she comes back, I have some news to report."

"Oh?"

"The property is owned by someone other than Brent Mitchell."

Lawrence shrugged. "Shouldn't be a problem, should it? Offer the same deal to the real owners."

"I did. She was reluctant at first, but I think I can persuade her. It just may take a few weeks until I have her signed contract. The wrinkle is that Nicole Ingram is her business partner and friend."

"Nicole Ingram? That's no problem. She's in my employ."

For the first time, Poe appeared uncertain. "You know her?"

"She's part of the firm I hired to renovate some buildings. You know all about that."

"I know the firm's name. I didn't know the employees."

"What is this about?"

"She's the woman who found the cave."

It wasn't often that Lawrence was unable to speak. "What did you do with her?" Lawrence held up his hand. "Never mind. I don't want to know. This is getting more and more complicated. Just get the property signed and delivered. I want to break ground by the end of the summer."

Poe nodded. "My thoughts exactly. The thought of ten million dollars was quite an enticement to the owner."

"Just get it done," Lawrence snapped. He nodded toward his daughter, who was approaching with a smile. "You'll be part of my family soon if you get this deal settled."

Emotion flickered in Poe's eyes and his jaw hardened. "I'll do that, sir. You won't be sorry you trusted me with this."

Lawrence's good mood had evaporated. The property would be his no matter what he had to do.

———

The winds died by early afternoon. Alec stood surveying the storm damage in the heart of Hope Beach. Libby had insisted on coming with him and Zach when the sheriff called about all the damage. Alec thought she was afraid Nicole's body was going to be discovered floating in the debris, but he prayed she wouldn't be assaulted with such a sight.

At the first glimpse of his house, he thought it had been spared. Then he drove closer, and water sloshed to the top of the truck tires. "I'm flooded," he said, unable to keep the dismay from his voice.

Zach pointed. "Both boats look to be all right though. They're both still attached to their moorings. Listen, can I take out the old boat?"

"The sea is still too rough," Alec said.

Libby grimaced. "It looks like the entire town is a mess." She was staring out the window at the still-turbulent water. "There's no sign o-of Nicole, is there?" Her voice quivered.

He reached over and squeezed her hand. "Tom would have told us if there was." He released her hand and stared at his house. "Guess I'd better see how bad it is inside. You can wait in the truck if you like."

"I'll come." She shoved open her door and stepped into the water.

He took her arm when they reached the front of the truck. He waved at some of his Coastie buddies, who were down the street carrying belongings from a house. The water filled his boots, and he shivered as the cold soaked his jeans. The flood covered Libby's flip-flops and reached nearly to her knees. His spirits sank lower as he pushed open the door and saw the flooded living room. "Gonna be a lot of damage," he said.

"There's plenty of room at the hotel," she said. "Let's gather some things. I'll help."

"It won't take long. You can wait here." Alec went into his bedroom and pulled some jeans and T-shirts off hangers, then scooped up underwear from the bureau. In the bathroom he grabbed toiletries, then met Libby in the hall again. "Let's toss this stuff in the truck and check on the rest of the town."

She nodded and followed him back outside. People were assessing the damage along Oyster Road. He wondered if she knew which house had been her father's. Taking her arm, he pointed down the street. "Your father lived there."

She stared at the two-story house and he tried to look at it through her eyes. Ray had always kept it in top repair, but it was in sorry shape now. The storm surge still lapped a foot up the gray clapboard siding. The sea had deposited debris around the porch and the yard swing. The wind had torn some shingles loose, and they flapped in the last of the wind.

"Aunt Pearl said Vanessa was at a friend's, but is that her?" She pointed down the street.

He followed her finger. "Yeah, that's Vanessa. How did you know?"

"She looks a lot like me."

He glanced at her. Same high cheekbones, same expressive dark eyes. They wore their hair differently, and Vanessa always covered her face with a ton of makeup. Libby was much more natural. "Guess you're right. You want to meet her?"

She shook her head, but about that time Vanessa caught sight of him. "Alec!" She waved to him and sloshed through the water toward them. She was dressed in shorts and a red tank top. The tips of her short hair were purple.

"Sorry," he said. "Should I introduce you?"

"I—I don't quite know what to say. Give me a minute." Libby sounded breathless.

Vanessa reached them. "Is Aunt Pearl all right? I heard you rescued her last night." She gave Libby a curious glance, then her gaze went back to him.

"She's fine. Where did you ride out the blow?"

"At the church. Brent too. He's there now helping clean up. It's a mess."

"Looks like your house is hit pretty hard too."

She shrugged. "I figured we'd join Aunt Pearl at the hotel. At least it's still ours until the dragon lady comes to claim it." She blew her bangs out of her eyes. "I still can't believe Dad would give our property to some daughter who has ignored him all these years. I want to be out of town when she comes. I want nothing to do with her. Ever."

He tried to interrupt her fierce flow of words, but she barreled over him.

"It's a good thing my *sister* wasn't in residence yesterday, or Aunt Pearl would have been out on the streets."

He could see Libby take a step back. "Uh, Vanessa, there's something you should know."

Libby put her hand on his arm and shot him a pleading glance. He closed his mouth.

Vanessa's face took on a rosy hue, and her voice rose with every word. "I can just see her arriving and trying to lord it over us. I'm going to put her in her place the very first thing. She didn't know Daddy. *She* certainly didn't love him, or she would have come to visit. I hope she just sells the place and stays away. No one here wants to meet her."

"She might not be so bad," he said.

Vanessa's brows arched. "You think the best of everyone, Alec. I'm sure she's some money-grubbing landlubber who doesn't know the first thing about island living. I hope she realizes that and doesn't bother us any longer than necessary. When we hear she's coming, I think I'll take a vacation."

Libby's face was getting pinker and pinker. Alec didn't think she'd take much more before she blew.

ELEVEN

As Libby listened to her newfound sister rant, her emotions veered between anger and hurt. Why had she thought her new family would be as happy to meet her as she was to meet them? Her aunt Pearl had been welcoming, but Libby was an outsider in this small community.

Vanessa's diatribe finally ended. She turned her attention from Alec and stared at Libby. "I feel like I should know you. Have we met? I'm Vanessa Mitchell."

Libby forced a pleasant smile to her face. "I think I seem familiar because we look alike. And we should. I'm your sister, Libby Holladay."

Vanessa went white. Her mouth opened but only a garbled word came out. Red washed up her face, and she closed her mouth before finally opening it with the strangled statement of "Half sister." Her mouth looked like she'd just bitten into a bad oyster.

"I don't blame you for being upset," Libby said. "Please understand though. I had no idea my father was living. My mother told me he died when I was five."

Vanessa's eyes narrowed, but there was a flicker of uncertainty in them. "I find that difficult to believe."

"It's true. I . . . . I wish I'd known him." She held her hand toward Vanessa. "You can't imagine how thrilled I was to find out I have a large family. It's something I've always longed for."

"No cousins or other family?"

Libby shook her head. "My mother never talked much about my father. All she ever said was that he died when I was five, and it was good riddance as far as she was concerned."

Vanessa glared. "Daddy was a wonderful man!"

"So I've heard since I got here to try to find Nicole."

"Nicole?" Vanessa glanced toward the water, then back. "The woman who was kidnapped? You know her?"

"Yes. We're in business together."

Vanessa's glare was still wary. "I met Nicole. I was sorry to hear about what happened to her."

"She told me about you. I was watching on the beach cam to catch a glimpse of you. I saw her taken."

"That must have been hard," Vanessa said, her voice warming for the first time. "I was going to meet her and show her the old lighthouse ruins. I got held up. When I got there, she was gone. I liked her a lot."

"Please don't talk like she's dead," Libby said, tears starting to her eyes. "She's not dead. She's *not!*"

Vanessa bit her lip. "I didn't mean to say she was. I hope you find her."

Alec put his hand on Libby's shoulder. "Don't give up hope," he said.

"I will *never* give up," she said. "She's not going to be another woman who disappears without a trace from an island." The thought of never knowing what had happened to Nicole haunted her.

"Maybe you should contact the media," Vanessa said. "They can get word out. Someone might have seen something."

"That's a good idea," Alec said. "I know a guy who works for the Richmond newspaper. I'm sure I could get him out here."

Libby recoiled at the thought. "Nicole would hate to be the

center of a media circus." But would she, really? She'd probably revel in the attention.

Alec nodded. "But if the coverage could help find her . . ."

"We're going to find her soon. I know it." But even as she proclaimed her belief, Libby's pulse skipped. "Maybe you're right," she said, her shoulders sagging. "Make the call."

Alec squeezed her shoulder, then dropped his hand back to his side. "Want us to help you gather some things, Vanessa? We're going back to Tidewater in a little while. Let me call my friend first, then we'll help you."

Libby forced a smile to her face. "I'd like you to come to the inn too. I'm eager to get to know you."

Vanessa's stormy eyes revealed how torn she was. Libby knew the woman wished she could throw the invitation back, but if she did, she'd have nowhere to stay. Pearl's house was damaged as well. It only made sense to join the rest of her family.

"What about Brent?" Vanessa asked. "Is there room for both of us?"

"Of course," Libby said.

"We can stop by and introduce him to Libby too," Alec said. "I need to talk to Zach. I'll be right back."

Libby's stomach plunged at the thought. Zach had already mentioned how upset Brent was about the news that she had inherited.

Vanessa shot a glance Libby's way. "He's not going to be welcoming, just FYI."

Libby kept her smile pinned in place. A soft answer turned away wrath. She had to remember that. "I understand you are both dismayed to find out that you have a sister. I'm not going to push you. I hope you find that I'm not such a bad sister to have."

Vanessa shrugged. "Whatever. Don't say I didn't warn you. He's liable to go off on you. That's all I've heard since Horace gave us the news. Brent had plans for that property."

"I've heard that too. What kind of plans?" Libby asked.

"What difference does it make now? Unless you plan to split it with us?" Hope tinged her words.

"Horace told me our father left you both plenty of money," Libby said, refusing to be goaded.

"But the property you have is what Brent needs." Vanessa turned and squinted. "Here he comes now. He must be done at the church."

Libby turned to look and saw a young man jogging toward them. He wore denim shorts low and loose around his waist in the style she hated. His blond hair fell across his forehead, and his expression was sulky. She wanted to love this new family, but they were making it difficult.

Nicole's muscles were cramped from the night on the roof. The hurricane had blown itself out hours ago, but she remained atop the roof. The surge had covered the island, and the water was still a couple of feet deep. The shack was off its foundation, and she feared it was going to float off to sea with her on top of it. The table and chair from inside bobbed in the flood below. Her cot with her food and water also floated in the debris under her feet.

Her eyes burned, and she told herself not to cry. Someone would be along. Surely someone would come. That boy knew she was out here. Nicole would give anything to be in her own tiny room, to look out and see the tired houses across the street, to hear the traffic that she hated. She would never complain again if she got the chance to be home.

The sun was getting hot on the back of Nicole's neck, and her thirst was mounting. She was going to have to get down off this building and see if seawater had leaked into her jug. Staring at the brown swirling water, her courage ebbed. Who knew what was below that roiling surface? Poisonous snakes or spiders came to mind. Hugging her knees to her chest, she tried to talk herself down into the water. There were no snakes out here. Nothing that could hurt her. Though logically she knew that, she didn't want to test it. What if the storm had washed all manner of nasty creatures onto the island?

She licked her cracked lips. Dehydration would kill her if she didn't get down. There was no sense in staying up here out of fear. She rolled onto her stomach and scooted down until her legs hung off the edge of the roof. The plastic bucket was long gone. All she could do was lower herself as far as she could, take a deep breath, then let go.

Her bare feet splashed into cold water. The seawater rushed to enclose her legs up to her thighs. She forced herself not to look down into the swirling water as she slogged through it to her cot. She seized the jug of water. Still full. Hefting it to the light, she examined the cap. Tight. She exhaled with relief, then unscrewed the top and took a swig of water.

The moisture on her tongue revived her. She replaced the cap, then grabbed the cot and dragged it toward the shack. The door was cockeyed now and hung open. Practically swimming, she tugged the cot into the building and glanced around for some way to secure it. There was nothing, so she left it floating there in the water and grabbed her provisions. She would stay on the roof until the water receded.

TWELVE

When Alec crossed the street, Zach was sitting in the truck, thumping his hand on his leg in time with the blaring country music. He was oblivious to Alec's approach and jumped when his uncle touched his shoulder.

Zach bolted upright and turned down the radio. "I was about to go looking for you."

"Something wrong?"

Zach chewed on his lip. "I wanted to ask to take the boat out. I know you said no earlier, but the waves aren't all that bad. I have that job."

Alec lifted a brow. "It's still pretty rough out there, Zach. And it's getting late."

"I've been out in worse. In the dark too."

"True. Are the supplies that urgent?"

Zach's gaze cut away. "I need the money. And they're depending on me."

Alec fished in his pocket for the keys to the boat and handed them over. "Okay. Be careful. Wear your life vest."

Zach's smile was big as he jumped from the truck and jogged through the standing water to the pier. The sea had calmed considerably since they arrived. The flood from the storm surge had gone down a bit too. Now the water barely covered the tops of Alec's boots. But recovery was going to take awhile.

Alec opened the door of his truck and slid inside to make his call.

Earl Franklin answered after two rings. "I was going to call you, Alec," he said, wasting no time with a greeting. "How's it look out there?"

"Rough. Storm surge did more damage than you'd expect from a cat-1. Most of the houses in town have sustained considerable damage."

"Sorry to hear that."

Alec could hear the speculation in Earl's voice. The reporter was probably already planning a feature. "Listen, there's a bigger story here. I think you need to get over to the island as soon as possible."

"What's up?"

"A young woman was kidnapped right off the beach. Her friend was watching via one of the beach cams. So far we've found no sign of her."

"I heard about that. After we left town, I realized we'd given the woman's friend a ride to the island. Tom called to ask me about her."

"I thought you might want to do an article about the abduction, get some publicity rolling. It might help the case."

"You think the Holladay woman killed her and made up the story?"

"Why would you say something like that?"

"She didn't say a word about her friend's kidnapping to us. Seems suspicious."

Alec opened his mouth, then shut it again. He didn't have a good answer to that other than a gut feeling. His fingers curled into the palms of his hands. Surely the crime couldn't be a hoax. But no, Nicole's car was there at the beach. And her cell phone. It would show that a call had been connected to Libby's phone for several minutes.

Unless she had an accomplice.

"Alec? You there?"

"I'm here. All I can tell you is that we're investigating the kidnapping. If you give the case some attention, maybe someone will come forward with information."

"One way or another," Earl said, his voice deep with satisfaction, "it will be all over the national news. Maybe international. I'll head out there as soon as I can. Any chance you can come after me? My sailboat is being repaired. I heard quite a few charter boats were damaged. I might have trouble getting someone to bring me."

"Things are a mess here, and I need to work. If you don't find a charter, call me back and I'll have Zach fetch you after he delivers some supplies."

"Okay, I'll see what I can do first." Earl hesitated and didn't hang up. "Keep an eye on the friend, Alec."

"I will," Alec said. He ended the call. Libby couldn't be guilty of something like that. She was genuinely devastated by her friend's disappearance.

Maybe the hurricane had exposed new leads for Tom. Alec got out of the truck and headed toward the sheriff's office. His cousin was likely to be out helping the townspeople, but his receptionist would know where he was. He spotted Tom's SUV driving slowly away from the church and waved.

Tom stopped the vehicle beside him. The window came down, and he peered up at Alec. "Something wrong?"

Alec leaned on the side of the vehicle. "I got hold of Earl Franklin. He's coming out to do a piece on Nicole Ingram."

Tom uttered an expletive, and a frown wiped away his smile. "What'd you go and do that for? It will be a media circus. I was careful not to give him any information when I talked to him."

"Every hour that passes puts Nicole in more jeopardy, and you know it." He stared at the sheriff. "Listen, I have a question. Earl said something that got my attention. He seems to think Libby might be involved because she's close to Nicole. You don't suspect her anymore, do you?"

Tom shrugged. "Most homicides are crimes of passion. The murderer is usually someone known to the victim. And we still haven't seen the video of the kidnapping. The tech guy I hired can't find even a piece of that video. All we've got is what Libby told us."

"Well, you found Nicole's phone and car."

Tom nodded. "That's the only reason we're treating it as a real kidnapping." He stared at Alec. "You're in the perfect position to keep your eye on Libby. See if you notice anything suspicious."

"I don't believe she did anything to her friend."

"Well, you can be alert, can't you?"

"I guess so." Alec looked down the road, then back to his cousin. "Did you trace the call between the women?"

"Sure. It lasted four minutes. The only prints on the phone we found at the beach were Nicole's." Tom scowled again. "I wish you'd asked me before you called in the media. I've got enough on my plate with the hurricane damage."

"Sorry."

"I'm sending out a sketch artist to see if she remembers any details about the two men she saw. Let her know they're coming, will you?"

"Sure." Alec stepped back so his cousin could drive on. He watched the SUV's taillights come on, then wink out as Tom rounded the corner toward a group of people picking up the pieces that used to be the town library.

Could she be guilty of something unthinkable? He hoped not. Libby was the first woman who had intrigued him.

Libby's heart stuttered in her chest. She'd always wanted a brother, but Brent was not quite what she had in mind. He stared at her, then at his sister, as if he sensed the tension between them. Libby smiled at him, but he didn't return it.

"Hey, sis," he said to Vanessa. "You about ready to go out to the hotel?"

Vanessa sent her brother a warning glance. "I'd better introduce you, Brent. This is Libby. Dad's *other* daughter, Libby." She pressed her lips together as if the admission had pained her.

Brent took a step back. His glare pierced Libby, but she kept smiling in spite of the way her chest contracted. "I've been looking forward to meeting you, Brent." She held out her hand, but when he ignored it, she dropped it back to her side.

His gaze swept over her. "You look a lot like Vanessa."

His tone wasn't as hostile as his expression. Not yet anyway. Libby smiled. "I can see that. Vanessa is beautiful, so I take that as a compliment." Her statement didn't change Vanessa's scowl. "We must take after our father. You look more like your mother?"

He shrugged. "Are you staying at the hotel?"

"Yes."

"That woman who was kidnapped two days ago, Nicole? Libby is her business partner," Vanessa said.

His eyes widened. "I talked to her at the ice-cream shop. She didn't say anything about being connected to you. She just said she was looking to restore some of the downtown area for a client. And she asked about Tidewater Inn."

"You told her how disgusted you were about me inheriting, right? That's okay. I know it must have been a shock. I was surprised as well."

He frowned and crossed his arms over his chest. "Dad never mentioned that he was going to do this. So yeah, I was surprised."

"So you wanted to sell the land?" Libby asked.

"Sure. The inn doesn't even turn a profit."

"It doesn't matter now. It's not yours," Vanessa said. "Libby says her mom told her Daddy died when she was five."

"You never saw Dad all these years?" he asked.

"Not that I remember. I'm eager to hear more about him." She tried another smile on him. "I've always wanted a brother."

His eyes flickered. "This is a lot to take in."

He wasn't welcoming her with open arms yet, but she could live with guarded cordiality. "It's a lot for me too. Can I help you grab belongings from the house?"

He shrugged. "If you want." He pointed to the house just down the street. "We live there."

She followed him and Vanessa toward the large two-story, eager to see more than the cursory glance she'd had earlier. The shingle home had been allowed to go gray with the salt. It was newer than the hotel, built in the twenties. The home had been well taken care of and featured an expansive yard that had probably once been meticulously tended, but the floodwaters had left debris everywhere, and some of the shingles were missing. The shrubs and flowers would likely be dead by this time next week, killed by the seawater.

Brent held the door open. "It's a mess. The first floor was flooded. Bedrooms are upstairs."

They trooped through the small entry to the living room. The floor was still damp, and Libby feared the dark floors would warp soon. They were expensive teak, she guessed. One wall had a built-in oak bookcase filled with books. Libby winced to see how waterlogged the books on the bottom shelf were. She longed to examine the books and discover her father's reading tastes. The tables held a few pictures.

She picked up one of a man and a woman standing under a tree. The man had dark-brown eyes and light-brown hair like hers. She liked his open face and contented smile. The woman was lovely with nearly black hair and deep blue eyes. "Our father?" she asked.

Vanessa took the picture from her. "And our mother." Her tone told Libby she didn't want to answer any questions.

Libby wanted to linger and look, but Brent went on through to the stairway, so she had no choice but to follow him up. There were four bedrooms on the second floor, and she started toward the back one.

"That's Daddy's room. You can't go in there," Vanessa said.

Libby stopped with her hand on the doorknob. "I'd love just a peek. I want to know more about him."

Vanessa set her jaw. "Not today. My room is here." It was as if she was willing to expose herself to prevent Libby from invading their father's space.

Not hiding her reluctance, Libby turned and went into her sister's room. The scent of perfume hit her when she entered. Something so strong and flowery that it made her sneeze. Vanessa was feverishly pulling shorts and tops from a bureau and tossing them onto the queen-size bed. The room's polished floors matched the downstairs wood.

"Love the floors," she said. She grabbed a suitcase from the shelf and began packing it.

Vanessa didn't look up. "Thanks." She went to the attached bathroom, then returned moments later with an electric toothbrush and toiletries. She dumped them on top of the clothes in the suitcase. With her hands on her hips, she stared at Libby. "What do you expect from us anyway? That we're all going to be a big happy family now that you've arrived? Forget it! You're not my big sister. You're not anything to me. I don't know you and I don't want to know you."

Libby dropped the top she'd been folding. *Be generous with grace.* "I want to know my family," she said. "Is that so hard to understand?"

"The family has to want to know you too. You can't just force your way in here and expect us to fall on your neck."

Libby rubbed her forehead. "I'm sorry if I've been presumptuous, Vanessa. That wasn't my intention. If I back off, would you agree to trying to be friends?" She held out her hand.

Vanessa stared at Libby's extended fingers and shook her head. "I'm not promising anything. I think the only reason you're here is for the money. There's been ample time to get to know us before now if that's what you really wanted."

Libby dropped her hand to her side and struggled to keep the tears at bay. "I'll see you at the hotel." She turned and plunged through the door and down the stairs to the fresh air outside, free of her sister's vitriol.

She'd tried to honor her father's request, but she'd failed.

THIRTEEN

Every inch of the island was damp and covered with flotsam when Nicole finally descended from the roof. Her face and arms were sunburned from her hours atop the shack, and her tummy rumbled and twisted in its desire for food. She'd eaten half of a peanut butter sandwich, but that was all she'd allowed herself. What if no one came back for days? She would conserve her food and water as much as possible.

Libby had always preached that she should have foresight, but Nicole wasn't sure any kind of wisdom would get her out of this predicament. She kicked a palm frond out of her way and resisted the urge to cry. Tears wouldn't get her rescued. Glancing at the fallen palm fronds, she decided to gather them up. Maybe she could make an outdoor shelter from the sun. She wouldn't be cooped up in the waterlogged shack that smelled of mold and fish.

Once her arms were full of fronds, she deposited them under the palm tree and went back for more. After she'd gathered every frond from the island, she sat down to rest under the tree. The wet ground dampened her shorts almost immediately. Glancing at the water jug, she resisted the urge to drink.

She thought she heard a motor in the distance. Leaping to her feet, she ran to the edge of the water, but at first she saw nothing.

Then in the trough of a wave, she saw a boat carrying one person. Shouting and waving, she jumped up and down. The boat was heading for the island like before, and as it neared, she realized it was the same craft as yesterday. The same young man dropped anchor offshore.

She had to convince him to take her off this cursed island. Standing with her hands at her sides, she waited for him to splash ashore. He carried more supplies, so the pain in her stomach would soon be eased. And fruit! She spied apples and oranges in his arms. She salivated at the thought of their sweet taste.

"You're okay," he said. "I was worried the storm surge would carry you off."

"It would have if I hadn't climbed on top of the building." She couldn't take her eyes off the apples. Pink Lady, her favorite variety. "Can I have an apple?"

"Sure." He handed her one.

She bit into it, relishing the sweet yet tart flavor that flooded her mouth. It was all she could do not to moan at the taste. And while she was eating, she didn't have to talk to her jailer. Though she *needed* to talk to him, needed to convince him to let her go.

Wiping her mouth with the back of her hand, she smiled at him. "Were the seas rough?"

"Not bad. I caught some mullets. You want some?"

"I would love some. But how do we light a fire?"

"I brought a lighter."

She watched him slosh back to the boat and return with a box. Inside she spotted fish, a lighter, a knife, and other food items. If she could get the filleting knife, she'd force him to take her to the mainland.

"We'll need firewood. I should have thought of that," he said.

"I have palm fronds. Will that work?"

"No." He glanced back toward the boat. "I can cook it on board, though. There's a grill in the galley." He squatted and grabbed the knife, then began to clean the fish.

Nicole had never wanted anything as much as she wanted that knife. She wanted to leap on him and wrest it away, but he was muscular and she wouldn't have a chance. Even the lighter would do her no good without firewood to burn. She eyed the palm tree. Unless she could manage to set it on fire where it stood.

He finished cleaning the fish, then put the knife in his back pocket and picked up the fillets. "I'll be right back." As he walked toward the boat, the knife slipped to the sand.

She swooped down on the weapon. The handle felt substantial and deadly in her palm. Turning her back to the boat, she tried a few threatening swoops with it in her hand. Could she even bring herself to hurt him? He seemed to believe she was a danger to some imaginary brother. There was no malice in his treatment of her.

She glanced over her shoulder. He was intent on his task, and she caught a whiff of the fish beginning to cook. How could she get this to go down her way? After he returned to the beach, she could back out to the boat with the knife in front of her. He might be afraid to charge her for fear of getting cut. She would have to turn her attention away to get in the boat. Still, she should manage to get aboard before he could wade through the waves. But what if he boarded in spite of her efforts?

All she could do was try. Swallowing hard, she put the knife behind her back and turned when he approached with the cooked fish. "Smells good," she called.

"I'm not the cook my dad was," he said. "I hope it's done. And it's hot and filling."

"Was? Your dad is dead?"

His lips tightened and he nodded. "He died in a plane crash. He and my mom."

"I'm so sorry."

"Thanks." He set the tray of fish on a rock.

"Where do you live? In Hope Beach?"

He nodded. "With my uncle. He's a Coastie." His tone held pride. "I don't want to live anywhere else. I'm a commercial fisherman, like my dad. At least that's what I want to do, if my uncle will let me." He bent down to slide the fish onto a paper plate.

While he was bending over, she shoved him with her foot, and he toppled onto the sand. In a flash, she was running to the boat.

When her feet hit the water, she turned and brandished the knife. "Stay back!"

He'd gained his feet and already stood only five feet away. "You won't cut me."

"Try me!" She wagged the knife blade at him. "I've been kidnapped, half starved, left to rot during a hurricane, nearly drowned. I'm not someone you want to mess with."

She began to back through the waves toward the boat. He stood watching her with a scowl.

"You are just as crazy as they said," he called. "You don't even know which direction is land."

She stopped. "I'll figure it out."

"You don't have enough gas for exploring."

He was just trying to scare her. She continued to back toward the boat. Her bare foot moved and found nothing under it. The underwater hole made her lose her balance, and she fell back into the water. She came up brandishing the knife and sputtering, but he was already at her side.

He snatched the knife from her hand and grabbed her arm. "I was beginning to wonder about what I'd been told, but you just proved how dangerous you are. You tried to cut me like you did your brother." He dragged her back to the beach and left her there.

Brent and Vanessa were ensconced in rooms across the hall from Libby. After she'd helped to settle them, Alec called her to say a sketch artist was coming. Libby met the artist—a woman—in the parlor and did the best job she could. She could only pray the drawings helped find Nicole.

After the artist left, Libby went to see if she could help Delilah with dinner. The manager had a suite on the second floor and rarely left the property. Libby had the impression that Delilah had been here a long time and was content with her home. Maybe she could get some information out of the woman.

She found Delilah in the kitchen stirring something that smelled amazing. "Is that she-crab soup?"

Delilah smiled. "It is. This is a special recipe with whipping cream and butter. No flour to thicken it either. Want a taste?" Delilah held out a spoonful.

Libby sipped it and closed her eyes as the rich, buttery flavor hit her taste buds. "It's heavenly."

"I thought you'd like it."

"Can I help with anything? We have a lot of people to feed."

Delilah's eyes widened. "Really? You wouldn't mind? I let our cook take the day off to help with cleanup in town."

"I love to cook, actually. I don't get much opportunity since it's just me and Nicole. She's rarely around anyway. It's hard to cook for one." Libby lifted the CD player in her hand. "I need music though. That okay with you?"

"Of course. I sometimes listen to Beethoven."

"This isn't Beethoven." Libby plugged the player in and started the Counting Crows CD. The lyrics to "Big Yellow Taxi" made her pause. *Paved paradise.*

Delilah stared at her. "Is that what you want, Libby? To see this place become one big parking lot?"

Libby's smile faded. "I don't want that to happen any more than you do."

"So what are you going to do?"

"I don't know yet." She pulled the notebook out from under her arm. "Do you have a menu plan for the next week? I assume our guests will be here that long?"

"A few weeks, most of them," Delilah said. "It sounds like Ray's house is pretty bad, so your brother and sister might be here longer, maybe months."

Months. It would be expensive to feed all of them. Libby mentally counted up the residents. Eight. "Are they chipping in for food?"

"Alec was quick to give me some money for him and Zach. I doubt Vanessa and Brent will contribute. They consider the inn home." Delilah's glance held curiosity. "They know who you are, right?"

"They were less than pleased to meet me."

"Don't take it to heart, honey. It's just a shock. Especially to Vanessa. She's always been a daddy's girl, and she's just jealous."

"Jealous? I didn't even know him."

"But he loved you," Delilah said. "Vanessa realizes that. She never wanted to share Ray with anyone, not even her mother. She's been obsessive about him. So much so that Ray had her in counseling when she was fifteen or so. It got a little better, but this has got to send her reeling."

Was their mother anything like her own? Libby had noticed people often chose the same kind of mates when they remarried. "What about their mother?"

Delilah smiled. "Everyone loved Tina. Ray was nuts about her right up to the day she died." She pointed to the refrigerator. "If you want to fix some salad, go right ahead. We're having grilled lobster, soup, and salad tonight."

Libby winced at how much that must cost. "For so many?"

Delilah stirred the soup. "Zach brought me the lobster and crab. I only had to buy veggies for salad. This is a cheap dinner."

"That was nice of him. Most young men wouldn't have thought of that."

"Alec's brother raised him right. Most folks in Hope Beach look out for one another. Zach's a little troubled right now, but he'll be all right. He's basically a good boy. Trying to find his place in the world."

Libby almost asked about the intriguing Coast Guard captain, but she didn't want to reveal her interest to Delilah. It was much safer to talk about her family.

"How long have you worked here?" She put the salad ingredients on the butcher block in the middle of the kitchen and found a chopping knife.

"Fifteen years. I came here when I was eighteen. I was in foster care and had nowhere to go when I got out of high school. Ray found me crying my eyes out on the pier. When he heard what I was going through, he offered me a job on the spot. At first I was a housekeeper, but I worked my way up. I've been manager ten years in October."

"How many employees are here?"

Delilah stopped and thought. "Three in housekeeping, a groundskeeper, and me."

"I wish I'd known my dad. He sounds like a really great man."

Delilah's eyes glistened. "He was the best."

"You sound a little in love with him."

"Maybe I was." Delilah put down the soup ladle. "I could never take Tina's place, but I would have been willing to try. He never looked at another woman though. Even though I let him know I was available."

"You're much younger."

"I'm thirty-three," Delilah admitted.

"He was in his fifties when he died?"

"Yes, he was fifty-two. But he looked much younger." Delilah shrugged. "The age difference never bothered me. A man like that doesn't come along often."

Libby mixed the greens and vegetables together. "So everyone says." She went back to the refrigerator. "No avocados?"

"There's one in that bag." Delilah pointed to a paper sack on the counter.

"We'll have to get more. I like avocado in everything. I'll make my special avocado dressing for tonight too."

"Sounds great. What about your mother?" Delilah asked. "Do you know much about their marriage?"

"Only that it lasted a short time. They were both young. My mother said he lit out when I was three. I was bitter about it when I was a teenager. Now I find out that my mother lied all those years. She told me he died when I was five. It's pretty devastating."

"I'm sure it is. One thing I know about Ray—he would never shirk his responsibility."

"My mother tried, but she was a kid at heart herself, even at fifty. I was more a parent than she was sometimes. We moved around a lot. I think I went to ten schools in twelve years."

Delilah winced. "Some of Ray's old letters and albums are in the basement. You might want to go through them."

"Oh, I would!" Libby began to chop the avocado.

The thought of learning more about her parents and their lives appealed to her. So much of the time she felt alone, as if a piece of herself was missing. She'd assumed the cause was some dim memory of her father. Even now that she knew he was an honorable man, his abandonment still hurt.

FOURTEEN

The huge living room table felt crowded with so many around it. Alec had never eaten here at the Tidewater Inn when there were so many guests. A white linen tablecloth covered the mammoth table, and fresh flowers made a bright centerpiece. Platters were heaped with steaming lobster, and a white tureen contained the soup he'd just tasted.

"Great meal, Delilah," he said. "No one can make she-crab soup like you."

Delilah smiled and ladled soup into a bowl for herself. "Libby helped. Wait until you taste the avocado-ranch dressing she made from scratch."

Libby was to his right, and she brightened at the praise. "I hope everyone likes avocados."

"Is there any store-bought dressing?" Vanessa started to rise from her seat directly across from the table.

Her aunt Pearl shot her a look that made her sink back into her chair. "I've bought too many avocados for you to think your tastes have suddenly changed, Vanessa."

A dull red crept up Vanessa's neck, and she tipped her chin up. "I'll try it, I guess." The glance she shot Libby was full of challenge.

Alec wanted to tell her to stop acting like a spoiled brat, but he tucked his chin and took another sip of the soup. "I could live on this, Delilah. But I'm not going to. The lobster looks great."

Libby glanced at Zach. "I hear we have you to thank for this fabulous dinner."

Zach shrugged. "I had a good afternoon on the boat."

She smiled at him. "Modesty. I like that in a man." She turned to her other side to listen to Thomas Carter.

Alec suppressed a grin at the way Zach's shoulders squared when she called him a man. Libby had a way about her that made every man in the room want to impress her. Even old Thomas was busy telling her about the days when he built boats. She listened with the kind of attention that would make any person feel important. Why had she never married? But maybe that was a false assumption. She could be divorced.

Thomas finally ended his story. Libby glanced across the table at her siblings. "Brent, I met Kenneth Poe this morning. He told me about his client's interest in buying the inn."

Brent stiffened and looked up from his plate. "Did he make you an offer?"

"He did." Libby broke off a piece of French bread and dipped it in her soup. "I had no idea this place was worth so much money."

Everyone seemed to freeze. Alec shot her a quick glance. Was she trying to see what kind of reaction she would get? The strain in the room seemed to grow. How much money had she been offered? A million or two? That would be enough to tempt most people.

"You're not going to sell, are you, honey?" Pearl asked.

"Of course she is," Vanessa said. "She doesn't care about the family. She just wants the money."

"I don't know yet," Libby said. "I haven't had a chance to even think about what should be done. *You* were going to sell," she said, directing a level gaze at Brent before glancing at Vanessa again.

"Why is it all right for your brother to sell but not me? Why don't you characterize him as a money grubber?"

"Brent knows this island. He would have done what was best."

"The offer is from the same person," Libby said. "So there is nothing different except who is benefiting."

"Children, let's not argue," Pearl said. "Your father would be very displeased by your attitude to your sister, Vanessa. I'm disappointed myself. We are all family, but you're not acting like it."

"I haven't done anything," Brent said. "Libby, you can do whatever you want. It's your property. Dad seemed to want it that way."

Alec winced at the coldness in Brent's voice, but Libby just nodded.

"Thank you, Brent," she said. "I don't know what I'll do yet. It's a lovely old place. I wish I had the money to keep it. It needs a lot of repairs." She glanced at Alec. "What do you think about a resort going in here?"

He raised his brows. "Resort? We'll need ferry service or a very long bridge to draw in enough people to support it."

"The ferry service is coming," she said. "That's why Nicole was here. We had a client who wanted us to restore some of the more important buildings and make Hope Beach more attractive to tourists."

"It hasn't been announced if it is." He glanced at Brent. "You've heard this?"

Brent nodded. "From Poe. I doubt his investor would be spending that kind of money if he wasn't sure it was happening."

"The island will change," Alec said. "We'll be like Ocracoke. Which is better than Myrtle Beach at least. The tourists aren't overwhelming. It's still a fishing village. We'll survive, whatever you decide."

Delilah's spoon clattered into her bowl. "Easy enough for you to say! This place is my home. It's my *life*." She stared at Libby.

"Don't think for a minute that they won't tear this place down. That's what he told you, isn't it?"

Libby nodded. "That's the only thing holding me back. I would have to compromise my passion for historic preservation if I let them do that."

Libby's soft answer defused Delilah's anger. The red faded from her cheeks, and she slumped back in her chair. "Don't do this. I can't bear to leave my home."

Libby bit her lip and looked down at her plate. "I can only promise that I'll consider everything, Delilah. I'm in a hard spot. I don't have the kind of money it would take to restore the inn. Without a major investment, it's going to fall down around your ears." She glanced at Brent. "Why did our father not keep it up? The house in the village is in great condition."

"I can answer that," Pearl said. "The place was due a paint job when Tina died three years ago. Ray had a small stroke, then started letting things slide. The sea is hard on buildings. They need constant maintenance. I told him he needed to spend some time here and make a project list, but he didn't do it. Then his illness turned chronic, and he decided to transfer all his liquid assets to the kids. He wanted to make sure everyone was taken care of."

"I can understand that," Libby said. "But he left me no money for upkeep. It was as if he wanted me to sell it."

"I'm not sure I believe that," Alec said.

"Then why leave me saddled with a house that's in need of so much?"

"Maybe he wanted to see what you were made of."

She absorbed his comment, then nodded. "I suppose we'll never know."

"What you're made of?" Alec raised his eyebrows.

"No. What he wanted me to do."

"If anyone can figure it out, it's you," he said.

Vanessa's head came up and she gave him a sharp glance. He realized he'd let too much of his admiration show. If Vanessa hated Libby before, it was going to be worse now.

———

The basement stairs creaked as Libby eased down them. The dank smell was nearly enough to make her turn tail and run, but the promise of the prize contained in the trunk below was stronger than the claustrophobia squeezing her lungs. The bare bulb in the ceiling put out enough light to see the old leather chest right where Delilah had told her it would be, against the wall beneath the shelves lined with jars of canned vegetables.

She was going to grab the albums and letters and run right back to her room with them. The place gave her the creeps. The distant sound of dripping water added to her unease, though the stone floor was dry. The place was free of cobwebs too, so Delilah must keep it swept out.

Libby hurried to the trunk and lifted the lid. The fabric-lined interior smelled of disuse. The trunk was packed with bundles of old letters and photo albums. Her pulse thumped in her throat. Would there be any mention of her or her mother in these old letters? Any photos of her?

A framed picture was in the very bottom of the trunk. Libby held it up to the light. She barely recognized the smiling young woman as her mother. Why had her father kept it all these years? His marriage to Tina seemed to have been ideal. Her mother looked like she was about twenty-five. Young and carefree. Her long, straight hair was on her shoulders, and she wore a buckskin dress covered with beads.

Her mother had been happy but never content with any situation or with any man. She was always striving for the next big thing. Everyday choices had molded her mother. Libby touched the beads at her neck. Her own choices could make her a better person if she chose wisely.

She sorted the contents, then lifted the pile of albums and letters and carried them back up the stairs and to her bedroom. There was no one around. The sun was setting, and she'd arranged to meet the reporter with Alec, so she dropped the mementos on the bed with a regretful glance and went to find him.

FIFTEEN

Libby and Alec sat on the expansive porch at Tidewater Inn after sunset and listened to the ocean. "I thought he'd be here by now," Alec said.

"I don't mind waiting," she said. "It's a beautiful night."

The stars were bright in the night sky, but the moon hadn't risen yet. He kept shooting glances Libby's way. She seemed so at home here.

"What?" she finally said. "Do I have soup on my nose?"

He grinned. "Sorry. I was staring, wasn't I? It's the offer for this place. Would you really sell it, or were you just trying to see what you could find out from Brent?"

"I don't want to sell," she said in a low voice. "But I don't see that I have any choice."

"There's always a choice."

She stiffened. "What would you do?"

"Turn over every rock to find a way to keep it."

"Well, I have another life. The place is gorgeous and historic, I give you that. But sometimes sacrifices have to be made. The money will change my life. And I have a stepbrother who needs help. He was hurt in Afghanistan and is on disability. I could do a lot of good there." If he would let her. He wasn't eager to have a relationship with her. He'd been a teenager when their parents married, and he had no time for her.

"Life isn't all about money."

"Spoken by someone who has always had enough."

She wasn't going to listen. He peered at the dock as a boat approached. "Looks like Earl is finally here. You ready for this?"

"I'll do anything to help find Nicole."

"You can wait here." He rose and went to the dock. When the boat neared, he caught the rope and tied it to the pilings.

"I'll be back in about an hour," Earl told the captain.

The young man in shorts nodded. He plugged in earphones and settled back in his chair.

Earl was in his fifties with a paunch. His one pride was his thick head of red hair. It had faded with the years, but he still wore it over his ears like an aging Beatle. "She up there?" he asked, jerking his thumb toward the house.

"Yes. Go easy on her though. She's had a rough few days."

Earl chewed on his ever-present toothpick. "Sounds like you believe her story."

Alec shrugged. "I know what it's like to be accused of something you didn't do. I don't want us to assume she's guilty until proven innocent."

"Is Tom going to ask the state for help?"

"Yes. With the hurricane, I think he's overwhelmed." He fell into place beside Earl, who was walking up the boardwalk to the hotel.

"My story will get some action."

They reached the grand steps. Libby was standing on the porch waiting. Her expression was one of dread. This wouldn't be easy for her, airing her life to the world. Alec sent her a reassuring smile. "This is Earl Franklin," he said when they reached her.

The two exchanged a long look. "It's you." She glanced at Alec.

"Earl and his wife gave me a ride to the island," she said. "Naomi thought I was Vanessa."

"You never said a word about your friend having gone missing." Earl's voice held accusation.

She bit her lip. "There was just so much to explain. It seemed easier to say nothing."

Alec already had an uneasy feeling about the exchange. It did seem odd that she wouldn't have told Earl and Naomi anything. Especially Naomi. If any woman had the warm manner that invited confidence, it was Earl's sweet wife. And Libby hadn't made any secret of the incident to him. Alec could see the suspicion on Earl's face.

"There's iced tea," she said, pointing to the table with the refreshments. She resumed her seat in the swing. Tucking one leg under her, she sipped her tea and regarded them over the rim of her glass.

"Don't mind if I do." Earl poured himself a glass from the sweating pitcher. "Ah, nothing like sweet tea." He settled in the rocker and took out a pen. "Hope you don't mind if I record this? It's easier than trying to write it all down." He clicked a switch on the pen recorder without waiting for her to answer. "Can you take me through the events that led up to your friend's disappearance?"

She blinked. "Okay."

She plunged into the story about the client who wanted restoration estimates and ended with what she saw on the beach cam. She broke down again when she got to the part about the men taking her friend. Alec couldn't imagine how he'd feel if he saw someone he cared about being kidnapped and couldn't do anything to stop it.

Earl leaned forward. "Ms. Holladay, did you harm your friend?"

She sat upright, sloshing tea over the side of her glass onto her shorts. "Of course not!"

"You didn't kill Nicole, dump her body in the Atlantic, then call the sheriff with some far-fetched story about an abduction?"

"No, no! You can't possibly believe that." She stared wildly from Earl to Alec, then back again. "Nicole is my friend. I would do anything to find her. Anything!"

"Yet the website with the cam is blank during the time your partner was supposedly kidnapped."

How had he found that out? He must have talked to Tom. Alec wanted to interrupt, but he bit his tongue and let Earl continue his questioning. She'd survive. It *was* strange that the tape had been messed with.

Earl smiled. "I did a little research. You're a computer expert. A person at the historical society said you're their go-to person when they have any computer issues. It's not out of the realm of possibility that you hacked into the cam data and erased that portion of the tape."

"It was an accident." She gulped and held his gaze. "I was trying to save the video. It wouldn't let me, so I . . . I hacked into the system and tried to save it that way. Something happened, and the next thing I knew, the data was gone."

"I see. I must say I thought you'd come up with a more believable story than that," Earl said.

"It's the truth."

Alec watched her face, the way it crumpled, the way tears formed in her eyes.

"I think you've made enough accusations, Earl."

Her fingers inched toward him but stopped before she touched his hand. "I didn't hurt Nicole, Mr. Franklin. If you write a story suggesting that I did, you'll only aid whoever took her."

Earl turned off his tape recorder. "Let me know if you remember anything else." He tucked the recorder into his pocket and strode to the waiting boat.

———

The boat carrying Earl back to Kitty Hawk cruised away, and none too soon for Libby. She wanted to throw something, to scream about the injustice of anyone even thinking that she might have hurt Nicole. His blue eyes watching her somberly, Alec continued to sit on the porch with her. He probably still suspected she had done something criminal.

She set her iced tea on the table and paced the expansive porch. "You said you'd give me the benefit of the doubt."

His sip of tea seemed deliberate, as though he was fishing for extra time before answering. "I am. But it seems strange the data would be missing from the cam."

His doubt was written on his face, and she fought to keep her voice level. "I swear to you I didn't do it on purpose. Yes, I might have caused it. I don't know." She clasped her hands in front of her. "Did you talk to your cousin when we were in town? I want to *do something*! I have to find Nicole."

"With the hurricane, Tom's going to have his hands full. And to be honest, this kind of thing is much more serious than the domestic disputes and traffic tickets he normally deals with. He's my cousin, but I think this is way over his head."

"I'm going to have to find her myself. It's clear no one else is going to do it."

He raised a brow. "You? What do you know about looking for a missing person?"

"Nothing. But I can retrace her steps. Talk to everyone she spoke with. Surely I'll find a clue somewhere. I can't just sit here and wait!" Her voice broke, and she turned her back on him.

She was alone here, and it was time she faced it. The people in the inn shared only her blood. They cared nothing about her. Well, maybe Aunt Pearl cared a little, but her warmth might only be curiosity. Libby refused to entertain the thought that Nicole might be dead.

She sensed rather than heard his approach. His hand came down on her bare arm, and its warmth made her shiver. She didn't turn to look at him. He had brought that reporter here.

"I'm sorry," he said. "Reporters and law enforcement are trained to look at the person closest to the victim."

She whirled, jerking away from his touch. "Don't call her that! She's not dead, she's not!"

His hand dropped to his side. The wind ruffled his dark hair. "I'm sorry. I didn't mean it that way. She's still a victim of violence. Kidnapping is a violent act."

She shuddered and moved farther away from him. "Earl is going to write a piece suggesting I hurt her, isn't he? He really thinks I killed her and dumped her body in the ocean."

"I'll talk to him. I think he'll be fair."

The breakers rolled over the beach in a hypnotic rhythm. She turned to stare at him again. "Is that what your cousin thinks too? Is he going to taint the state's investigation by implying that I'm guilty?"

"I don't know what Tom is thinking. Look, I'll help you, okay? I'll take some accrued leave. I know everyone in town. It's a good idea to trace Nicole's movements. Someone has to know what happened."

His words were so gentle. Even though she'd screamed at him, he stayed calm. "Why would you do that for me?"

He shrugged. "I was falsely accused once."

"What happened?"

He folded his arms across his chest and moved back a step. "My older brother drowned. We were mulletting with a neighbor. I was about Zach's age. My older brother was named Zach too. He was twenty."

She heard the pain in his voice and wanted to tell him he didn't have to describe what happened, but she found herself holding her breath and wanting to know more.

"Giles, our neighbor, was with us. He was supposed to have checked the fuel in the boat. We were pretty far out and the engine died. No gas. The ship-to-shore radio had broken the week before, and we couldn't call for help. My brother was the strongest swimmer, so he decided to swim for help."

"Oh no," she said softly.

He sighed. "His body was never found. A fishing trawler found us the next morning. As soon as we got to land, Giles started railing at me, saying it was all my fault. If I'd filled the tank, my brother would still be alive. Everyone believed him. The pain and disappointment in my parents' eyes haunted me for years. Still does. They believed Giles instead of me."

"Have you talked with them about it since you've been grown?"

He shrugged. "Pointless now. Even if they believed me, it wouldn't make up for their condemnation back then."

"That's so sad, Alec. It has to have been so hard for you to lose two brothers. And then your parents, in a way."

He went silent for a moment. "Mom keeps the house like a shrine. Everywhere I look I see pictures of my brothers from babyhood to the year they died. In Mom's eyes they are saints now. Something I'll never be."

"And your father?"

"He doesn't say much. Mom rules the household. Her hero worship eventually drove Beth away too. Beth is my younger sister. I don't think she's been home in three years."

"I'm so sorry." She touched his hand. "I've always felt a little unlovable since my father abandoned me. I *thought* that's what he did anyway. Now everything I believed is all jumbled."

He held her hand in an easy grip. "You'll figure it out."

"So will you. I'm already sure that you're a good man, Alec."

A tinge of color stained his face. "Hardly. I was a wild kid. I guess that's why I want to help Zach avoid my mistakes."

"Most of us have to learn the hard way."

Her skin was still warm from touching his hand. He knew what it was like to be misunderstood. She wasn't in this by herself.

SIXTEEN

The rest of the house slept, but Libby paced the rug in the parlor. The grandfather clock in the corner chimed two, but she wasn't a bit sleepy. She should have been. Her last full night's sleep had been before this nightmare started.

What was she going to do if everyone began to look at her as a suspect? How could she clear herself?

"Libby?" Pearl stood in the doorway. A pink nightgown covered her bulk, and her hair was in a long braid. "Are you all right?" She stepped into the room. "You've been tense ever since dinner."

"You'd be tense too if you were accused of harming Nicole."

"What? Who accused you of such a thing?"

"Earl."

"Oh, honey, he's just snooping for something sensational. The truth will come out. You'll see." She beckoned for Libby to come with her. "You're tall. I need some help in my room, if you don't mind."

Libby followed her up the stairs. Helping Pearl would give her something to focus on besides what other people thought of her. When they reached Pearl's room, she looked around. It was very different from the way it had been when Nicole's things were here. Now there were angels everywhere, spilling out of boxes, perched on the dresser top, and heaped on the bed.

She picked up one that held a child in its arms. "How many angels do you have?"

"Oh, I've lost count. Well over two hundred, I'm sure."

"Did you bring them all?"

Pearl picked up an angel still in its box, which was lying beside the bed. "I could hardly leave them in the house, now could I?"

Libby smiled. "Of course not. Why angels?"

"I've always loved stories about angels. I'm sure I saw one once."

Libby found she believed Pearl. "What did he look like? And how did you know?"

"I was ten." She gestured to the window. "It was right out there in the water. I wasn't a very strong swimmer and I got a cramp in my side."

"Oh no."

Pearl nodded. "The surf was high and I couldn't keep my head up. I finally decided I would give up and just go to heaven. My grandpa had died two months earlier and I missed him anyway. So I quit swimming. I said, 'I'm going to heaven now.'"

Libby sat on the edge of the bed with the angel in her hands. "What happened?"

"I felt a hand on my arm, and the next thing I knew I was on my knees in the sand vomiting seawater. I looked around and a teenage boy was walking away. I called out to him and he turned around and smiled." She paused and her eyes were moist. "I've never seen a smile like that before or since. He said, 'You'll be fine now. It's not your time.' Then he turned and jogged away."

"You'd never seen the boy?"

Pearl shook her head. "He wasn't a real boy. There was something special about him."

Libby wanted to believe her aunt. Even more, she wished she could have an experience like that. She touched the beads at her neck. Somehow God felt more *real* here, on this island. Almost as if he could whisper in her ear at any moment.

Pearl smiled. "How'd we get on that subject? You need to get some rest and I'm blathering about something that happened fifty years ago."

"What can I help you with?"

Pearl pointed to the closet. "The disorder is driving me crazy. It's why I'm still awake at this crazy hour. I want to put some of the boxes of angels on the closet shelf, but I'm too short. There are some boxes in there that could go to the attic. That would leave me enough room. Can you reach?"

"I think so." Libby opened the closet door and eyed the boxes on the shelves. She stood on her tiptoes and pulled down the first box easily. "I think I need a chair for the one in the back."

Pearl brought her the desk chair, and Libby climbed onto it. "Can you flip on the closet light? It's dark in here." When the light came on, she peered to the back of the shelf. "What is this?" She reached in and brought out an envelope. "It's an old letter." She climbed down from the chair and sat on the edge of the bed where the light would allow her to read.

The bed sank as Pearl settled beside her. "It looks like it's addressed to Tina."

Libby opened it. "Did she ever stay in this room?"

Pearl shrugged. "Not that I know of."

Libby pulled out the letter inside the envelope. The writing was in a bold hand that suggested it had been penned by a man. The style was a little hard to read. She held it under the light and read aloud.

"'Tina, I will ruin Ray. You'll see what a huge mistake you've made.'"

Libby stared at her aunt. "Does this make any sense to you?"

Pearl gave a faint gasp. She snatched the note and crumpled it. "It's so old. I don't think we can possibly know what it means."

When Pearl fanned herself, Libby knew her aunt was hiding something. "What do you know?"

Pearl pulled her braid over one shoulder. "Ray had some financial problems a few years back. I never heard what went wrong. He lost about half of his money."

"He still had plenty to leave my siblings."

"He'd already put that money for them in trust funds."

"You suppose someone set out to harm him financially?"

"I can't imagine something so sordid."

"What wrong choice could Tina have made?" Libby wished she'd had the chance to look at the back of the sheet. "The letter is yellowed, like it's old. How long were Dad and Tina married?"

"Twenty-five years the month before Tina died."

"My father didn't wait long to replace my mother."

Pearl started to speak, then closed her mouth and shook her head.

"Was anyone else interested in Tina?"

Pearl rubbed her head. "I think there might have been, but it was so long ago. I just don't remember."

Libby sighed. It didn't matter anyway. This was old news and had nothing to do with finding Nicole.

———

Libby lay in the comfortable bed with her eyes open. She'd expected to sleep until at least eight, but something had awakened her. Birds sang outside her window, though the sun was not yet up. The air had the sense that sunrise was just around the corner. She rolled over and glanced at the alarm clock on the bedside table. Five thirty. The sun would be up in half an hour.

She listened again to the sleeping house. What had she heard? Or had it been a dream? She sat up. "Is someone there?"

The sound of running feet came from beyond the door. Her first inclination was to cower under the covers, but she wasn't going to give the person the satisfaction of thinking she was frightened. It was probably Vanessa. Or Brent. She forced herself out of bed and went to the door. There was a folded sheet of paper lying on the carpet. Something inside made it bulge.

Libby nudged it with her foot, and the paper opened to reveal a black blob. She leaped back until she realized it was a dead jellyfish. Why would someone leave this for her? Though she hated to get close, she lifted the paper and carried it into the attached bathroom, where she dumped the jellyfish into the trash. The paper was blank.

She balled up the paper and tossed it into the wastebasket, then pulled on shorts and a top. Whoever had left the creature couldn't make her cower in her room. The beach called, and she could watch the sun come up over the ocean.

The sky was lightening as she stepped onto the porch. A figure loomed to her left and she jumped, then realized it was Alec. "What are you doing up so early?" Mercy, he was handsome in his crisp white shirt and the khaki shorts that showed tanned, muscular legs.

He grinned. "I could ask you the same."

She told him about the jellyfish. "I'm not going to let her scare me."

He lifted a brow. "Her? You think it was Vanessa?"

"Probably. Does a jellyfish have any symbolism?"

He shrugged. "The obvious one is that she's calling you spineless. But that doesn't apply to you. It's clear to all of us that you've got backbone."

She had to smile at that. "I'll admit that it scared me this morning when I found it. But if you tell anyone, I'll deny it."

He grinned and made a zipping motion across his lips.

She pointed toward the whitecaps. "Want to take a walk?"

He pulled his hands from his pockets. "My thoughts exactly."

They jogged down the steps and down the slope to the beach. "I found an old letter last night in the room where Aunt Pearl is staying." She told him what the note contained.

"All that was before my time, but someone would probably know if Tina had another beau. I don't see how that matters now though," Alec said.

"It probably doesn't. I guess I'm just interested in all the history." She paused to peer at a black blob on the beach. "What's that?"

"A mermaid's purse," he said, steering her around it. "Technically known as a skate's egg sack."

She shuddered. "Looks creepy, like some kind of alien." She fell into step beside him again. The murmur of the sea was balm on her soul, and she ran into the gentle waves as far as her knees, letting the water wash away her worries.

"You look happy," Alec said, watching her.

She splashed him with water. "The water's warm!"

He grinned and jogged into the waves with her, then splashed her back. She licked the salt from her lips and smiled. "I'm not going to let Earl's suspicious nature rob me of my peace of mind. I know I'm innocent."

He sobered. "That's good. Because he could do a lot of damage."

"Maybe. But I have to believe the sheriff has enough integrity to look for the real criminals."

"I think he does, but sometimes it's tempting to take the easy way out."

"I'll keep pushing back until he finds the truth." Her high spirits began to sink. Alec's sober demeanor reminded her that she still faced many problems. She didn't even want to see Earl's article.

"What are the plans for today?" she asked. "I want to get started on finding Nicole."

"I thought we'd take the cutter out with my friends. I got permission to search for her, and I talked my boss into allowing you to be on the boat."

"I wish we would find her today." She stared out at the water, which shimmered with gold and orange as the sun lifted its head above the horizon.

He touched her arm. "Don't give up hope."

"I haven't." She rubbed her head. "What made you decide to join the Coast Guard?"

He smiled. "That's an easy answer. I'm happy when I'm on the sea. The Coast Guard rescued us when I was a kid, like I mentioned."

She sobered. "When your brother died."

He nodded. "Riding on that cutter back to land, I knew I wanted to snatch people from the jaws of death the way we'd been rescued. It seemed very noble."

"And is it?"

"Sometimes. When we're successful. Sometimes we're not though. We're not always in time to save lives. Then it's hard, and I feel like a failure."

"I don't think you could ever be a failure." She held his gaze for just a moment, then turned back toward the house. "I think I'll fix coconut pancakes for breakfast."

She couldn't think of a man she admired as much as she did Alec. He was quite a guy. The strain between them was gone this morning, and she prayed it meant he fully believed in her now.

SEVENTEEN

It was ten by the time Alec drove Libby to town to go searching. While Libby ducked into the store to buy some sunscreen,
Alec walked across the street to step into the sheriff's office. He
found Tom at his desk filling in paperwork.

"Got a minute?" Alec closed the door behind him.

Tom leaned back in his chair. "You bet. What's up?"

"You heard from the state boys on the search for Nicole?"

Tom pursed his lips. "Yeah. There are two detectives coming
first of the week."

"Why so late?"

"The state is still reeling from the hurricane, I guess. And their
best detective is in Saint Croix on vacation. They're sending him
and his partner out when he gets back."

"I guess it will have to do."

"You find out anything by hanging around Libby?"

Alec shook his head. "I think you were right about Earl
though. He came in with guns blazing for her last night. He found
out about the missing video. Did you tell him?"

Tom frowned. "You know better than that. I wouldn't do anything to compromise the investigation."

"I wonder how he found out, then."

"He might have a contact in the Virginia Beach office. I guess it doesn't matter. It's going to come out sooner or later."

Alec fell silent as he tried to think of how he could convince his cousin to drop his suspicions about Libby. "This morning she said she was sure you had the integrity to dig for the truth. Don't make me think you're less of a man than we both know you are."

Tom flushed. "Come on, Alec, you're letting yourself be fooled by a pretty face. I admit she's a looker, but use your head. Stay neutral and consider that she might be implicated."

"I am. What other evidence have you found about the two men?"

Tom leaned back in his chair. "Two men in a small boat with an outboard motor were seen offshore."

"That reminds me of what Mr. McEwan said." He told Tom about the old man seeing a boat with two men and a sleeping woman.

"Might be our perps," Tom said.

"Did you get a description of the boat? Libby could say if it's the same one she saw. We might be able to track it."

"It was too far for my witness to make out the name or make. Did you ask McEwan?"

Alec nodded. "He said he thought it was a Sea Ray, but he wasn't sure. Said it had some wear and might be a charter boat."

"I'll check out the marinas on the mainland and at Kill Devil."

It sounded like Tom was going to stay objective. The tension eased out of Alec's neck. "Promise me one thing, okay? That you won't prejudice the state boys against her. Let them come in and look at the situation with fresh eyes."

Tom hesitated, then looked down at his desk. "They are already looking at her, Alec. She wiped out the video."

"I believe her story about doing it accidentally."

"I don't know what to believe yet. But we have to consider all possibilities. I need you to promise to keep an open mind and report anything suspicious you see about Libby."

"I know the meaning of duty," Alec said. "I'm not going to hide anything. But we need to find Nicole. Every hour that passes is bad news and you know it."

"I'm doing my best. We're looking too. You have to consider that we may never find her though, Alec."

"I don't want to give up too soon."

"Neither do I."

———

The Coast Guard boat rode the waves so well Libby barely felt the swells left from the storm. Nicole had been gone three days. Was she even still alive? Libby stood at the bow of the craft and scanned the sea for any sight of her partner. Alec stood shoulder to shoulder with her and lifted binoculars to his eyes. He'd stopped to change into his uniform.

"We've got the boat for three more hours," he said.

Libby moved restlessly. "I don't think she's out this way. There's nothing here." She'd seen nothing but gulls and whitecaps.

"I don't either."

"If it was the kidnappers the old man saw, could they have had a destination in mind?"

"There isn't much out here but open sea."

"No islands?"

He shrugged. "Just uninhabited bits of sand. Nothing that would withstand a hurricane or support life. Some people picnic on the small islands, but there's no food or water on most of them."

She held out her hand. "Can I borrow your binoculars?"

"Sure." He handed them over.

She adjusted them to suit her and studied the whitecaps. Nothing. Every hour that passed left her feeling more and more hopeless. Where could they turn for information?

She handed back the binoculars. "Could we check the little islands?"

He spoke to Curtis, and the boat veered toward a tiny spot of land to the west. "It will take days or weeks to search them all. It would be insanity to put her on one of them."

"I'm not going to give up. She has to be somewhere. What do you think they did with her?"

He pressed his lips together, then shrugged. "Hard to say. They could have veered toward land at any point and put ashore."

"You don't think they did though, do you? I hear it in your voice. You think they dumped her."

"Libby, we don't know what happened or why they even took her. Anything is possible."

She felt a rising tide of distress and clamped down on it.

"It's too early to give up," he said. "We're going to keep looking." His tone held determination. She smiled at him. "Thank you."

The craft reached the tiny island. Alec ordered the anchor lowered and the raft readied. "Want to go ashore?"

She eyed the island. It looked deserted. "I'll go."

"It's likely full of bird offing," he warned. "The pelicans like this island."

"I'll manage. Are they nesting?"

"Yes. They breed from March to November. So we may see some fledglings." He helped her into the raft with the others, then rowed ashore. The raft touched bottom and he jumped out, then dragged it to the sand. "Stick with me, just in case." He asked his friends to go the other direction. Josh and Sara went east.

She and Alec went west toward a patch of spindly trees. "Oh look!" She pointed to the ground. "Is that a pelican nest?"

"Yes. There are two eggs. That's common. The parents take turns incubating the eggs." He grinned. "That's the way it should be. The mom shouldn't have to do it all."

"Nice of you to admit it," she said. She glanced at him out of the corner of her eye as she turned away. Did he feel that way about raising kids? He handled Zach well.

It took less than five minutes to meet up with the other two Coasties. Gulls scolded them as they searched, but the island held nothing.

Sara fell into step beside her. "You doing okay?"

Libby liked the other woman's manner. Calm and confident. "I'm fine. Alec says you're the EMT? Is it hard to work with mostly men?"

"I used to think I had to prove myself, but the guys are fair. They let me pull my own weight." She smiled. "Most of the time."

"Does anyone ever stay on these little islands?" Libby asked.

"Sometimes fishermen will camp out, or teens will party on one. Once in a while a foolhardy mainlander will get it in his head to build a house on one, but it never lasts. The isolation gets to them after a while. Nothing is convenient either. One accident and things can get hairy quickly."

The four of them walked to the center of the island, where Sara pointed out a stash of beer bottles, both empty and full. A cornhole game had been set up, and someone had carved the words *I love Carrie* onto a tree trunk.

"Kids," Josh said. He and Sara headed back to the boat.

"What's that?" Libby pointed to the ground. "Looks like someone built a fire here."

"Probably kids cooking fish," Alec said.

She prodded the ashes with her foot. Nothing but pieces of charred wood.

"Wait." He knelt and sifted with his fingers, then his hand came up holding a pocketknife. He stood, his mouth pinched.

"What's wrong?"

"It's Zach's."

"How do you know?"

He showed her the name carved into the side of it. "He told me he dropped it overboard. This must be a hangout. I'm going to have to have a talk with him."

"You sound discouraged. You're thinking of the beer, aren't you? Boys generally experiment with alcohol."

His mouth was pinched. "He knows better. And he's driving a boat, which makes it worse."

She wanted to ask more, but there was a wall up in his manner. "He seems to love you."

He shook his head. "He's been a handful since his parents died."

"I know they were killed in a small plane crash. Do you know the cause?"

"Dave was an amateur pilot. Their plane went down over a lake in Minnesota. The authorities think clouds rolled in. He wasn't certified for instrument flying."

"I'm sorry."

They boarded the boat and got under way again. She strained to see the next island. Maybe Nicole would be on that one.

"We'll check there too," he said. "But I don't think we're going to find her on an island."

She jutted out her chin. "We have to try."

He glanced at his watch. "Two hours. Then we have to go back. Zach is bringing in fish to feed the town. We'll all need to help."

She wanted to scream that finding her friend was more important than fish, but she swallowed hard and nodded. This man and his friends were helping her. She would be grateful.

Eighteen

The cutter docked at the Coast Guard headquarters in the bay. Alec pointed Libby to the ladies' room, then he walked with his friends across the grassy field toward the parking lot.

"Buddy, you better watch out," Curtis said.

Josh grinned and moved his hand like a diving airplane. "Kaboom! You're about to crash and burn."

Alec stopped and stared at them. "What are you two idiots talking about?"

Josh poked Alec's arm. "We're talking about you, my friend. And that pretty lady. You're already halfway smitten."

"That's ridiculous. I've only known her a few days." He started walking away.

Josh exchanged a long look with Curtis. "We're too late, Curtis. He's gone past denial to defensiveness."

Alec wanted to scowl, but he couldn't hold back the bark of laughter. "I'm just helping her, guys."

"That's what they all say," Curtis said. "I get to be best man though, right?"

"No, I get to be best man," Josh said. He punched Curtis in the arm. "Just because you're a month older, you think you get to do everything."

"No one is best man," Alec said. "There's no wedding."

"You mean we get to come to your house and watch the Dodgers play forever?" Josh whooped. "Now you're talking."

Curtis was grinning as he watched Josh cavort along the lawn. "What do you really think of Libby?" he asked Alec. "Any news on the case at all?"

"Not that I know of." He told his best friend about the disastrous interview with Earl, and Libby's admission about erasing the video.

"That's bad, Alec," Sara said. "You're *sure* it was accidental?"

"I believe her. Why are you asking? Do you know something about hacking?"

Curtis gave an innocent smile. "Well, this is all hearsay, you understand. I've never actually done it myself."

Alec grinned. "Okay, spill it. When did you hack a website?"

"Well, in college, there was this girl I liked. She had a website and I thought it would be cute to hack it and put up a poem I'd written for her."

Sara punched him on the arm. "Get out! You didn't. Poetry? From *you*?"

Curtis grinned. "I did. But the next day I wished I didn't. She wouldn't speak to me. So much for that relationship."

"How'd you learn to do it?" Alec asked.

"I was taking website design. If you know a little, you can do a Google search and get the directions on how to do it. As long as the website doesn't have a good firewall. And many don't."

"What about the cams here? Do they have good firewalls?"

Curtis shrugged. "I'd think so, but with the budget cuts, it's hard to say."

"So maybe a college student could have done it. Or just anyone with a little knowledge."

"Maybe."

"Is IP tracing always accurate?"

Curtis shook his head. "A trace can be misdirected. So you need more evidence than a trace."

Alec gestured to the building. "Here comes Libby."

"When are you going to take her out on a real date?" Josh asked.

"Where would we go? Get a grip, Josh."

"You've got a boat. Take her for a nice, romantic dinner in Kill Devil Hills."

His friend had a point. Maybe Alec would do just that.

———

Zach's face was set and strained. Alec eyed his nephew's expression as they stood on the church lawn filleting fish with half a dozen men. Residents from all over the village had brought their gas grills and skillets. Griddles stood ready to cook the seafood, and news of the fish fry brought most of the townspeople to the church with dishes the women had prepared.

Curtis threw a mullet into the bowl. "You think that's enough? We're not going to clean *all* of these, are we? Where'd you get a haul like this, Zach?"

Zach shrugged. "Out past the sandbar. I knew the fishing would be good."

"I think that nephew of yours can read fish minds," Josh said to Alec. He pursed his lips like a fish. "Come catch me. I'll be good eating."

Zach's smile didn't reach his eyes. "Ha ha."

"When are you going to join us in the Coast Guard?" Curtis asked.

"Like, never," Zach said. "I just want to fish."

Josh poked a scale-covered finger at Alec. "Look at your uncle. He serves his country and fishes too. A perfect combination."

Alec wanted to tell them to lay off, but he was curious to see if their ribbing would get Zach to reveal why he was in such a rotten mood. He placed another fillet on the growing mound in the big stainless bowl. But Zach hunched his shoulders and continued to work on the fish. He didn't look at either of Alec's friends.

Pearl hurried across the lawn toward them. "We're going to start cooking the fish. This was wonderful of you to do, Zach. You're a thoughtful boy, just like your dad. He would have done this too."

Zach straightened and smiled. "Thanks, Mrs. Chilton."

She patted his cheek. "So polite."

Zach grinned and so did Alec. Pearl could change anyone's frown into a smile.

"I think we're ready to start cooking," Pearl said. "Zach, would you carry the bowl for me? It's about as big as I am."

Zach carried the big stainless bowl overflowing with fish fillets to the grilling station. A dozen men stood by, ready to start the cooking. The aroma of charcoal made Alec's stomach rumble. Side dishes covered the tables that had been hauled from the church basement.

He loved Hope Beach. It was a gift from God that he'd been able to live here all his life. Good people, good friends—what more did he need in his life? His contentment vanished when he caught a glimpse of Libby. Okay, so maybe he was a little lonely.

Josh nudged him with his elbow. "Look away. Resist the pull."

Alec grinned. "Maybe I don't want to resist."

"Be like me. A confirmed bachelor."

"Right. I've seen you looking at Sara."

Josh folded his arms across his chest. "I don't know what you're talking about."

"No?" Curtis knocked Josh's hat off. "I don't know why you don't ask her out, man."

Josh retrieved his Dodgers hat. "It would mess up the working relationship. What if it didn't work out but we still had to work together? Besides, it's better to be alone. Then I can do whatever I want, when I want."

"In Genesis God says man was not meant to be alone," Alec said, "that a woman completes him. My mom always reminded Dad of that when he complained about something." Alec grinned at the memory.

"All my parents did was fight," Josh said. "Until my mother lit out for somewhere else with another guy. I never saw her again."

"Sara's not like that," Curtis said. "If you don't ask her out, I will."

Josh stiffened. "Oh, come on now, that's not playing fair. She wouldn't go with you anyway."

"Want me to ask and see?"

"No. Just lay off, okay?" Josh's good-natured grin was gone. "I'll ask her if I get good and ready."

Alec had never seen his friend so serious. Who knew Josh's joking hid so much pain? He put his hand on his friend's arm. "Okay, we'll lay off. But think about Sara, okay?"

"Someone mention my name?" Sara was smiling as she joined them. She looked different out of her uniform, happy and carefree with her honey-colored hair blowing in the wind.

Josh shot them a warning glare. "We were just wondering where you were."

She lifted the dish in her hands. "I made my famous sweet-potato casserole. It's about the only thing I know how to cook."

Josh's face was red and he didn't look at her. Alec decided to take pity on him. "Hey, Sara, would you make an effort to be a friend to Libby? I think she feels a little out of place. Her family has been less than welcoming."

"I'd be glad to." A smile hovered on Sara's lips. "We talked a little out on the island today. I'm glad you're interested in her. I like her."

He wanted to protest that he wasn't interested, but they'd all know he was lying.

NINETEEN

L ibby stood slightly apart from the happy crowd populating the churchyard. She wanted to be part of the group, but so far no one had taken notice of her. What was it the Bible said about friends? *A man who has friends must himself be friendly.*

She pasted on a smile and approached the closest group of women. "Can I help? I have a really great coating recipe for fish." She targeted her question to the only familiar face, Sara, who'd been on the Coast Guard boat.

Sara smiled. "Hello, Libby. I'm glad you're here. I'm terrible at cooking. What do you need for your breading? I'm a good gofer and I can rustle up the ingredients."

"Cornmeal, flour, paprika, pepper, and onion powder."

Sara held up her hands. "Whoa, whoa, I need to write that down." She pulled a scrap of paper from the purse at her feet and jotted it down. "Be right back."

The other ladies smiled and spoke to Libby as she waited for Sara to return. Their friendliness was a balm to her, and several told her they'd been praying that Nicole would be found. Her pulse blipped when Alec came across the lawn toward her.

He smiled when he reached her. "You any good at cooking fish?"

"I can fix fish that will have you begging for more," she said.

"I have a special breading I use. Sara went after the ingredients for me."

"I can't wait to taste it."

Surely he hadn't come over to make small talk. She searched his expression. "Any news?"

"I've been thinking about that beach cam website. Can we retrace exactly what you did? Did you copy the video to start to save it?"

She shook her head. "I tried to save it to my laptop and it wouldn't work. So I decided to look at the coding and copy it that way. I had just gotten in when it blipped, and everything was gone."

"Maybe someone else was there too. And the trace got misdirected to you. Curtis says it's possible."

"I wish I could believe that. I hate that something I might have done has hindered finding her kidnappers. How can I prove my innocence to the sheriff and everyone else?"

"I don't think you can unless we find the men responsible."

"It feels impossible." She glanced around. "This might be a good time to question people, don't you think?"

"Good idea."

She nodded toward Horace's secretary. "I thought of a few other questions for Mindy."

Mindy was sitting on a lawn chair by herself with a glass of iced tea in one hand and a novel in the other. She seemed oblivious to the hubbub going on around her. Libby had to speak her name for the woman to look up from her book.

Though Mindy smiled, her gaze wandered back to her book, then up again. "I thought you two would be around here somewhere."

"Did your house have any damage?" Alec asked.

She shook her head. "Mine's on a hill. The storm surge didn't reach me."

Alec glanced around. "Is Horace here somewhere too?"

"He and his son both came. His wife is in Virginia Beach." She looked at the book in her hand again.

Libby took the hint. "I am trying to figure out what all Nicole did when she was here. Did she mention any of her activities when you talked to her?"

Mindy thought for a moment. "She went parasailing."

"Who took her out?" Alec asked.

"Brent. I think he was a little smitten."

Libby gasped, and Alec straightened. She stared up at him. "Don't you think Brent would have mentioned that to us? He only mentioned talking to her in the ice-cream shop."

"Yeah, that seems odd."

Libby glanced across the lawn to where Brent stood talking with friends. "I'm going to ask him about it. What day did she go out with him, do you remember?"

"I think it was last Saturday."

Libby started toward Brent, then saw Sara standing by the grills with a basket of items in her hands. "I'd better do my part with the fish first. Sara went to all the trouble to get me the ingredients."

"I think I want to watch this," Alec said. His lips twitched.

"You think I can't cook?" She tried to put indignation into her tone, but her smile gave her away. "You had plenty of my avocado dressing. Did *you* bring a dish?"

"I can make a mean bowl of microwave popcorn, but that's it," he said. "I don't think there's much demand for popcorn." He took her arm and steered her back to where Sara waited. "I think everyone wants something more substantial."

"I like popcorn," she said. The moment the words left her lips, she wanted to recall them. They sounded flirtatious, as though she was angling for an offer. His fingers seemed to warm as they tightened on her arm, but it had to be her imagination.

He cleared his throat. "Listen, I know your mind is on finding Nicole, but when this is all over, you want—"

"Alec, I need your help," Pearl said. "We need a few more tables hauled up from the church basement."

"Sure thing, Pearl."

Did he sound relieved? Libby watched them go and wished he'd finished his question. Had he been trying to ask her out?

———

Brent seemed to be deliberately avoiding him. Alec tried to catch him alone several times during the fish fry. Every time Alec neared him, Brent moved off to talk with another friend.

Libby's fish was a success. She stood talking recipes and food with several of the women from town. It warmed Alec to see how quickly she had made connections. Maybe she wouldn't sell out and leave. She gave a little wave when she saw him, and then spoke to a couple of women before joining him.

"Everyone liked my fish," she said, a trill in her voice.

"It was terrific." He took her arm and moved her out of the way of men carrying chairs back to their cars. "I've tried to talk to Brent, but he's jumping from place to place like a nervous cricket."

"Where is he now?" She glanced around. "There he is. Heading to the street. And he's alone."

"Let's get him." He grabbed her hand and they hurried after Brent. "Brent, wait up!"

Brent appeared not to hear, but he broke into a jog. Alec let go of Libby's hand and ran after him. He reached Brent as the younger man opened the car door. "Hang on there, Brent. We need to have a little chat."

"I'm in a hurry," Brent said. His gaze went past Alec to Libby, who was rushing toward them.

"This will only take a minute."

Her cheeks pink, Libby reached them. "Glad we caught you, Brent. We heard something today and wanted to ask you about it."

"Yes, I took Nicole parasailing, all right?" He shrugged. "It was no big deal."

"Mindy mentioned that she'd told us?" Alec wished he'd instructed her to keep a lid on it. He would have liked to gauge Brent's reaction to their discovery.

"Yeah. So what?"

The kid was cool. Too cool. Alec couldn't put his finger on why it bothered him. "It's odd you never mentioned it. Were you afraid you'd be implicated in her disappearance?"

"No. I was out of town the day she was kidnapped. Is that all?"

"No, that's not all!" Libby put her hands on her hips. "What is *with* you, Brent? You're oh-so-smooth. Can't you just say what you think for once? Every time I talk to you, I can tell there is so much going on in your head."

"I'm thinking of nothing but my future," Brent said. He pushed his car door open wider.

"I get that my coming derailed some plans. It derailed my life too, but you all seem to forget that. And the other thing you ignore is that none of this is my fault! If I had lobbied for our father to leave me that property, then I could see your attitude. But I didn't."

Brent started to get in the car, but Alec blocked him. "Why didn't you tell us you spent time with Nicole? You never answered that."

"It didn't seem important." For the first time, Brent looked uncertain.

"What are you hiding?" Alec stood in the way of the door shutting. "Come on, Brent. We're not letting you go until you tell us the truth. What did Nicole have to say that day?"

"We didn't spend that much time talking. We were parasailing."

"You traveled together. Did you know who she was?"

Brent's jaw tightened. "I didn't know she was Libby's business partner, if that's what you mean. She asked me about the property, said she had someone interested in buying it. I already had their offer on the table though, so that was no big news."

"Why do you want to sell it instead of keeping it in the family?" Libby asked. "Did you disagree with our father's goal of preserving Hope Beach's peace and quiet?"

"I want to get off this podunk island," Brent said. "With that kind of money, I could go anywhere, do anything."

"You have quite a large amount of money coming even without the inn," Libby said.

"A million dollars will be gone in a heartbeat," Brent said. "That's nothing in today's economy."

What planet was this kid living on? Aware his jaw was hanging open, Alec shut it. "You could go to Harvard, start a business. Buy a house just about anywhere. What do you want to do that would require more than a million?"

Brent's eyes flickered. "You wouldn't understand."

"Try me."

"I'd like to build ships. Cruise ships."

It was a goal Alec could admire. "So get a job doing that. You don't really know anything about building ships. Start at the bottom and work your way up. There's virtue in that. Starting a business when you're ignorant of how to go about it is sure to result in failure."

"It doesn't matter now, does it? I'll have to make do with my paltry million. But don't worry. I'll figure out a way to accomplish my goal." He gave Alec a cold stare. "If you'll move away, I'd like to go."

Alec shrugged and backed off. The guy wasn't going to tell them any more. They watched him leave.

"I think there was something more between him and Nicole," Libby said.

"Me too. Let's talk to Vanessa."

TWENTY

The TV blared in the rec room, where Brent had apparently been in a hurry to watch some kind of shoot-'em-up film starring Bruce Willis. Libby and Alec walked through the inn in search of Vanessa. When they failed to find her, Alec stopped to snag bottles of water from the kitchen. Delilah was whipping cake batter and handed over the spoon when Alec begged for it.

"Have you seen Vanessa?" Libby asked.

Delilah slid the cake pan into the oven. "She said something about going for a swim."

"It's after dark," Libby said. "Isn't that dangerous?"

Delilah shrugged. "She's done it for years."

"Sharks are out now." Libby shuddered at the thought.

"The most dangerous time is just as it's getting dark," Alec said. "That's when they go out to feed."

"Does she know this?" Libby asked.

"Sure. Anyone who lives here knows the danger. But Vanessa isn't one to let anything stand in the way of what she wants to do." The spoon was licked clean and he put it in the stainless dishwasher. "How are you doing for money, Delilah? There are a lot of us to feed."

She hesitated. "Okay."

He pulled out his wallet. "Here's another hundred." He pressed it into her hand.

Libby caught a glimpse of his wallet and realized he'd given her all the cash he had. It shamed her to realize she'd given nothing toward food. Yes, the place was hers, but still. Alec didn't owe them anything. No money had been requested, but he'd handed it over without being asked. More than once.

She had a hundred tucked back for emergencies. This wasn't an emergency, was it? But her fingers dived into her wallet and pulled out the folded bill tucked behind her driver's license. "Here, take this too, Delilah." She had to force herself to release it into the other woman's hand.

When Delilah smiled, Libby felt lighter somehow. Her chest was warm. So this was how it felt to give. When was the last time she'd given so freely? Had she ever done it?

Delilah blinked rapidly and bit her lip. "Thank you, both of you. You're very generous. Some of the folks can't afford to give anything. Old Mr. Carter, for instance. All his pension money is in the groceries that have spoiled in his refrigerator. He feels terrible about it too, poor guy. And Vanessa and Brent can eat me out of house and home. Especially Brent. He expects peanut M&M'S to be in constant supply."

"I'll tell them to kick in some money," Libby said.

"Oh no, don't do that! They'll know I said something."

"I'll just ask if they have," Libby said. "I'll be very diplomatic."

Delilah began to smile. "There's cocoa fudge in the fridge." She pulled open the refrigerator door and pulled out the pan.

"Is this from the box of Hershey's cocoa?" Libby asked. She took a piece and bit into it. The flavor took her back to a time when she'd stand at the stove on a chair and stir the fudge while her mother gave directions. "Oh my goodness, I haven't had this kind of fudge since I was a little girl." She licked her fingers. "I'd better leave before I eat the whole pan."

"You could use a little fattening up," Delilah said.

"I think she looks pretty perfect," Alec said. His face reddened when Delilah laughed. "We could watch the movie with Brent while we wait. Maybe he'll say something more about Nicole."

Libby started to agree, then had another thought. "Which room was my father's when he stayed here? I'd like to look through it."

"Of course." Delilah wiped her hands on her apron. "He had a big suite on the third floor. In fact, his room was the only finished space on that floor." She grabbed a ring of keys hanging on a hook by the back door. "It's locked, so use the red key. It's clean. I make sure of that every week."

Libby's pulse skittered as she took the key ring. "Where are the stairs to the third floor?"

"At the end of the hall, down past my quarters. Take your time. Vanessa won't be in for another hour." Delilah pointed. "Use the back stairway."

Libby led the way up to the second-floor hall, then back to the third-floor stairs. "Why would he put his suite up there?"

"I think he wanted a retreat where he could play the piano without disturbing anyone," Alec said.

"Piano?"

"He played beautifully. There are some tapes of him playing. They must be around here somewhere."

"I would love to hear one. All of them, actually."

The attic stairs were steeper than the main flights. The stairwell was closed as well. Alec reached past her to flip on the light. The steps creaked as she mounted them to the landing in the attic. It had been beautifully restored to highlight the maple floors, exposed rafters, and large windows that let the starlight shine in.

"How nice," she said, taking in the decor. The chairs went well with the camelback sofa and antique tables. "He had good taste. Chippendale chairs?"

"I think so. You would know better than I would."

There was a flat-screen television mounted on one wall. A bookcase filled with books was on the opposite wall. There was a small kitchenette with a microwave and coffeemaker beside it.

"Looks like his bedroom was through there." Alec pointed to a door on the other side of the cabinets. "Or do you want to look around here first?" He walked over and switched on the table lamps.

The warm glow illuminated the table. Libby frowned and went to inspect the purse. "That looks like Nicole's bag." She picked up the Brighton bag and opened it. Nicole's favorite lipstick, Burt's Bees Fig, was in the top pocket. She pulled out the wallet and glanced at the driver's license. Nicole's face smiled back. "It *is* Nicole's! What was she doing up here?"

———

The contents of the purse lay strewn on the coffee table. "Nothing out of order?" Alec asked Libby. The find had shaken her. Her high spirits vanished.

She picked up a piece of paper. "What's this about? It's a note from Mindy asking her to meet Brent for parasailing. Look, Mindy was going to go with them. She didn't mention that. I think we need to ask her how many times she saw Nicole. She hasn't been up front with us."

"I'm going to tell Tom about it too. Something isn't right about all of it. I think Mindy knows more than she's telling. Brent too." He stretched his arm across the back of the sofa. She was sitting close to him. Was it on purpose?

"I'm so tired of trying to figure this out."

Her hair tickled his arm. All he had to do was drop his arm

around her and pull her close. What would she do if he tried it? Slap him? He felt as though he'd known her forever. They'd spent more time together in the past four days than he'd spent with the last woman he'd dated for two months. The fragrance in her hair was wonderful. Vanilla maybe? Sweet and enticing. He leaned a fraction of an inch closer and inhaled.

She must have heard him, because she turned her head and lifted a brow. "Is something wrong?"

"I was just smelling your hair," he said, his voice soft.

She didn't slap him. In fact, she leaned a little closer. "Vanilla shampoo," she said.

Her breath whispered across his face. With his right hand, he reached out and twisted a curl around his finger. "Nice," he said. With the back of his hand, he caressed her jaw. His gaze was caught by the glimpse of a necklace under her collar. "Is that Ray's?"

"You recognize it?" She pulled it free of her shirt and held it up. "WWJD. I've been trying to figure out how Jesus would act if his siblings hated him."

"So that's how you've been keeping your cool so well." Ray's legacy continued, even now. The realization stunned Alec.

"I don't know that I've been doing a good job of it. It's hard. My dad's letter asked me to be generous with Vanessa and Brent. I think he meant more than money."

"I'm sure he did. Money never mattered much to him."

"He said to be generous in grace. It would be easier just to share the property with them. Neither of them make it easy. But I'm trying."

No wonder he was so drawn to her. She was remarkable. "Back at the fish fry, I was going to ask you if—"

"What are you doing up here?" Vanessa shouted from behind them. She stood at the top of the stairs.

Libby sprang to her feet. "I'm looking around. How was your swim?"

Nice way to keep her cool. Alec managed not to grin. Her soft answer did nothing to calm Vanessa, who stood with her hands on her hips. Her wet hair hung down her back, and she wore a blue cover-up.

"See any sharks?" he asked.

Her gaze skewered him, and she ignored the question. "This is my father's personal space. You have no business here."

"I own it," Libby said, a steel undercurrent in her voice.

Vanessa strode across the floor to stop two feet from Libby. "So you keep throwing in my face! You may own the property, but you don't own the personal contents."

"Oh, but I do," Libby said. "Ask Horace if you don't believe me."

Tears hung on Vanessa's lashes, and Alec realized she was genuinely hurt. It wasn't anger that drove her. She was covering her pain with outrage.

"You miss your dad, don't you?" he asked her. "Do you come up here often?"

Vanessa burst into tears and covered her face with her hands. "She didn't even know him or love him." She ran to the bedroom and twisted the knob, but it didn't open. She pounded on the door and shrieked, "It's not fair. It's not!"

Libby went to her and put her hand on her shoulder. "Vanessa, I'm sorry. I wish I'd known him. It's not my fault, you know."

Vanessa flinched away. "Don't touch me! It wasn't my fault either, but I'm paying the price."

Libby said nothing. Her hand fell to her side. She bit her lip and turned away.

"You two are sisters, Vanessa. You can build a relationship if you work on it."

Vanessa folded her arms across her chest. "It's too late. I don't want to." She rattled the doorknob. "Give me the key. I want to go in. By myself." Her eyes narrowed, and she stared at Libby's neck.

"That necklace. Where did you find it? Up here?" She swiped at Libby's throat.

Libby leaped back. "Our father left it to me."

Vanessa went even whiter. "That's impossible. He knew I wanted it."

"I'm sorry," Libby said. "I can show you the letter. He wanted me to think about the meaning of the necklace every day as I'm working to try to get to know you and Brent."

Vanessa's face worked and her eyes filled again. "That belongs to me. You have no right to it."

Alec winced when he realized what Ray had intended for good was causing more division between the sisters.

TWENTY-ONE

The beads were warm and smooth under Libby's fingers. *What would Jesus do?* The necklace was just a thing. Yes, her father had left it to her, had wanted her to have it. But did it mean even more to Vanessa? Her father had asked Libby to give mercy and grace to Vanessa and Brent. What exactly did that mean?

Libby studied her sister's face. Were those tears of pain or of anger?

Vanessa covered her face with her hands. "Don't look at me like that."

"Like what?" Libby asked. "I'm trying to understand."

"I don't want your understanding. Or anything else from you. I just want my daddy back!" Vanessa whirled and rushed out of the room.

Tears sprang to Libby's eyes too. Alec put his arms around her, and she buried her face in his chest. "What should I do?" she choked.

"What do you mean?"

She pulled away and touched the beads. "About this? Should I give it to her?"

"I don't think I can tell you the right thing to do. What does your heart say?"

"I think Jesus would give it to her." Her voice broke, and she swallowed hard. "It's only a thing. I think I may have already gotten out of the necklace what my father hoped I would. But he wore it for over twenty years. I feel close to him when I'm wearing it. It's all I have of him. So I want to keep it."

"No one is making you do anything. It's your choice."

She studied his kind eyes. "You think I should give it up, don't you?"

He shook his head. "I think Vanessa is acting like a spoiled brat, and I wouldn't give in to her. But she's not my sister. I'm not the one trying to be part of a family the way you are. I don't know what the right answer is."

"I don't either. Vanessa *is* acting like a brat. But I see her pain too. I think I'm going to have to pray about this and see if God will give me some clear direction."

"Let's pray together." His head touched hers.

She closed her eyes and listened to him pray for wisdom and discernment on how to best handle the family dynamics. No other person had ever prayed with her like this, about concerns that mattered so deeply to her. Her spirit bonded with his as they asked God for help.

"Amen," she said when he was finished. "Thank you, Alec. You're a good man."

He shook his head. "I've got lots of faults, believe me."

"I'm not seeing them," she said, holding his gaze. "Thank you for caring enough to pray. I don't know anyone else who would do that."

His fingers touched her chin and tipped her face up. He leaned forward and his lips touched hers. Warmth spread through her belly and up her neck. His lips were firm and tender. No kiss she'd ever experienced affected her like this one. In his arms she felt safe and treasured. She palmed his face, relishing the feel of the stubble on his cheek. He was all man, yet the tender side of him was so godly, so strong.

She pulled away when Delilah called up the stairs. "Alec, phone call."

"Sorry," he said with obvious regret. "I'll be back." He went down the stairs.

Libby stared at the door to her father's inner sanctum. There was no reason not to go inside. Before she could talk herself out of it, she fitted the key into the door and unlocked it. Her hand shook when she twisted the knob, and her knees were weak. She pushed open the door.

There weren't many windows, so she flipped on the lights to illuminate the dim room. It contained a king-size bed with tan and blue linens. Pillows were heaped at the head of the bed. The walls were painted a creamy tan. The wood floors gleamed. Libby wandered around the room, picking up pictures and examining details. There were many photos of her father with Vanessa and Brent. Also ones of him on a big yacht with his wife.

If only she could have been part of his life. If only there was even one picture of her with her father. Libby turned back toward the door and spied a brown leather Bible on the bed stand. She picked it up and settled on the edge of the bed. The ribbon marked a passage in Hebrews 13. She skimmed it until she saw verse 16 highlighted in yellow.

But do not forget to do good and to share, for with such sacrifices God is well pleased.

She clutched the beads. God didn't mean the necklace. She could share other things with Vanessa. But even as she argued with herself, a sick roiling in her belly told her the truth. God had answered Alec's prayer with a clear message.

The question was whether she could make herself give up something so precious to her.

Debris still littered Oyster Road, and folks were out cleaning their yards. It was going to take a long time before Hope Beach looked like it did before the storm. Mud puddles were everywhere, and gulls swarmed the area, scavenging sea creatures that the waves had left behind. The air reeked of rotting fish and seaweed.

She sniffed the air. "Smells like the sea on a really bad day."

"Careful." Alec put out his hand to stop Libby from stepping in front of a kid on a motorbike.

The wind tugged strands of her shiny hair loose from the ponytail. She sure was pretty. He'd lain awake for hours last night reliving that kiss. Their attraction felt God-ordained to him.

He nodded toward a neat white bungalow that had been converted into a small café. "Mindy is usually getting an egg sandwich for her and Horace about now. Let's see what she has to say about the note in Nicole's purse."

They crossed the street to the courtyard. Live oak trees shaded tables draped with red-and-white cloths. Inside, several residents spoke and nodded greetings to them as they threaded their way to where Mindy sat with lunch in one hand and a novel in the other. Her attention was on the book as she absently took a bite of her egg sandwich.

She looked up when Alec cleared his throat. Her gaze went from him to Libby and back again. She finished chewing and swallowed, then dabbed her napkin to her lips. "You looking for Horace? He's not here."

"Nope. We wanted to talk to you. Mind if we join you?"

She put down her book with obvious reluctance. "I don't have long. Horace will be wanting his egg sandwich in another fifteen minutes."

"This won't take long." He pulled out a chair for Libby, then settled into the one beside her. "We want to ask you a few more questions."

Mindy hunched her shoulders. "I already told you everything I know."

Alec brought out the note they'd found in Nicole's purse. "I don't think so."

Mindy's face went white. Her gaze darted from him to the note.

"Why didn't you tell us you went parasailing with them?"

Mindy bit her lip and looked down at her hands. "It didn't seem important."

"Every detail is important. We have to retrace Nicole's tracks and find out what happened to her," he said.

Libby leaned forward in her chair. "What did you all talk about?"

Mindy took a sip of her pink lemonade. "Mostly business stuff. She talked to Brent about the sale of the inn."

Libby shook her head. "By then he would have known I owned the inn, not him. So why would Nicole discuss it with him?"

Mindy looked down at her lap. "He wanted to know if she could talk you into giving up your inheritance. He thought she might have enough influence."

"What did Nicole say?" Libby asked.

"That no one would be that stupid."

Knowing Brent the way he did, Alec could only imagine how well that went over. "I'll bet that ticked Brent off."

"Yes." Her admission was barely audible.

So that's why Brent brushed them off when questioned about the parasailing event. If they knew there'd been an argument, he would draw suspicion.

Mindy glanced at her watch. "I need to get back to work." She signaled to the server, who brought her the bill and a white lunch sack. She left money on the table and rose. "You aren't going to tell

Horace, are you? He wouldn't like it if he knew I'd gone out with them. She was a client."

"If Brent had anything to do with Nicole's disappearance, it's going to come out sooner or later," Alec said. "You should tell him yourself."

Mindy shook her head violently. "He'd fire me in a heartbeat. I know Brent had nothing to do with it, so I'm safe." She scooped up the bag and headed out through the dining room and into the courtyard.

Alec sat back in his chair. "I think we'd better talk to your brother. He knows more about this than I thought."

TWENTY-TWO

The last of the clouds had rolled away when Libby got out of Alec's truck in the circular drive by the old hotel. She was struck again at the structure's beauty. Someone moved on the expansive columned porch, and she saw Brent leaning on the balustrade. Vanessa was at a table with a coffee cup in her hand.

Libby's stomach tightened at the thought of the coming confrontation. She wanted to love her siblings. That they might be involved in Nicole's disappearance was too horrible to contemplate.

"Steady, let me handle this," Alec said when she drew in a deep breath.

She knew he would be calmer than she was, so she nodded and followed him up the sweeping steps to the grand porch. At the moment, she was glad she hadn't given the necklace to Vanessa.

Brent straightened when they drew near. Libby studied his handsome face. Vanessa was beautiful as well. Their adversarial situation showed no signs of changing. Libby touched her necklace. *What would Jesus do?*

Brent's smile melted away when he glanced at Alec's face. "Something wrong?"

"You tell us." Alec stared at him. "You tried to persuade Nicole to talk Libby into giving up her inheritance. And when

Nicole refused, you argued. Two days before she disappeared. That looks bad."

Vanessa joined them at the railing. "Who told you this?"

Alec folded his arms across his chest. "That's not important."

"It had to be Mindy. She was the only other person there," Brent said. "So what? It's no crime to try to convince Libby to do the right thing."

"The right thing." Libby shook her head. "It was the right thing for you. Not for anyone else."

His eyes were cold. "I didn't know you. I still don't. You're a stranger to us and to this town. You don't understand."

"So help me understand! I know it's too much to ask to be part of the family, but the least you could do is treat me with common courtesy."

Vanessa and Brent exchanged a glance. Was it Libby's imagination or did her sister look a little shamefaced?

Alec narrowed his eyes. "So why didn't you go meet her to show her the lighthouse, Vanessa? Because the two of you'd made plans to do away with her?"

"We had nothing to do with her disappearance," Brent said.

The screen door opened and Pearl stepped out. For someone so rotund, she was light on her feet. "What's going on out here?" she asked. "Your voices are carrying to our guests."

"Brent and Vanessa may know more about Nicole's disappearance than they've been willing to tell us," Alec said.

"Oh dear me, that's not true, is it?" Pearl's gaze went from her nephew to her niece. "What do you know about that girl's kidnapping? Tell the truth now."

Pearl's appearance took all the bravado out of Brent. "We didn't have anything to do with her disappearance, Aunt Pearl."

Pearl's gaze narrowed on him. "Did you ask some friends to put a scare into her?"

He flushed. "I wouldn't do that."

Pearl lifted a brow. "No? I think Jennifer Masters might disagree with that."

"That was different."

Libby didn't like the way he looked down, or the color that came and went in his face. "You've done this before?" If he'd played a prank, then maybe she would have Nicole safe and sound yet today.

He shrugged. "It was just a trick on an old girlfriend."

"Way I heard it, you had two friends grab her and take her to the mainland, where they left her to find her own way back home," Alec said. "I'd forgotten about that. Is that what you did with Nicole? Tell us the truth. We can have her picked up."

"I didn't do anything!"

"Quit harassing Brent," Vanessa snapped. "He had nothing to do with this. Neither did I."

"It still seems odd that you didn't meet her when you said you would," Libby said. "I was watching on the cam. When she was taken, you were already ten minutes late."

"Being late is not a crime." She glanced at her brother.

This was getting them nowhere. The two weren't budging, but Libby didn't get the sense that they were guilty of harming Nicole. "How do you get to the lighthouse ruins you were going to show her?" she asked. "Maybe that's a place to start looking."

"She wasn't taken there," Alec said. "She was on the boardwalk."

"True enough, but we don't know anywhere else to look." Libby wasn't about to let any of them dissuade her. If she had to go by herself, she would. "Can someone direct me to it?"

"I'll take you whenever you want," Alec said. "I think it's a waste of time though. The site is down the shore in an area where no one ever goes. The fastest way to get there is by boat."

"How was Nicole going to get there?" Libby asked. "Were you meeting her in a boat or what?"

They both stared at Vanessa, who put her cup down on the railing and stared out to sea without answering. Libby curled her fingers into her palms. "Vanessa, I've had enough of your attitude. My friend is *missing*. She's been kidnapped. Do you get that? I saw two men forcibly take her away. She was kicking and screaming. One of them poked a needle in her arm." Her voice broke and she took a deep breath. "You'll help me find her or you can get out of my house."

Vanessa's eyes widened. So did Pearl's. Brent just continued to look bored.

"We have no place to go," Vanessa said. "I've spent more time in this house than you can imagine. Dad would roll over in his grave if he heard you threaten us like this."

Her sister's words brought Libby up short. Extend grace, he'd asked. She hardened her jaw. "All that matters to me is finding Nicole. Conflict like this is fruitless."

Vanessa's lips tightened. "I'm not the one who declared war. You think you can breeze in here and take over, but as you pointed out, you didn't even know Daddy. You're no real daughter."

"Maybe not," Libby said evenly. "But I own this place and I say who goes and who stays. So you choose which side you're on and let me know." She slapped her hand to her head. "What's the use? I'm going to go do something useful."

As she walked into the house, she fingered her necklace. Would Jesus have been so harsh? Maybe. He did confront the money changers in the temple. Figuring out how to act in a godly manner was even harder than she thought it would be.

———

Libby changed her clothes. Heat gun in hand, she attacked the layers of chipped paint on the trim around the front door. There were easily ten layers of paint on the wood. When it softened and melted, she scraped it off with a putty knife and deposited it in a metal coffee can the gardener had found for her.

"That almost looks fun," Alec said from behind her. "Want some help?"

"I only have one heat gun or I'd take you up on it."

A white SUV pulled into the driveway. A slim woman with auburn curls stepped out of the passenger side. Moments later a stocky man with dark hair was out also and opening the back door on his side. A young boy of about ten joined the woman in the drive.

Libby put down the heat gun. They must be new guests. "Hello," she said, smiling at the family. "Welcome to Tidewater Inn."

The woman was staring at the inn with clear admiration. "I always forget just how beautiful it is until I get here again." She transferred her attention to Libby and held out her hand. "I'm Bree Matthews. You're expecting us."

Delilah had mentioned the family's arrival. It was their third visit in as many years. "We've got your room ready," Libby said. "Can I help you with anything? Call one of the men to help with luggage?"

"I'll help them," Alec said.

Bree pulled the boy beside her. "This is Davy. He's ten now and my big boy. That's my husband, Kade."

Kade was lifting toddlers from car seats in the back. "Be ready," he called. "They've been cooped up and will want to run for the water." He set a little boy and girl on the ground.

"How old are they?" Libby asked.

"Almost two. They're named Hunter and Hannah." Bree smiled and scooped her daughter up as she ran past. "You don't have your swimsuit on yet, honey," she told the child.

"They're beautiful." But Libby's attention was caught by the gorgeous dog that hopped out of the hatch. "Nice dog." Did they allow dogs in the inn? Delilah had never mentioned their policy.

"This is Samson, my search dog."

Libby watched Alec pet the dog. "Search dog? He finds lost people, like on TV?"

"He's the best." Bree snapped her fingers and the dog rushed over to lick them. "Good boy," she crooned.

Libby stared at the dog. He looked like he had quite a bit of German shepherd in him. "I don't know if you've heard anything about it, but we have a missing woman here. She happens to be my business partner."

Bree's gaze sharpened. "What happened? I haven't watched the news. We've been driving from Michigan and have been playing videos for the children."

Libby told her about Nicole's abduction. "You think he can find her?" Libby petted him and he nosed her leg.

"We can let him try." There was a shadow in Bree's green eyes, but she held Libby's gaze. "A water search is always harder. I want you to understand that. But he has a good nose. We'll do what we can, okay?"

Libby had hoped for utter assurance, but she managed a smile. "I appreciate anything you can do."

Bree glanced around. "Any idea of where to start the search?"

"I can show you where she was taken, but I also know Nicole was down the beach a ways, at some old lighthouse ruins. We haven't searched there yet, and I thought we might look at the ruins too. But let's get you unpacked first. I'll show you to your room."

Delilah had arranged for them to have the only two-bedroom suite so the children would have plenty of space. Libby hadn't been around kids much, and as the men unloaded the back of the SUV, she found her gaze lingering on the twins. Their dark hair was soft and curly. The little girl had Bree's pointed chin and hairline. The little boy was stocky like his handsome father.

"I want to see the water," Davy announced.

Hannah ran to Alec's leg and tugged on his jeans. "Water," she said, pointing toward the waves.

"We're going, bug," Kade said, touching the boy's hair.

Libby liked Kade already. The way he looked at Bree made Libby glance at Alec from the corner of her eye. Alec was tossing little Hannah in the air while she giggled and screamed, "More!" He seemed to be a natural with the kids. And he'd willingly taken on the raising of his nephew. That couldn't have been easy. Only a rare man would be willing to alter his life that much.

The women corralled the children while the men took the luggage to the room. Bree's mouth curved in a smile. "I like your fellow."

Libby stopped petting Samson, then resumed. "He's not my fellow. I haven't known him very long."

"Sometimes it doesn't take long. He seems like a nice guy."

"He's a good man," Libby agreed.

The men came back out. Kade had a vest in his hand. The dog began to prance around Bree when she took it from him. "Hold still, Samson." She knelt and slipped the vest onto the dog. His tail came up and he looked even more alert. "Someone is ready to go searching."

Samson's ears pricked at the word *searching*. He whined and looked down the beach. "He knows what we're talking about?" Libby asked.

"Oh yes. He loves his job. He acts differently when he's working. Let's go to the location where she was taken. Can you get me something that Nicole has worn? Put it in double paper sacks." Bree handed her two bags. "Our best chance is to go out on a boat and see if Samson can get a scent. But, Libby, it's going to be a long shot, okay?"

Maybe so, but it was a better chance than any other Libby had. She ran inside to grab one of Nicole's shirts. Having another ally had given her new courage.

Twenty-Three

Alec stood on the boardwalk with his hands in the pockets of his shorts and watched the freshening wind blow Libby's hair in tangles. As soon as they let the dog out of the SUV, he ran in circles, then back to Bree, who held the bags containing Nicole's shirt. Alec had heard of search dogs, but he'd never seen one in action.

"Where was she when she was taken?" Bree asked. She stood looking around the area.

"Right there." Libby pointed out the camera and the spot where her friend had been standing.

They scanned the same sand dunes, the same rolling ocean that Alec had seen earlier in the week when he'd come here with Tom. The only new items were a crumpled cigarette pack, an empty potato chip bag, and a few Marlboro butts.

Bree knelt and opened the bag. Samson thrust his nose into the bag. "Search, Samson!"

The dog pulled his head from the bag and barked. He ran back and forth across the beach with his nose in the air. Alec's jaw dropped as he watched the dog work. Samson clearly seemed to know what he was doing. When the dog stiffened, so did Alec, though he didn't know what it meant.

"He's got a scent!" Bree ran after the dog.

Alec and Libby followed. Libby's expression was intent and hopeful, so he rushed ahead of her, just in case whatever Samson was smelling was something Alec didn't want her to find. Samson trailed the scent to the parking lot. He ran to a trash barrel and began to bark.

Alec's gut clenched, and he prayed they wouldn't find Nicole's body in it. "Stand back." He motioned for the women to move back a few feet. Once he got the top off the garbage pail, he put on plastic gloves and began poking through it in spite of the stench. It was only about half full, so he relaxed, sure he wasn't going to find anything at all. The dog had probably gotten sidetracked by the food smells.

"That's hers!" Libby's arm shot past him and grabbed a pink straw hat. She shook off the debris. "I told you I saw it fall off her in the struggle."

"You're sure?" Bree asked.

Libby nodded. "I bought it for her for her birthday. What's it doing in the trash?"

"You shouldn't have touched it." Alec took it in his gloved hands. "Maybe the killers handled it."

The animation on Libby's face ebbed. "It came off her head in the struggle. I don't think they touched it."

"You said they took her right to the boat and offshore," he pointed out. "You saw them throw her into the boat and move off? They didn't come back for the hat?"

"I saw them leave." Her mouth drooped. "So this means nothing."

"We know the dog can smell her," he said. "Pretty amazing. I guess they could have come back and just thrown it away so nothing looked out of place on the beach. Anyone could have tossed it."

Bree called the dog back to her and had him smell the sack again. "Search, Samson!"

Samson sniffed the air, then ran back to the beach. He barked and raced to a spot near the water, where he began to dig. Alec and the women ran to see what he'd found. Alec knelt to help Samson, but he woofed and nosed at a pair of sunglasses before Alec could dig his fingers into the sand.

Alec held them up. "Nicole's?"

Libby nodded. "I think so."

The dog whined and pressed his nose against Bree's hand. She went through the process of letting him smell the bag again. He ran back and forth on the sand for ten minutes before going back to Bree's side. He whined, then laid at her feet.

"I think this is all he's got," Bree said.

"It was worth a try." Libby glanced at Alec. "Could you take us out tomorrow in the boat?"

"Sure. You think he can find something in the ocean?" Watching the dog work was interesting, but Alec didn't see how Samson could possibly find Nicole in that ocean.

Bree shrugged. "I won't lie and say it's likely. There's a lot of ocean out there and we really don't know where to even look. But Samson has done many other amazing searches successfully, so I want to try."

He appreciated Bree's honesty. Alec nodded. "We'll take my boat out first thing in the morning."

Libby was too restless to watch the movie playing in the living room. Bree was bathing the children and getting them to bed, so Libby slipped away from the group and went to the third floor again. Her interest in finding out how Nicole's purse had ended up there had resurfaced.

She flipped on the light, then stood in the main living area of the third floor and glanced around. The stairs creaked behind her and she whirled to see Brent stepping into the space.

"What are you doing up here?" he demanded.

"Looking around." She decided against reminding him that she owned the property and could go anywhere she pleased. She'd written in her journal that she hadn't extended much grace after their last encounter.

He scowled at her. "These are Dad's private quarters."

"I know." She gestured to the table. "Nicole's bag is here. Do you have any idea how it got up here?"

"*She* was up here?"

"It appears so. Unless someone put her purse here."

"Have you asked Delilah about it?"

She should have thought of that. "No. But you didn't answer my question. Did *you* know about it?"

His gaze was steady. "You really think I had something to do with her disappearance, don't you?"

She'd had enough of his evasiveness. "Why do you always answer a question with another one? Just answer me, yes or no. Did you see Nicole's purse up here?"

"No. This is the first I've been up here since Dad died. Your turn. You think I'm guilty of something bad, don't you?"

He looked so innocent, so hurt. Was any of it real? Libby wanted to believe him. He was her brother, after all. "I honestly don't know. I'd like to believe you did nothing to hurt her, but you have to admit your lies look bad."

"I didn't do anything to her. It was an innocent outing."

Libby reminded herself how young he was. Maybe she was overreacting. "I know you weren't one of the men who took her. I saw them. But you could have hired the men."

"I could have, but I didn't."

She wanted to know this brother, but she couldn't seem to get through. "You're hard to read, Brent. I want to believe you." She decided that Jesus would lay it all out there, so she gathered her courage. "What do you want, Brent? Do you even care that you have another sister? We're family, you know. We share our father's blood. I want us to learn to love each other."

His eyes flickered when she mentioned love, but then he folded his arms over his chest. "I'm sure you're a very nice person, Libby, but I have one sister and that's enough. You don't belong here. I'm sorry to be so blunt, but you can't show up here and announce you're part of our family and expect it to be so. To us, you're just a stranger."

Though she agreed with the gist of what he'd said, his cold gaze cut her. Her eyes filled, and she turned away so he wouldn't see. "I see. Thank you for being honest." He was still standing there when she regained her composure, so she turned back toward him. "In Nicole's journal, she mentioned that someone whispered to her outside her door. Was that you?"

His jaw tightened. "You're determined to pin something on me, aren't you?"

"Who else would have access here? And it was a male. Be honest with me, Brent. I've learned enough about our father to know he valued honesty and integrity."

His lips flattened. "Fine. I tried to scare her off. Satisfied? But I had nothing to do with her disappearance."

"Why did you want to scare her off? She wasn't hurting you."

His sigh was heavy. "Look, she told me she wanted you to keep the property and develop it yourself. I felt the honorable thing for you to do was to bow out. I still feel that way."

"She wanted us to develop it? That's crazy. Where could we come up with enough money?" Maybe Nicole had been making a play to squeeze more money out of the buyer. Poe seemed determined to have the land.

She held Brent's gaze and found truth there. "I believe you."

His eyes flickered. "Really? Or will those doubts surface again?"

She shook her head. "We've gotten off to a really bad start. Friends?" She reached out her hand.

Brent stared at her extended hand, then quickly touched his fingers to hers and withdrew. "Let's say acquaintances for now."

It was a start.

The steps creaked behind them, then Delilah stepped into the room. She stopped short when she saw them. "I went to the storage shed to look for something and saw the light on up here. I thought someone had forgotten to turn it off. Is everything all right?"

Libby nodded. "I do have a question though." She picked up Nicole's bag. "Do you know how this got here?"

Delilah's lids flickered. "I assume Nicole left it."

"She was up here? Why?" Libby didn't like the thought that Nicole had been poking through her father's things. Maybe this was how Vanessa felt.

"She'd asked to explore the house. I didn't give her any keys and had no idea she would find her way up here, but I must have left the door unlocked when I cleaned the last time. I found her here and chased her out."

"Did she say what she was doing?"

Delilah shook her head. "I think she just wanted to see what was here. She didn't seem to have an agenda, if that's what you mean."

Nicole was as much of a history buff as she was. Libby could see her wanting to poke into every nook and cranny of the attic.

So the purse was a dead end. "I'd like to be alone for a while," she said.

Brent and Delilah exchanged a glance. Brent shrugged. "You're the boss." He went down the steps and Delilah followed.

Libby exhaled and sank onto the sofa. In this place she could sense her father. It would be the perfect spot to have her devotions every day too. His Bible was still on the table where she'd left it. She hadn't had a chance to go through it much. When she picked it up, she realized there was a folded paper, stiff with age, under it.

She unfolded it and discovered it was a map of the island. The old lighthouse site was marked on it. Holding it under the light, she saw someone had written the word *cellar* with an arrow on it near the house structure. Another X marked the wellhead. The place once had several outbuildings too. She was eager to see how much of it still stood. And whether it harbored any clues to Nicole's whereabouts.

TWENTY-FOUR

The sun was barely up, and haze still hung over the waves. Sea spray stung Libby's cheeks and filled her nose with the salty scent of the ocean. She crouched behind the windshield of Alec's boat to avoid a large wave that threatened to wash over the bow. "The sea is strong today."

Bree and Samson rode up front. The dog had his nose in the wind and wore an ecstatic smile. "It's gorgeous out here," Bree called. "Not quite the same as Lake Superior where we live, but close enough. Where are we going?"

Alec pointed to the shore. "The lighthouse ruins. We'll land there. I'll drop anchor, and we'll have to wade to shore. It's got a sandy bottom though, so no danger of getting dunked."

"I'm not afraid of the water," Libby said. In fact, she couldn't think of anything she enjoyed more than being on the sea. Well, other than digging into the history of a gorgeous old house.

The spit of land was narrow, only about twenty feet across. Scrubby bushes and vegetation that had stood up to the salt clung to the sparse soil. The small peninsula widened at the base and joined the main part of the island, where heavier vegetation hid whatever ruins they'd come here to see. Libby scanned the area for a hint of the cover-up Nicole had been wearing. She wasn't sure

163

if she was relieved or sad to see no sign that her friend had ever been here.

The boat touched bottom, and Alec tossed the anchor overboard. Samson dived over the side and swam toward shore. Alec clambered into the shallows, then held out his hand to assist Libby and Bree. Kicking off her sandals, Libby slipped into the water with him. The sea was chillier than she'd expected. The storm must have stirred up the cold from the bottom. She held her shoes out of the water and waded to shore. The sand was firm and smooth under her bare feet. When she reached the beach, she slipped her feet back into her sandals, then looked around.

"Where are the ruins? I don't see anything," she said.

He pointed. "This way."

He led them north, away from the finger of barren peninsula, deeper into the vegetation. Samson barked and ran ahead. Sea oats waved in the breeze, and beach grass fought to hold on in the dunes. Skate cases littered the sand. The sand began to run out and was replaced by thin soil that supported a maritime forest of straggly live oaks pruned by the salt into wedge shapes. Palmettos and loblolly pines marched along the forest.

Libby spied the ruins before he said anything. "There," she said, pointing. The area was still flooded, and she could see only the tops of brick and mortar. "It was a lighthouse once? There's not much left of it. I expected a standing structure."

"It was knocked over in a big hurricane in the late eighteen hundreds. Legend has it that Blackbeard stormed the lighthouse and captured the keeper's daughter."

"What happened to her?" Bree asked, shuddering.

He shrugged. "No one really knows. Some say Blackbeard loved her and carried her off to his lair in the Bahamas. Others say she jumped overboard and drowned rather than face dishonor. But it's just a legend. There may be no truth to it at all. People have come out here from Hope Beach for generations. Weddings have been held here, ashes have been committed to the sea from here, and babies have been dedicated on this spot. It's almost a shrine to the town."

Libby glanced around. "Why? The place seems so barren."

He propped one foot on the ruins. "Over the years it gained the reputation of bestowing good luck on residents. The first marriage here that I know of was at the turn of the century. That marriage lasted sixty years."

She lifted her chin and sniffed the sweet-smelling air. "It has a welcoming feel in spite of all the ruins."

Advancing to the base of the building, she examined the debris. "Nicole was wearing a pink cover-up over a brown bathing suit. She had on pink flip-flops too. And her hair was in a ponytail."

"I'll take Samson and we'll nose around," Bree said. She pulled a bag of pistachios from her pocket. "Want some?"

Libby grinned and shook her head. She dug into her pocket and held up her jalapeño jellybeans. "I have these."

Bree wrinkled her nose, then she and Samson headed toward the line of vegetation. The dog had his nose down.

Alec walked the perimeter of the ruins and back. "I don't see anything but a few Coke bottles. We'll come back again when the water recedes."

"I'd wondered if she came out here on her own, but I don't see any sign of her."

"How would she get here? It would take an hour to walk from the house," he said.

"She's an avid runner. I imagine she could run along the beach and get here in forty-five minutes. She's not the type to wait for someone else to show her something of interest. I thought she might have come out here the day before to scout it out before coming with Vanessa." She turned and looked out to sea. "Would they have taken her to the mainland? I don't know where we should look."

"The state has put out a bulletin about her. If she's there, someone will see her. This is summer. The coastline is crawling with tourists. It would be hard to take her anywhere without being seen."

"But not impossible if they did it in the middle of the night," Libby said.

"She was taken late in the afternoon."

Libby felt so hopeless. "They could have holed up somewhere."

"True enough."

Libby realized she was grasping at straws. "What about farther out? Are there any uninhabited islands on this side of the island?"

He nodded. "Plenty of them. Some of them barely as big as a postage stamp. I thought we'd check out as many as we can. We can go out in the boat and ask fishermen if they've seen anything too."

"You think she's dead, don't you?" The question tore from Libby's throat.

He stared down at her. "We both know that the longer it goes since she's been spotted, the scarier it is. But I haven't given up hope yet. Someone has to have seen something."

She searched his expression. "You really believe that?"

"I do."

His certainty strengthened her. She glanced back at the ruins. "Are there any photos of the lighthouse before it was destroyed?"

He nodded. "Your dad has quite a library at the old hotel. He was a history buff, and the information about the island and Hope Beach that he has is more extensive than anything the town library has."

It appeared she had something in common with the father who left her.

Alec led Libby across the street from the harbor to the Oyster Café. It was lunchtime and there would be plenty of townspeople around who might have met Nicole during her stay. Bree had taken Samson to meet Kade and the children for lunch at Captain's Pizza.

"This is such a darling village," Libby said when they stopped outside the café. "I love it. So quaint."

He pushed the door open. The waitress seated them by the window that looked out onto the street where bicyclers zipped past.

"Why do so many people ride bicycles here?" she asked.

He hadn't thought much about it. "Gas is high, and it costs to get a car over here. I guess progress hasn't caught up to us."

"I like it. I'd like to get a bike."

"Your dad has one in the basement of the inn. I'll show you where it is."

She brightened. "I'd like to use his." Her smile faded. "Though it's likely to be one more source of contention with Vanessa and Brent. They don't want me to have anything personal of my father's."

"They'll get over it." He watched her toy with the necklace. "You still have the necklace, I see. I wondered if you would give it to Vanessa last night."

"I think God is telling me to do it, but I'm fighting the idea."

"It's never a good idea to fight God."

"I know." She gave a heavy sigh. "I don't want to do it. I've been praying he makes me willing to obey."

"Good prayer." He looked at the menu. "I think I'll get shrimp grits."

"Crab linguine sounds good," she said, staring at the menu. "Have you had it?"

He nodded. "It's good."

She glanced around the crowded space. "Who might have talked to Nicole?"

He scanned the tables. "I guess anyone in here could have. This is a popular place to eat."

"Maybe the waitress will remember her."

"Maybe." He motioned to the waitress, a pretty woman who was about twenty-five. He should know her name, but he couldn't remember it. All he knew was that she'd moved here from Kill Devil Hills about six months ago.

"What can I get for you?"

He gave their orders. "Did you meet the young woman who was kidnapped earlier this week?"

"Sure did. She sat at that table right there." The waitress pointed to the corner table behind them. "I didn't know her name, but I recognized her face when I saw it in the paper."

"Did she eat alone?" Libby asked.

The waitress shook her head. "Some slick city guy was with her. Real dark hair. Kind of reminded me of Elvis."

"Poe," Libby said. She shot a glance at Alec.

"Could you hear what they talked about?" Alec asked.

"I overheard them arguing a little," the woman said. "She said she thought he wasn't paying enough."

"For what?" Alec asked.

"I don't know. I didn't hear that." The server stuck her pencil behind her ear. "I'd better get this order in."

When the woman walked away, Libby leaned forward. "So maybe she was negotiating for more money for my land."

"Looks like it. When are you supposed to hear from him again?"

"I told him to give me a week. But we didn't set a specific time."

"Did he give you his card?"

Her face lit. "He did. I forgot about it." She dug in her purse and came up with a card and her phone. "My cell doesn't have any bars."

"Neither does mine. We can go over to my house and call after lunch though." Alec's head came up when Tom walked in the door. "Hey, Tom," he called.

Tom had been starting toward a free table, but he changed directions and headed toward them. "Mind if I join you?"

Alec shoved a chair out with his foot. "Have a seat. We just ordered."

Tom motioned to the waitress and gave her his order. He stared at Libby. "I heard you got a search-and-rescue dog team helping. I would have appreciated it if you'd let me know what you were doing before you did it."

She flushed but didn't look away. "I have the right to try to find my friend. You don't seem to be looking."

His jaw tightened. "I'm doing things you don't see."

"No harm in looking on our own," Alec said.

Tom's eyes were dark when he glanced Alec's way. "If you found anything, you contaminated evidence. You know better than that. I would have sent a deputy along with you to retrieve anything you found."

"Fair enough." Though Alec was sure the items they'd found had been dropped by Nicole, what if he was wrong? "We found a couple of things last night, but I'm sure they aren't evidence."

Tom's mouth was pinched. "What?"

Alec told him about the discarded hat and sunglasses. "Someone threw them away. Could have been the kidnappers covering their tracks, or it could have been someone cleaning the beach."

"Where are they?"

"In my truck."

"Alec, that was just plain stupid. I hope you didn't destroy something that might have led us to Nicole."

Alec exchanged a long look with Libby. He had been suitably chastised.

TWENTY-FIVE

B ree and Kade took the kids to explore the town and harbor, and Alec went with Zach back to town to buy some jeans. Worry had drained Libby, and searching for Nicole left her feeling hopeless. What if she never found her friend? Though she tried to kill the thought, it refused to go away.

For days the box of letters from her father had been in her closet. Libby fingered his necklace and decided to gather her courage and read some. But not alone in this room. Maybe with Pearl. She lifted the shoe box from the shelf and stepped into the hall where she practically ran into Vanessa.

Vanessa's eyes narrowed. "What's in the box? That's my father's handwriting on top."

Libby had studied those words for days. *For My Oldest Daughter.* "They're letters he wrote to me."

Vanessa made a grab at the top and flipped it off. "Let me see."

Before Libby could pull away, Vanessa had one of the envelopes in her hand. She stepped out of reach. "I want to understand what this is all about. How could my father prefer you over me and Brent? Surely you can see how I need to figure this out."

Short of snatching the letter back as rudely as Vanessa had taken it, Libby watched as her sister pulled the sheet of paper from the envelope. It took all her self-control to stay calm. "I haven't read it myself. Please give it back."

The other woman lifted a brow but made no move to return the note. She unfolded it.

"Vanessa, that's enough." Pearl stepped from the doorway of her room. "You're being incredibly bad mannered. That was not meant for your eyes. If your sister wants to share it, that's up to her, but the choice is hers, not yours." When Vanessa kept the letter, Pearl stepped closer, plucked it from her hand, and handed it to Libby. "I'm sorry for her rudeness, my dear."

Libby stared at the page. This was an experience she'd wanted to savor, but if she wanted to be part of this family, she was going to have to make an effort. *What would Jesus do?* "Would you both care to look at these with me? We can go back to my room."

The expression on her aunt's face warmed, and the approval Libby saw there convinced her she'd done the right thing. Libby glanced at Vanessa, who shrugged and followed her back into the bedroom. Vanessa glanced around and made a beeline for the four-poster bed that dominated the large room. She kicked off her flip-flops and climbed onto the bed, curling her feet under her.

"This used to be my room whenever we came here for the night." Her tone made it clear what she thought of Libby staying in the room.

Libby opened her mouth to offer to switch rooms, then closed it again. Vanessa was not going to manipulate her. "It's a nice room." She glanced at the space beside Vanessa, then glanced at Pearl.

Pearl shook her head. "You sit there, honey. It's too high for me." She took the Queen Anne armchair at the foot of the bed.

If not for the tension coming off Vanessa in waves, Libby could almost imagine they were really friends holed up on a rainy night. She looked at the letter in her hand. "This is the oldest one.

I would have been fifteen when this came. So he evidently didn't try to contact me before this." She continued to stare at it. Did she even want to know what it said? These communications from her father were a clear sign of how much her mother had lied to her.

"Want me to read it aloud?" Pearl asked.

Libby reached across the bed and handed it to her. "It seems appropriate."

There was something in Pearl's face that caught at her heart. It was as if she knew Libby was about to hear something life-changing. Then Pearl glanced at Vanessa, and that expression intensified. Vanessa's head was down as she traced the pattern in the quilt. Libby tried to summon sympathy for the young woman, but Vanessa's prickly manner made it difficult. It was hard to remember they were sisters.

Pearl unfolded the letter and cleared her throat. "'My dear Libby. I know I'm breaking the custody agreement by trying to contact you, but I miss you so much. As time has gone on, I've been more consumed by grief over what we have done to you girls. It was wrong. I should never have agreed to the custody split. At the time, it seemed the best for you and Vanessa, but I've regretted it every day of my life.'"

Libby caught her breath. "Vanessa? What does he mean that it's best for me *and* Vanessa?"

Pearl put down the letter. "At last, it's out in the open. I always thought it was the most terrible thing I'd ever heard, but it wasn't my decision."

"What wasn't your decision?"

Pearl glanced from Libby to Vanessa, who was staring at her with the same horror on her face that Libby felt. *Custody split.* Did he mean that she and Vanessa were full sisters? Surely no parent would be so cruel as to split up siblings.

Pearl sighed heavily. "Vanessa is your younger sister."

Libby rose to her knees on the bed. "No, you don't mean we're *sisters*! Full sisters? Not half?"

Pearl nodded. "Vanessa is a year younger than you."

Vanessa scrambled off the bed. "You're lying!" She shot a glance of utter dislike at Libby. "I don't know what you're trying to do here, but this is some kind of scam."

"Vanessa, sit down," Pearl said in a weary voice. "You too, Libby. I can't believe Ray left this for me to untangle. Do you honestly think I'd be part of something unsavory, Vanessa? You know me better than that."

"It's not true, it's not!" Vanessa sobbed. She ignored her aunt's outstretched hand and rushed from the room.

Her knees too weak to support her, Libby sank back onto the bed.

———

Several people darted across the street in front of Alec's pickup as he drove slowly through the debris-strewn streets toward the sheriff's office. While he and Zach were at Skipper's Store looking for jeans, a deputy had stopped in to ask Alec to come to the jail. His tone was somber, and he'd said not to tell Libby. Alec feared some new evidence implicated Libby even more than the missing video had.

His cousin was leaning against the doorjamb smoking a cigar when Alec parked and got out of his vehicle. Tom straightened and blew a puff of smoke Alec's way. "Thanks for coming right away."

Alec waved the smoke out of his face. "What's up?"

"I'll show you. Come with me." Tom yanked open the office door.

Alec followed him to the evidence room, down a green hallway. A table in the corner held items that made his heart sink. Bright-pink flip-flops and a cover-up in a matching color. "Those are Nicole's?"

"Seems likely. They washed up on shore a few minutes ago. That woman and her dog found them."

"Doesn't mean she's dead," Alec said quickly.

Tom lifted a brow. "Come on, Alec, you and I both know the odds aren't good. Yeah, she might have lost her shoes in the struggle, but her cover-up is a different matter."

Alec winced. "You call Libby yet?"

"No."

"Why not?"

Tom headed for the door, and Alec followed. His cousin's closed expression sent a prickle of unease up Alec's spine. Tom went directly to his desk and jiggled his mouse. After a few clicks, he motioned to Alec. Alec stepped around the desk and peered at the screen. It displayed the video of the boardwalk where Nicole had disappeared. It displayed only sand and surf at first, then abruptly went black.

Alec frowned. "This the recording of the time she disappeared?"

"Yeah. I checked when Libby arrived in Kitty Hawk. She went to the harbor and tried to rent a boat about nine in the evening. That means she didn't leave Virginia Beach until seven, two hours after she made the call to 9-1-1. Yet she said she rushed off so fast that she didn't talk to the police."

"She may have waited that long for the police, and when they didn't show, she finally took off."

"Maybe." Tom leaned back. "I think we have to consider her as a suspect. And with the items that washed up, we have to treat it as a homicide."

"I can ask Libby why she didn't leave for a couple of hours."

"Don't show your suspicion. Maybe you can trip her up in a lie."

"You really think she harmed her friend?" Alec shook his head. "I don't see it, Tom."

"You and I have both been around long enough to know the likeliest culprit is usually the most obvious one."

"But not always. I think we need to give Libby the benefit of the doubt." Alec could see by the closed expression on the sheriff's face that he was wasting his breath.

Tom stood. "Look, are you going to help me or not? Or are you too afraid to find out the truth?"

"The truth is never something to fear. But I'm not going to be part of any scheme to railroad Libby."

"I'm not asking you to. Just be on the lookout for anything suspicious."

"I already am."

Tom twirled a pencil in his fingers. "There's more, Alec. I talked to Earl Franklin a little while ago too. Libby's mother died under mysterious circumstances. Libby was held twenty hours for questioning."

Mysterious circumstances. "So? The police were doing their job. She was never charged or you'd have mentioned that first."

Tom banged his fist on the desk and swore. "You're being just as pigheaded as usual, Alec. There's a lot in her past that's questionable."

Alec leaned over the desk toward his cousin. "So investigate, but don't assume she's guilty without getting facts! Otherwise, you're letting a murderer walk."

Tom's face was red. "Let's go tell your lady friend what we've found and see what her reaction is. Maybe that will convince you."

"I'm not the one who needs convincing," Alec said. He hoped that was true.

Twenty-Six

Nicole paced the tiny island. Fifty steps to the left of the hut and thirty steps to the right. Then around the back. She was going to go stark raving mad out here. The boy had been here yesterday, so she doubted he would come today. Not when he left enough food and water to last her for several days. She was stuck here under the blazing sun by herself.

She had to get off this island. What would happen if the boy never came back? Or another storm came? She eyed the clouds drifting across the brilliant blue sky. Was there anything she could use for a raft? She darted across the island so fast that her bare feet kicked up sand. Inside the shack, she paused long enough to let her eyes adjust to the dim light filtering through the open doorway and single window. There was no flooring to pry up, only sand. The cot was metal, so it would sink immediately. There was a wooden table. Maybe it would work.

She curled her fingers under the edge and dragged it to the door. It was too wide to pull through the doorway so she turned it on its side and maneuvered it out onto the damp sand. With difficulty, she managed to drag it to where the surf broke on the beach. The waves crashed so hard she wondered if she would manage to get it out to sea. The legs would make it more difficult too. She scoured the beach until she found a rock about eight inches in diameter. Once she got it back to the table, she lifted it over her head and brought it crashing down on the table leg closest to her. It took four whacks to dislodge the first leg. She rolled the table around and continued to batter at the legs until she had all of them free of the top.

Now she had the makings of a raft. And if she could tie the legs together, she might have something that would work as oars. She stared at the trees. There were no vines. She wandered the beach again but found only flotsam and seaweed. Nothing strong enough to take on the crashing waves. Returning to the table, she looked from it to the foaming water. Using single table legs was going to have to do. There was no choice. And she needed to bring water and food with her, but how did she keep it from tumbling overboard while she got the raft out past the breakers?

The sound of the sea rolled over her, powerful and frightening. But she couldn't let fear deter her. If she did nothing, her death was almost certain. If she died in the attempt, at least she was doing *something*. She turned back toward the shack and ducked inside to get peanut butter and water. The peanut butter jar fit in the bra of her bathing suit. She tucked one bottle of water in the front of the bottoms and one in the back, but she didn't have high hopes that they would stay put. If only she had some rope.

Sighing, she grabbed an edge of the tabletop and dragged it into the water, then seized two table legs and tried to hang on to them as she tugged the wood farther into the water. The sea foamed around her ankles, and she waited for the right moment to pull the table through the waves. When the crashing wave receded, she lunged through the water with her fingers gripping the makeshift raft. The waves tried furiously to rip the raft from her fingers, but she managed to hang on. When the water reached her waist, she flung herself atop the table. Tucking the table legs under her, she paddled with her hands for all she was worth. It seemed for every foot she managed to propel herself forward, the surf flung her back toward the island two feet.

The breakers were crashing just ahead of her. She paused her paddling until the right moment, then tried again with all her strength. The waves lifted her, then flung her past the breakwater. The ride smoothed out and the waves didn't threaten to tip her into the sea at every moment. She sat up and examined her circumstances. One bottle of water had been pulled from her bathing suit. The peanut butter had survived the experience, but she had only one table leg. It would be useless by itself. She nearly tossed it overboard, then reconsidered. Her resources were limited out here. She might need it for something.

The island was receding. She flopped to her stomach again and began to paddle with her hands. A fin appeared in the water beside the boat, and she snatched her hands back, then smiled when she realized it was a dolphin. If only the dolphin realized her distress and could help her find land.

The dolphin nosed her makeshift raft. She reached out and touched the mammal's skin. It felt like a warm inner tube. "Can you help me?" she whispered.

The dolphin bumped at her raft again, then flicked its tail and shoved at her raft. The table floated back toward the island. "Hey, that's the wrong way," Nicole said.

The dolphin pushed the raft with its nose again, and Nicole sat up. "Cut that out!" She glanced back at the island. Surely it was much closer. Her chest tightened and she grabbed the table leg and hit the water with it. The splashing didn't deter the dolphin. It continued to shove her back toward the island. Nicole didn't have the heart to actually hit the animal with the table leg. All she could do was splash and scream as the dolphin moved the raft back to the island.

The waves were suddenly higher, and she flung herself to her belly and clutched the sides as the breakers grabbed the tabletop and flung it toward the island. She heard a tearing, grinding sound and was suddenly in the water with salt water burning her nose and throat. She couldn't breathe as the waves rolled her over and over until she came to rest in a foot of water with her knees stinging from scraping the sand.

She sat up and cried out as the waves offered up the pieces of her raft, useless now.

———

Pearl carried a silver tray bearing delicate blue-and-white china into the bedroom. "Here you go, honey." She put the tray on the bedside table. "The tea will make you feel better."

"Thank you, Aunt Pearl. You're very thoughtful." Libby stared again at the letter in her hand.

Several hours had passed since Libby realized Vanessa was her sister, but the shock had not lessened. How could her parents have done such a heinous thing? To separate sisters until they were combative strangers was a crime that could not be forgiven. Libby found no charity in her heart toward her parents. God said to forgive seventy-times-seven times, but in this case, even one time was too many.

She fingered the necklace. *What would Jesus do?* Right now, Libby couldn't seem to summon the desire to care.

Pearl touched her head. "There are homemade cookies with M&M'S in them."

Libby flung a letter aside that had contained three pictures of Vanessa winning a swim competition. "Not even chocolate can heal this. We have missed so much of each other's lives. It's monstrous."

Pearl eased her bulk into the chair. "There's nothing you can do to change what is, Libby. All you can do is go forward from here."

"Have you talked to Vanessa?"

Pearl's expression clouded. "She won't open her bedroom door."

"She hates this as much as I do. Maybe more."

"Ray spoiled those children. He would be heartsick if he could see how she is treating you."

Libby rubbed her throbbing forehead. "I can't blame her."

"This is hardly your fault."

Libby stared at her aunt. "Did you try to talk him out of this?"

"Of course." Pearl sat heavily in the armchair. "When he arrived here on Hope Island with Vanessa in tow, I begged him to go back for you."

"Did you know my mother?"

Pearl's eyes filled and she nodded. "She was very naïve and childlike. Once she made up her mind, there was no talking her out of anything. Your mother had been adamant that she wanted no contact with Ray. The only way to do that was for each of them to take a child. She argued that it would only be difficult in the beginning. Once you both forgot, everyone could have a fresh start."

Libby's throat closed. "No wonder I've felt so abandoned. I lost a father and a sister in one blow."

"Your father mourned your loss all his life. Not a week went by but he spoke of you."

Where her aunt's pity had failed to move her, Pearl's words about Ray opened a flood of pain. Libby tried to compose herself. "I don't have any memories of him. What did he like to do?"

"Come with me. I'll show you his pride and joy."

Curious, Libby rose from the bed and followed her aunt into the hall and up a narrow flight of stairs to the third floor. It was a different staircase from the one that led to her father's suite. This space smelled of disuse and dampness.

Libby glanced around the stark space. "No one lives up here, do they?"

Pearl fiddled with a key in the lock of the first door to the right. "Oh no. Once upon a time it was the servants' quarters, but since it became an inn back in the sixties, it's been used only for storage." With a final click of the knob, she flung open the door.

Their feet had left prints on the dust in the halls, but not a speck of dust was in this chamber. Ceilings soared to fifteen feet. The walls were painted a pale lemon, and the wood floors were polished. "What is this place?" Libby asked, peering through the gloom.

"One moment." Pearl felt along the wall, then light filled the room.

Libby's eyes took a moment to adjust, then she gasped as the paintings came into view. "A-Are those real?" She moved close enough to see the brushstrokes. "They look like Washington Allston originals."

"They are. Ray loved the religious ones. He said Allston always chose obscure events in the Old Testament to illustrate how we should live out our faith."

Libby stared at the picture of a young woman sleeping at the feet of an older man. "Ruth and Boaz?" This one was hardly about an obscure event.

Pearl nodded. "He loved it, though it also reminded him that he had failed you. Boaz always did the right thing, in the right order. Ray felt he would never aspire to that high mark."

Libby glanced around the room. "How many did he collect?"

"Five in all."

"They're worth a fortune."

"They are indeed. I'm surprised you recognized them."

"I'm a huge Allston fan. I have a tiny print that's sat on my dresser ever since I can remember." She put her hand to her throat. "Did my father give that to me?"

"The one of *Moonlit Landscape*?" Pearl nodded. "It was his favorite. Though he could never own the original, he has some prints stored in another room."

"So that's why I love Allston," Libby said. "I inherited the love from him."

"He used to take you to art museums, starting when you were six months old. We laughed and told him you were too young, but he carried you from picture to picture, explaining what each painting was and why it was significant."

Libby wished she remembered. How much of her personality and passions had she absorbed from a father she never knew?

"Why did my parents divorce? Why did he leave me behind? Did he love Vanessa more?"

Pearl took her hand and squeezed. "Never think that, honey! Your mother flipped a coin. He got Vanessa, and she kept you."

Libby shuddered at the word picture her aunt's description evoked. "Why would he agree to that?"

"He wanted to take you both, but back then it would have been impossible to get custody of both of you without her agreement. He had no grounds. She told him she only had the energy for one child, that he could take one. It was the luck of the draw."

"So they flipped a coin and ripped a family apart."

Libby didn't want to be bitter. She didn't. But it was hard to come to grips with what had been done to her and Vanessa.

A dog barked. Bree and Samson must have come back. "I think I'll go for a swim and clear my head."

"I'll pray for you, honey. You need to forgive and let go of this."

Easier said than done.

TWENTY-SEVEN

The water beckoned like a lover. Libby dug her toes into the soft sand and watched the waves for a moment. Samson had wanted a walk, so she'd taken him with her. Bree had taken the children to get cleaned up for dinner.

A swim would clear Libby's head, though she knew she should march right back inside and demand Vanessa talk to her. In Libby's wildest dreams she'd never expected to find a sister who hated her. This could have been such a wonderful day. Instead it was a nightmare that she couldn't awaken from.

She pulled off her cover-up and tossed it on the sand. "Want to go for a swim, Samson?" The dog's ears perked at the word *swim*. He danced around her and barked wildly, then ran toward the waves and snapped at the foam.

"Moron," she said, laughing. The dog barked excitedly in answer.

She kicked off her flip-flops and ran into the waves. The shock of the cold water made her gasp, then giggle like she was ten. A breaker rolled toward her, and she waited until the right moment before diving into it. The force of the current rolled her along the bottom, but she relished its power. When she was in the water, she forgot all her troubles. She surfaced and tossed her hair out of her face. The sea didn't feel so cold now that she was fully immersed.

She broke into a breaststroke and crested the next wave. Samson kept up with her as she swam out.

When she turned to look back, she was a hundred yards out. There didn't seem to be a riptide, so she flipped onto her back and let the waves float her along. Sheer heaven. It would be sunset soon, so she wouldn't stay out too long. Sharks would be out.

When the first nudge came on her leg, she thought it was a fish. She straightened to a vertical position and looked around. Then something grabbed her leg and yanked her under the water. She managed to gasp oxygen into her lungs before her head was submerged. Though the salt water burned, she opened her eyes underwater and saw a diver in a black wetsuit. It was too dark to see much detail, but she could make out the person's masculine build and the air tank on his back.

She kicked out with her right foot and hit him in the chest, but the blow didn't make him turn her loose. His fingers squeezed her leg so tightly that it was beginning to go numb. Bubbles rose around her as he dragged her deeper under the waves. He reached the bottom and stood on the sand. She floated just above him with his hand still holding her fast.

He's trying to drown me. The shock of realizing his intention made her release a bit of her precious air into the water. Her lungs began to burn. She flailed to free herself, but he was stronger. Samson would not be able to dive down to help her. If she wanted to live, she had to escape this man. Panic drove all thought from her head for a few moments, then she forced herself to focus.

Think, Libby! Her only chance was to deprive him of oxygen. She lashed out with her foot, aiming for his face. Her heel struck his mouthpiece and it flipped out of his mouth. Bubbles escaped in a flurry. He let go of her legs and grabbed the mask. Lungs burning, Libby shot for the surface. He would be right behind her. She had to get to safety. Her feet pumped, and she rose toward the light.

She didn't think she could hold out much longer. Her vision began to dim, then her head broke the surface. She filled her lungs with air and shook her head to clear it. Shore was more than a hundred and twenty yards away. She struck out for the safety of the sand, vaguely aware that Samson was snarling. A hand grazed her ankle and she kicked hard, then swam to the right and then back toward shore. The diver had the advantage of seeing her from below. It would be a miracle if she escaped him.

Help, Lord! Her muscles were beginning to tire from the exertion, but she kept up the pace. Her starved lungs wanted her to pause and gather in more oxygen, but there was no time. Not if she wanted to live. She dared a glance back and saw a head pop up. The sight galvanized her into swimming even more frantically. The dog growled to her right. He left her side, but she didn't look back until the snarling reached a ferocious level. The dog had his teeth clamped on the man's arm. The diver struck at Samson, but the dog held on.

This was her chance to escape. She swam for all she was worth. The shore grew closer and closer until her knees scraped bottom. She staggered to her feet and practically fell onto the beach. There was no time to recover though. She sprang back up and turned to stare out to sea. Where was the dog?

"Samson!" She screamed his name into the wind. The harsh caw of a seagull was the only answer. She half turned to run to the inn for help, then she saw his head break the waves. He was swimming for shore. There was no sign of her attacker.

She ran a few feet into the water to greet the dog as he struggled to shore. Sinking to her knees, she threw her arms around his neck. He licked her cheek weakly and she half guided, half carried him the rest of the way. They both collapsed onto the sand. Panting, Samson crawled onto her lap.

"Good dog," she crooned. She'd wanted to see an angel, just as Aunt Pearl once had. Samson was that angel today.

The sun had colored the clouds with red and gold when Alec found Libby sitting on a piece of driftwood. Her face was turned toward the sunset. Her arm was around Bree's dog. They'd been for a swim. He could see that her hair wasn't quite dry and neither was the dog. Alec paused to shake sand from his sandals, and Tom nearly bowled him over in his haste to get to Libby.

"Ready?" Tom whispered.

"I guess we have to be. Libby," Alec called. She turned her pensive face toward them. He knew when she saw Tom because her eyes widened and she inhaled. "Tom has some news," he said.

Her lips tightened and she got up. "You've found her body?" The dog pressed against her leg as though he sensed she needed comfort.

Alec paused to reflect on her answer. He knew Tom would assume she'd asked because she knew for a fact that Nicole was dead. He didn't believe that. "Not her body but some of her clothing. Bree and Samson found it."

"Where? Why didn't she come to tell me?" She'd thought Bree had acted a little strange. She'd been quiet before rushing the children in to get cleaned up, then off to dinner in town without Samson.

Tom grunted. "I ordered Bree to let us tell you." He put his hands on his hips. "What we found were her sandals and cover-up, Miss Holladay. They match the description you gave us."

"Oh no," Libby whispered.

"You were quick to ask if we'd found her body. I suspect it's because you dumped her body out there."

She went white and her fingers stilled in the dog's fur. "That's a terrible accusation. You were both so somber that I assumed the worst."

"Her shoes and cover-up indicate that she's no longer alive," Tom said, his voice harsh.

"I don't believe it." Libby's lips trembled. Her gaze sought Alec's.

Alec saw no guilt in her face. "Tom needs you to identify the belongings he found."

"Pink flip-flops and cover-up?" she asked.

He nodded. "Shoe size matches."

"Where did Bree and Samson find them?"

Tom shot a fierce glance at Alec that warned him to be quiet. "They found one shoe in some rocks and the other twisted with seaweed a few feet away. The cover-up was fifty yards down the beach."

"Maybe the things aren't Nicole's." Libby's voice rose. "Pink is a common color for beach items."

"I want you to take a look," Tom said, gesturing back at his truck in the driveway.

Libby nodded and they trekked back to Tom's SUV. He stuck his head through the open window and withdrew a plastic evidence bag. Without speaking, he handed it to Libby.

The bag crackled when her fingers tightened around it. She loosened the top and pulled out the clothing and flip-flops. "They look like hers. I bought her the cover-up for Easter." Her voice quavered. She turned the shoes over. "See this nick out of the bottom? Her mom's dog chewed them the weekend she got them."

Alec nodded. "Looks like teeth marks."

She closed the top and handed it back. "I think I can say without any doubt that these belong to Nicole."

Tom tossed the bag into the SUV. "I think we have to assume we're investigating a murder, Miss Holladay."

She visibly wilted. "I don't want to believe she's dead." She turned a beseeching glance toward Alec.

He didn't want to give her false hope. "You have to face facts, Libby," he said, gentling his voice.

"If she's dead, where is her body?" she asked. "Wouldn't her body have washed ashore too?"

Tom shrugged. "I know it's hard to hear, but it's rare to find a body. Fish take care of the remains."

Her eyes filled and she backed away. Alec glanced at his cousin and saw Tom narrow his eyes. Did he think her distress was put on?

"I'd like to ask you some questions, Miss Holladay," Tom said. "What happened to your mother?"

She reeled as though she'd been slapped. "What do you mean?"

"How did she die?"

Libby wetted her lips. "She fell down the basement steps."

"Isn't it true that the police suspected you pushed her?"

"I didn't!" Libby blinked rapidly. "She was drunk."

"You were held for questioning," Tom said.

"They let me go." Her eyes pleaded for them to believe her. "I had nothing to do with it."

"But you were home?"

She sighed and leaned against the SUV. "I was home," she agreed heavily. "But I was upstairs working on some paperwork."

"You lived at home?"

"Someone had to take care of her. If I wasn't there, she wouldn't have bothered with food." She tipped her chin up. "I took care of her. I cared for her for years."

Tom took a step closer to her. "What happened?"

"I heard a clatter. I jumped up and ran downstairs calling for her. When I found the basement door open in the kitchen, I rushed down the steps and found her lying at the bottom of the stairs. Sh-She was lying there with her eyes open. I tried to help her up, but I knew as soon as I touched her that she was gone."

"The policeman I spoke with seemed to think your story was fishy," Tom said. "Why was that?"

Alec could tell Tom already knew the answer but wanted to see if she would tell him the truth. He prayed for Libby to be honest and put to rest any doubts his cousin might have.

She looked at her hands. "We'd had an argument in town earlier that someone overheard."

"And you threatened to kill her."

"It wasn't like that!" She lifted her head and stared at Tom. "I said, 'I could just kill you when you act like that.' That wasn't a threat. It was just a figure of speech. A really awful figure of speech."

"What had she done?" Alec asked gently.

"She insulted the grocery store owner, then threw tomatoes at him. It was an ugly scene. I tried to stop her, but she was like that when she'd been drinking. There was nothing anyone could do. She was the sweetest person when she was sober."

Alec heard the ring of truth in her voice. She'd loved her mother. He glanced at Tom and saw compassion. Tom could tell truth when he heard it.

TWENTY-EIGHT

Libby felt like she'd been tossed around by a tidal wave. Could the sheriff actually suspect that she'd killed her own mother—and that she'd disposed of Nicole? Couldn't he see her heart? She'd started to tell Tom that someone had just tried to drown her, but then she saw the suspicion in the sheriff's eyes. He would think she was making it up to divert suspicion. What a mess.

It was none too soon for her when Sheriff Bourne's vehicle left the driveway and headed back to town. Alec stood at the bottom of the porch steps with his hands in the pockets of his khaki shorts. She'd been hoping to tell him about what she'd discovered from Pearl, but now she didn't have it in her.

Her eyes burned, and she rushed up the steps before she could disgrace herself by showing how much the sheriff's accusations had hurt her. Samson whined and trotted after her.

"Libby, wait! Tom is just doing his job."

"His *job* is to find out who took my friend, not to railroad an innocent person!"

He mounted the steps to the porch and stopped in front of her. "Look at it from his point of view. Can't you see why he would have some suspicions?"

She was in no mood for his placating tone. "While he wastes his time investigating me, the real criminals are walking free. Don't you worry that the men might take another girl? Someone *you* know and love?"

That stopped him. She could see him processing her question.

"You're saying you don't think it was personal? That Nicole just might have been in the wrong place at the wrong time?" he asked.

"I don't know what to think. You hear of human trafficking though. Who knows but that's what these men intended? How did they know she would be there at that time? Maybe they just came ashore and saw a lone girl and decided to grab her."

He stared at her. "You didn't try to rent a boat until nine."

"What?" She didn't understand the sudden change of subject.

"The night Nicole disappeared. That means you didn't leave Virginia Beach until a good two hours after you called 9-1-1. Why?"

"No. I threw some clothes in a suitcase and left right away. Then I got stuck in a traffic jam from a jack-knifed truck." Her ire rose. "Do you want to check with the state patrol? I came as quickly as I could."

There would be no end to the suspicion and accusation. She was going to have to do this on her own. The realization made her pulse jump. But it wouldn't be impossible. She had years of experience uncovering the history of houses, interviewing previous owners, delving into the secrets of dusty pages. While this would be a different investigation, she had determination and love on her side.

"I can see I'm on my own now." She turned to leave.

"You're thinking about doing this yourself? You'll just make Tom and the state detectives mad," Alec said.

"What other choice do I have? The story Earl wrote is going to hit the papers soon, and we both know it's going to be slanted toward my guilt. The state isn't going to look any harder than the sheriff is. If I want to stay out of jail, I'm going to have to do this myself and find those men. And quickly. Before everyone in town is convinced I'm some kind of killer."

"Let's start with a sketch of what you remember."

"Are you going to help me or accuse me, Alec? I'm having trouble keeping it straight." If he doubted her, she didn't think she could stand it. His opinion mattered way too much.

"I told you I'd help. We've already started. I haven't changed my mind."

She searched his face. "For my father's sake?"

He nodded. "And for the sake of truth. Truth matters."

She relented. Should she tell him about today's attack? "It doesn't seem to matter to anyone but us," she said.

"What do you mean by that? Has something happened today?"

He had an uncanny perception. Where did it come from? She pointed to the rockers on the porch. "Let's sit down. This is going to take a few minutes." What would he think when she told him what their parents had done to her and Vanessa? Would he still idolize her father? And would he believe a diver had really tried to drown her?

———

A breeze lifted the strands of Libby's light-brown hair, and the porch light glimmered on her tresses. A few bugs buzzed the lamp. Alec stretched out his legs in the rocker and petted Samson, who rested his head on Alec's knee. The dog huffed with pleasure. If only people were so easily pleased. Libby had her legs tucked under her on the swing. He waited for her to explain what was going through that beautiful head of hers.

He noticed red marks on her ankle. "What happened there?" he asked, pointing.

Her gaze searched his face. She rubbed her ankle. "A diver tried to drown me a little while ago." She studied the marks. "I didn't realize he'd left marks."

He sat forward. "What? Someone tried to *kill* you?"

She nodded. "Samson and I went for a swim. A diver in a black wetsuit dragged me to the bottom and tried to hold me there. I managed to get away, and Samson helped until I got to shore."

He clenched his fists. "Why didn't you say anything to Tom?"

She shrugged. "He has his mind made up."

He pointed to her ankle. "You have proof."

"I didn't realize he'd left marks. And the sheriff would say I scraped it on something anyway."

Alec leaned forward and studied the marks on her skin. "Looks like fingers. We need to show Tom."

She rubbed her ankle, then shook her head. "He'd say I did it myself."

"No, he won't." He grabbed the portable phone on the swing and called his cousin. When he explained what happened, Tom told him to take pictures and bring her into the office tomorrow.

She was watching him talk with shadowed eyes. "What did he say?"

"He believed me. He wants pictures tomorrow and said to take some tonight too. He wants to get to the bottom of this, Libby."

She bit her lip and her head went down. Alec pulled out his phone and snapped several shots of her injury.

The screen banged open and Vanessa stomped out onto the porch. Her hands were curled into fists and her mouth was pinched.

She glared at Libby through narrowed eyes. "Don't think this changes anything! You'll never be part of this family."

"This isn't my fault, Vanessa. Mom and Dad did this, not me."

"Don't call him that! He was Daddy, always."

Alec found their conversation impossible to decipher. "What's going on?"

Libby sighed and leaned back. "It appears Vanessa and I are full sisters."

"You've got to be kidding." He eyed them both. There was a definite resemblance. They'd look alike whenever Vanessa lost the petulant expression she usually wore.

Libby tucked her hair behind her ears. "When our parents divorced, they each took a child. Our mother wanted nothing to do with our father and insisted this was the way it had to be."

"That's nuts," Alec said. This situation gave credence to her story of an atypical mother. "And neither of you knew?"

She shook her head, then glanced up at Vanessa. "Sit down, Vanessa. Standing over me like that isn't going to solve anything."

"Neither will talking." But Vanessa took a hesitant step forward.

Alec left the chair and moved to sit beside Libby on the swing. Vanessa shot him a grateful look. He liked being this close to Libby. The vanilla fragrance on her skin was enticing. "Did you remember another sister at all? Weren't you three when your parents split?"

Vanessa knotted her hands together. "I remember an imaginary friend. Her name was Bee."

"Bee. Lib-BEE," Alec said. "Maybe that was your nickname for her."

Vanessa frowned and shook her head. "I'm sure she was imaginary. She had a monkey named Fred."

"I had a monkey named Fred," Libby said in a low voice. "I still have him. He was a sock monkey."

Vanessa straightened. "He had an eye missing."

Libby nodded. "And his ear had been chewed by the cat."

"I remember that," Vanessa said in a stunned voice. "Do you remember me at all?"

Libby frowned. "I don't have very many memories from

childhood. Things were so rocky and constantly in flux. I have only snippets of things, and most of them aren't pleasant."

Vanessa's face clouded and she looked down at her hands. "You'd think you would remember a sister!"

Alec could feel Libby tense beside him. "Stress can damage memories, Vanessa," he said. "Doesn't mean she didn't love you."

"I don't care if she did or didn't," Vanessa snapped.

The screen door opened again and Pearl came out. Her feet were bare under her housedress. "I thought I heard voices out here." She chewed on her lip as she glanced at Vanessa. "Everyone doing okay?"

"Don't tiptoe around it, Aunt Pearl," Vanessa snapped. "How could you keep this from me?"

"If you would have opened your door, I would have talked to you about it."

Alec got up to offer his seat to Pearl, but she waved him off so he sat back down. She leaned her bulk against the porch post. "I'm not staying. This is something the girls have to work out on their own." Her gaze stayed on Vanessa. "I just wanted to assure Vanessa that this is true. I was there. I tried to talk them out of it, but your mother was adamant."

"My mother," Vanessa said, her voice stunned. "I just realized. Tina wasn't my mother!" Her voice broke, and her eyes filled with horror.

"She loved you as much as she loved Brent," Pearl said. "You know she did."

"I can't believe this," Vanessa said. She turned to stare at Libby. "Tell me about our mother. And what was her name? I don't even know her name!"

"Her name was Ursula." Libby held her gaze. "My childhood wasn't like yours, Vanessa. We moved around a lot. Mom was always looking for the rainbow over the next hill. She married again and divorced, then we had a revolving door with men coming and going. She was never happy. She always wanted more and more but never got it. Possessions were important to her, maybe because of her childhood. Still, she loved me more than her things, more than her men. But maybe not more than her beer. In spite of that, my childhood wasn't bad. Just constantly disrupted."

Vanessa winced and turned her attention back to Pearl. "Why did Tina agree to the deception?"

Pearl patted her shoulder. "You started calling her Mama as soon as they were engaged. It just gradually happened. I think your father thought you'd be happier if you didn't remember another mother and sister."

Alec had idolized Ray Mitchell forever. To find he had such feet of clay was indescribably shocking. This kind of tangle was going to be hard to unravel. Alec doubted the women would ever manage to be close. It would take a miracle from God's hand.

Vanessa jumped to her feet and rushed back into the house. Pearl followed, calling Vanessa's name. The seaside cicadas filled the silence as Alec and Libby were left alone on the porch.

Alec stretched his arm across the back of the swing, not quite daring to embrace her, though the thought strangely crossed his mind. "How are you dealing with this?"

She leaned back and her hair brushed his arm. "I don't quite know what to think. It's hard to realize I have a family but that I'm about as welcome as a bedbug. But I don't care about any of this, really. I'm finding it hard to care about anything since Bree found Nicole's belongings. I don't want to believe she's dead."

He hugged her. "I'm sorry, Libby. I wish I could change things."

She swallowed hard and sighed. "Thanks for being here, Alec."

"Does Brent know yet? About you and Vanessa?"

She shook her head. "He's been gone all day. I suppose Vanessa could have called him, but if she did, I don't know about it."

Headlamps pierced the darkness. "I think that's him now."

TWENTY-NINE

Libby could almost imagine they were friends, maybe more than friends, as she sat near Alec with his arm on the back of the swing. Did he feel the connection she felt? He'd offered to help her, and he'd kissed her. With a man like him, that had to mean something.

Brent would be here any minute, but she'd rather sit in the silence than endure more confrontation. Her brother was about to find out he was more alone than he'd thought. Would this change his relationship with Vanessa?

Brent's shadow loomed in the glow from the lamps along the walk, then he walked up the steps to the porch. "You're sitting here in the dark?"

"We have the porch light," Alec said, pulling his arm down.

Libby felt cold without his warmth radiating to her back. Or maybe it was the way Brent's lips pressed together at the sight of her.

"Have a seat, Brent. You've been gone all day and a lot has happened," Alec said.

Brent still stood in the shadows. "I'll stand, thanks. What's up?"

"Libby and Vanessa are sisters," Alec said.

"Sisters? That's not news."

"*Full* sisters. Not half."

Libby listened to Alec explain what they'd discovered today. The deep tones of his voice soothed her. She was still jumping at every sound. Was her attacker out there even now, watching and waiting for the next time? And why had he targeted her? She eyed her half brother. Could Brent want her out of the way so he could inherit? She didn't have a will in place, so by law he and Vanessa would inherit as her closest relatives.

She hated to suspect her own brother, but someone in this town wanted her dead. That someone had already killed her friend, it seemed. Tears welled in her eyes at the likelihood that she would never see Nicole again. She became aware that Alec had asked her something. "I'm sorry?"

"I wondered if you had anything to add?"

She stared at Brent's expressionless face. Though they had only been around each other a few times, she got the impression that he took in everything behind those calculating eyes.

He shifted and she saw what dangled from his hand. Tanks and a regulator. She caught her breath. "Where have you been, Brent?" she asked, noting his broad shoulders. Could he have attacked her himself?

"What's that got to do with anything?" he demanded.

"I see you dive," she said, pointing to his dive equipment.

He glanced down at his equipment. "Yeah, so what? It's the Graveyard of the Atlantic out there, remember? Diving mecca."

"Where were you diving today?"

He gestured. "Out at a wreck offshore. What difference does it make?"

"A diver tried to drown me. Right offshore here. He wore a black wetsuit."

If the thought of her being drowned bothered him, he didn't show it. "Most wetsuits are black."

She stared at him. "Do you hate me, Brent?"

"I don't know you well enough to like or dislike you."

"Did you try to kill me?"

"No." His face was expressionless.

"Can I see your arms?"

He frowned, then shrugged and held both arms out where she could see them under the porch light. The skin was smooth and unmarked. "Samson bit my attacker."

"As you can see, I have not been bitten."

He could have hired someone, but she might as well let it go. Even if he was guilty, she'd never be able to tell.

Tires crunched up the drive. Samson stretched and yawned, then bounded down the steps to meet his owners. Libby followed.

Bree held out her arms. "I'm so sorry, Libby," she murmured. "I wanted to tell you myself, but the sheriff wouldn't let me."

"She can't be dead," Libby moaned, burying her face in her new friend's shoulder.

"Samson and I will do what we can," Bree promised. "We'll help you get to the bottom of this."

Libby lifted her head. "Someone tried to drown me tonight, Bree. A diver grabbed me and took me under. I'm frightened."

Bree went still. "But what could be the motive?"

Libby pulled away. "Money, property? I don't know."

"Don't go anywhere alone until we solve this mystery," Bree said. "I'm afraid for you."

Libby nodded and lifted Hunter from his car seat. "I'm going to stay close to Alec from here on out."

———

Libby sat on the porch by herself. It was well past midnight, but she couldn't sleep. She'd seen light coming from under Vanessa's door as well, so she knew her sister was likely just as conflicted. Libby rolled the bead necklace in her fingers. *What would Jesus do?*

God had made it clear what she was supposed to do, but she didn't want to. This necklace meant the world to her. Vanessa only wanted it because she didn't have it. *Be generous with Vanessa and Brent.* Why did her father have to ask that of her? Why hadn't he asked that of them? They were the ones being hurtful. Why should it rest on her shoulders?

Alec's figure loomed in the doorway as he stepped to the porch. "Can't sleep?"

"No. Too much to process today."

He joined her and put his arm on the back of the swing behind her. "Anything I can help you with?"

"It's my dad!" she burst out. "Why did he ask so much of me and nothing of Brent and Vanessa? Why am I the one who is supposed to be generous? Why do I have to extend grace? I'm being pummeled with more than they are."

"I wonder if he knew that you're a Christian? I'm not so sure about Vanessa and Brent. Of course, it's impossible to judge another man's heart, but I've seen no evidence in their lives."

"To whom much is given, much is required." She paraphrased the verse from the book of Luke with a sigh. "Sometimes doing the right thing is so hard."

"What's the right thing you're reluctant to do?"

She pulled the necklace away from her neck and held it to the moonlight. "I have to give this to Vanessa."

"Ah." Alec's arm came down around her shoulders and he hugged her. "One thing I've discovered in my own walk with the Lord is this: when something is really hard but we do it anyway, the rewards are equally great. So if you just suck it up and do what you feel God is telling you to do, you're going to be really glad in the end."

She leaned up and kissed his cheek. He smelled good with some kind of spicy cologne. "Thanks. You're right. I have to do it."

His hand tightened around her shoulders, and before she could pull away, he brushed his lips across hers. The contact sent a warm rush through her. Surely he felt something for her. A man with his integrity didn't go around kissing women willy-nilly.

He pulled back and rested his head on the top of her shoulder. "I'll pray for you."

"That means more than you know." She kissed him again, relishing the stubble on his cheek. "I'm going to go do it now before I talk myself out of it."

"I'll wait here and pray. Come back down when you're done and let me know how it went."

"You're a great guy, Alec," she said, squeezing his hand. "I'll be back."

Before she could lose her nerve, she hurried inside and up the stairs to her sister's room. The light was still shining under the door. She knocked, hoping her sister wasn't asleep. That would get things off to a terrible start. "Vanessa? Are you still up?"

"I'm up." The door swung open to reveal Vanessa in a red nightgown.

"Can I come in for a minute?" Libby asked.

Her sister shrugged. "Suit yourself." She retreated to the bed, where she flopped on the edge and picked up a bottle of red nail polish.

The room smelled of nail polish too. Libby shut the door behind her. "You're up late."

"So are you. I imagine we're thinking about the same thing."

Was that a hint of warmth in Vanessa's voice? Libby decided to believe it was. "We're real sisters. I can hardly wrap my mind around it."

"Me neither. You might want to see that." Vanessa pointed to an old photo album. "Aunt Pearl gave it to me."

Libby picked it up and flipped to the first page. It showed a young woman smiling into the camera. She had a baby in her arms, and a little girl held on to her leg. "That's Mom. I'm the little girl. You're the baby?"

"I assumed so."

Why hadn't Pearl shown this to her? Libby tried to shove away her jealousy, but it crouched in her chest. She flipped the page to see several other photos. A baby in a crib with an older girl propping a bottle in her mouth, another with the toddler holding the baby on her lap on the floor, and one of a young man holding them both and smiling proudly. She recognized him as their father.

"They look so happy," she said.

"Aunt Pearl says the reality was far different." Vanessa looked up from painting her toes. "I don't remember her at all. Our mother, I mean. You'd think I'd remember my own mother! Do you have any pictures?"

For the first time, Libby looked at the situation from Vanessa's point of view. She'd been abandoned by her mother. She'd even been deceived about *who* her mother was. At least Libby had known the identity of both parents, even though her mother had lied about her father's death.

She nodded. "I have some back in Virginia Beach. I'll have some copies made for you."

Vanessa's expression hardened again. "I guess it doesn't matter. Tina was a real mother to me. She was wonderful. I still miss her."

"I've heard nothing but good things about Tina."

This wasn't going as planned. Vanessa seemed almost unapproachable. Libby inhaled and squared her shoulders. "I came here to give you this, Vanessa." She unfastened the necklace and held it out.

Vanessa's eyes widened and she held out her hand. Libby dropped it into her palm, and Vanessa's fingers closed around it. "But I thought you loved it."

"I have to admit I didn't want to give it to you, but God told me to." Her voice broke and she cleared her throat.

Vanessa frowned. "And you did it just because you thought you were supposed to?"

"I'm trying to obey what the letters mean. What would Jesus do? Jesus didn't care about possessions. The necklace is just a possession. So it's yours."

Vanessa held the hand with the necklace to her chest. "Thank you." Her gaze searched Libby's face. "Do you think we can have a real relationship?"

"I'd like that more than anything," Libby said. "I'm willing if you are."

"I'm willing." Vanessa fastened the necklace around her neck. "It's going to take time though. We have a lot of catching up to do."

"I have all the time in the world," Libby said.

She couldn't wait to tell Alec that he'd been right.

THIRTY

Alec gave the swing a push with his foot. Libby had been gone half an hour. He'd been praying that she would find favor with Vanessa, that a door to a good relationship might be opened between the two women. He had a sense that God was answering that prayer.

He heard a car and straightened. His stomach tightened when he recognized his truck, driven by his nephew. He rose to confront Zach for breaking curfew. This wasn't going to go well, but it had to be done. He waited under the security light.

The interior light came on when Zach got out of the truck. His whistle died on his lips when he realized Alec was standing on the walk. "Hey, Uncle Alec."

"It's nearly one," Alec said. "Your curfew is midnight."

"I'm seventeen years old. I don't need a curfew."

"Well, you have one anyway. Nothing good happens after midnight. Just things like this." He held out Zach's pocketknife. "I found this on one of the little islands. Along with beer bottles."

Zach snatched the knife from his hand. "I didn't do anything."

"You're saying you didn't have a little beer, have a little fun?"

"There's nothing wrong with that. You telling me you've never had a beer?"

"You're underage."

"And you never drank when you were my age? Come on, Uncle Alec. I've heard the stories about you. You were no saint."

"Which is why I'm trying to keep you from making my mistakes."

The security light illuminated Zach's angry face. He clenched his fists. "I don't have to listen to this."

Alec grabbed his arm as he started past. "You will listen. The next time you're not here at midnight, I'll come looking for you. I imagine it would be embarrassing to be hauled home in front of your friends."

"You wouldn't do that."

"I would and I will. This is a small island. I know every nook and cranny. You won't be able to hide from me."

Zach's eyes narrowed. "I'll run away."

"And you'll end up in a boys' home. Is that what you want? Look, Zach, I'm trying to help you. I know it hurts that your parents are gone. How do you think your dad feels when he looks down from heaven and sees how you're acting?"

Zach took a step back. "I'm trying to make sense of it, okay? I always wanted to be the kind of man my dad was. I idolized him. But what good did it do Dad to try to please God if he was just going to kill him?"

Alec tried to embrace the boy but Zach shook him off, so he dropped his arms back to his sides. "Integrity has rewards that are more valuable than how many days we spend on the earth."

The boy's face worked to restrain emotion. "If God cared, he wouldn't have taken both my parents. That's just plain cruel. Mom and Dad always told me that God loves me. I wish I could still believe it."

"I can see why you think he doesn't. Psalms says, 'Blessed in the eyes of the Lord is the death of his saints.' I know we miss them, but now they are alive like never before. God doesn't view death in this life the same way we do." Alec thought he saw a sheen of tears in Zach's eyes.

"Is that supposed to make me feel better? It doesn't. I want my dad. I want to come home and hear Mom's voice. No one could make peanut-butter cookies like her. And she *cared*. So did Dad." Zach's shoulders slumped. "I don't have anyone anymore."

Alec put his hand on the boy's shoulder. "You have me. And your grandparents. Plenty of us love you, Zach. Don't shut us out. We're all in this together. We're all hurting."

He opened his arms, fully expecting Zach to turn away. Instead, the boy buried his face in Alec's chest.

"I miss them," Zach said.

Alec hugged him. He struggled to speak past the lump shutting off his throat. "I do too. But we're still family. We will get through this."

Zach pulled away, looking a little embarrassed by his outburst. "I'll try to be home on time tomorrow."

"I'll wait up." He wanted Zach to know the rules still stood. "Time for bed, bud. We have church in just a few hours."

Zach made a face but said nothing as they walked to the porch. When Zach went inside, Alec settled back on the swing to wait for Libby. The front door creaked, and she burst through the opening with a smile on her face. He rose as she rushed toward him. She launched herself at him, and he caught her and hugged her. The scent of her vanilla shampoo filled his head. "I guess it went well?" He had to grin at her exuberance.

Her arms went around his waist and she hugged him. "It went super, Alec. You were so right."

He didn't want to let her go, but when she pulled away, he released her and led her to the swing. "So tell me about it."

Her face beamed as she told him about the pictures and

Vanessa's reaction to the necklace. "It was hard. Really hard. But you were right—my sacrifice opened a door between us. We may never be as close as typical sisters, but we're on the right path. We have a lot to get caught up on. She's going to tell me about Dad, and I'm going to tell her about Mom."

Her voice was full of excitement, and he smiled. "God always comes through."

"I think I've learned more about God this week than I have my entire life," she said. "And it's all thanks to you."

He hugged her. It was a habit he could get used to. "I'm not the Holy Spirit. He was telling you the right thing to do, and you obeyed."

He'd never been able to talk to another woman about God so freely. That had to mean something.

———

People of every age and description crowded the pews at church. Fishermen, stay-at-home moms, and shop owners mingled as friends and neighbors. Libby squeezed past Alec to stand in the aisle and shake hands. People eyed her curiously but were a little more standoffish than the last time she'd been in town.

If she were alone for a few minutes, she would slip up to the front and sit in the first pew. Not that God would answer her question of *why*. Libby wasn't ready to accept that Nicole was dead. Not yet. She didn't feel any sense of closure.

Alec touched her shoulder, and she realized most of the people had cleared out. She smiled at him. "Sorry, I was woolgathering."

"You okay?"

She nodded, her throat too full to speak. "I love this church. It was built in about 1890?"

He nodded. "You're good."

"Comes with the job."

His eyes were grave. "I wanted to wait until church was over to tell you. The article in the paper came out today. It's on the front page."

She examined his expression. "It's bad?"

"Yeah." He took her elbow and guided her down the aisle to the front where they settled on the pew. He opened his Bible and pulled out a clipping. "He basically implies you're another Susan Smith."

The woman who drowned her children. Numb, she took the clipping and scanned it. "He talks about my mother's death too, even though I was never charged with that. He's painted me as some kind of monster."

She was stunned. This was even worse than she'd expected. Why would Earl do something so vicious? She'd liked him on the trip from Kitty Hawk. Was this his revenge for her not telling him about Nicole's disappearance sooner?

Alec's expression was pained. "I'm sorry, Libby. This is my fault. I thought he'd help us, not hurt us."

He'd said *us* as though they were one unit. The realization that he sided with her was a comfort she could cling to. "What can we do about this?"

"Not much. Suing him for libel would just draw more attention to it. All we can do is try to find out who grabbed Nicole. And make him look stupid."

"Why are you doing this?" she asked, searching his face for clues.

"Doing what?"

"Helping me. Standing by me. Your own cousin thinks I might be guilty."

He was silent a moment. "You're Ray's daughter. He would expect me to help you."

Not quite what she'd wanted to hear. She'd hoped he'd tell her he liked her. That he believed in her. "You've never said why you idolized my father so much."

He closed his Bible. "Ray was my father's best friend. He was like a second dad to me. More than that, like a real dad. My father was often busy with his fishing boats. Dawn to dusk, he was out hauling in seafood. Lobster, crab, fish. He never had time to pitch me a ball or take me to the mainland for a game."

"He was working, providing for his family."

He nodded. "Sure. But Ray made time. And when I got into trouble when I was in high school, he turned me around. Forced his way through my rebellion with love and strength. It's because of him that I'm a Christian today."

"Why would he do that? Care about a kid that wasn't his own?"

"I honestly think he was trying to be Jesus in the flesh to me. To do what he could to share his faith through his actions." His gaze searched hers. "And maybe he was trying to atone for what he did to you. I know that's what you're wondering. Why did he help me and not you? Trust me though, Libby. Your dad was a good man."

"So he was a model Christian." She'd been more of a lax one. When was the last time she helped someone out just to bring praise to Jesus? Never. She wanted to do better, though, to shine like Alec did. Her hand went to her neck, but it was bare. No WWJD necklace anymore. Its impact hadn't faded though. She prayed it never would.

His smile was gentle. "Ray was more than a model Christian. He was a conduit for God's love to most everyone he met. I often saw him take bags of food to widows and give money to those in need."

She remembered turning away that woman who was collecting money for the house-fire victims. "He had plenty to give."

"Not in the early days. He always said God would provide for his needs. He just had to be faithful." He smiled. "Tina used to get so aggravated when he'd raid her larder and leave them without food. They couldn't always afford to buy more, so he'd trudge off to the store to buy peanut butter and bread. They always made it though. He would tell her that you can't out-give God."

She couldn't imagine that kind of generosity. If only she'd had a chance to know him.

THIRTY-ONE

N o, no, not that!" Libby stopped the workers from hauling the walnut wainscoting out of the lifesaving station. "I can restore it. It's native walnut."

The man made a face. "Looks ruined to me."

"Trust me, I can fix it."

She directed him to lean it against the far wall, then glanced at her watch. Alec was going to take her and Bree out searching on the boat this afternoon, but she had to get this project started. Once the renovations were complete, she was going to donate it to the town. Just being back to work in some way lifted her spirits. She might not be able to find Nicole, but she could help the town.

Libby wandered through the station. It practically boasted of its previous life. The boats that had carried rescuers to the seas were propped against one wall. One had holes in it, but two were in good shape. The bunks that housed the men were rusty and falling apart, but she could see in her mind's eye an exhibit that would explain the courageous work done here through the decades. The building was good and solid. It deserved to be saved, and her work would bring in visitors.

She climbed the old circular stairs, the iron clanging under her feet, until she stood in the widow's watch and stared out to sea. The lookout's job would have been monotonous until that moment when a ship broke to pieces on the shoals.

So much history here.

"Libby, someone here to see you," one of the workers called.

She turned her gaze from the sea to the parking lot. The sheriff's SUV was parked by the door. She gulped. The state authorities were supposed to arrive today. Sheriff Bourne had probably escorted them himself so he could watch her squirm. She prayed for strength as she clanged down the steps and found three men in the main room watching the activity.

"You're putting this place on the national registry?" the sheriff asked.

"Yes. It shouldn't be hard. There's so much important history here." She held out her hand to the two agents. "Libby Holladay."

The first man was in his fifties, skinny and wiry with a thin mustache and pale blue eyes. "Detective Monroe," he said, shaking her hand.

The other one also took her hand. His brown eyes were cold and judgmental. He was in his thirties and had an eager-hunter look about him. "Detective Pagett," he said. "We're here to find out what happened to your business partner."

"I'll do whatever I can to help you find her."

"Would you like to step outside so we can discuss this in private?" Monroe asked, glancing at the workers who were watching them.

"Whatever you say." She would not show any fear.

"After you." Pagett held open the door for her.

The hot sunshine on her face gave her strength. She heard the church bells ring out the time, as if God was telling her to take courage. There was a bench outside by the walk, so she headed for it and settled on it. "I've been working all morning, so I hope you don't mind if I sit down."

"Not at all," Monroe said. "Now, about your partner. We particularly want to talk to you about the day she disappeared. Where were you?"

"I was documenting a house for the national historic registry." She told them where it was located. "The new owner wanted us to do the restoration."

"Did anyone see you there?" Pagett asked.

She started to shake her head, then stopped. "There was a lady in the neighborhood collecting money for a family who had suffered a house fire. I don't know her name, but if you talk to the people who had the fire, they will likely know. I think the woman will remember that I was there."

Pagett's mouth grew pinched. "We'd like your permission to examine your bank account."

"That's fine."

His brows rose at her quick agreement. "You haven't withdrawn a large amount of money?"

She laughed. "Do you have any idea what I make? There was never a large amount of money to spend. It's all I can do to pay my expenses."

Monroe took out a notebook. "Let's talk about the call from your partner."

"She called while I was at the old house. She told me I had a sister here, and that if I could log on to my computer, I could have the chance to see her."

"There was an open wireless at your site?" the sheriff asked.

She shook her head, trying not to show her impatience. "No, but I have a card to tether my computer to my cell phone."

"I thought you didn't make much money. That would be an expensive gadget," Pagett said.

"It's part of my work and not that expensive. I get leads on the road all the time and I need to be able to pull up the maps. They're too small to see on my phone." She crossed her legs and clasped her hands over her knee. "Look, detectives, I can tell you think I did away with Nicole, but you couldn't be further from the truth. Find out who took her. It wasn't me. I saw two men."

The older agent had an expression in his eyes that made her hope he was listening, so she targeted her gaze at him. She described the kidnappers and everything she saw. As she talked, she remembered more about the boat and gave them details on color.

Monroe put his notebook away. "We'll get on it, Ms. Holladay. Thank you for your time."

"But don't make any plans to leave Hope Island," Pagett said.

"Trust me, I'm clinging to hope for dear life," she called after them.

With the sea spray in his face and the sun on his arms, Alec steered his boat toward a small cove down the shore from where Nicole's belongings had been discovered. He cut the engine. "I checked tide and current charts. I think there's a good chance the killers could have been out here when they threw her overboard. The currents would have carried anything placed in the water here to the shore where her shoes and cover-up were found."

Libby's face was pink with the sun, and she had her long hair back in a ponytail. The style made her look about eighteen. "She's not dead, Alec. I know it. We'll find her."

Alec smiled and said nothing. The day stretched out in front of them, and Alec found himself wanting to hang on to every minute. What did that mean? She was becoming way too important to him too quickly. He glanced at Bree and Samson in the front of the boat. The dog was enjoying the ocean breeze but didn't seem to have caught any kind of scent yet.

Libby lifted a pair of binoculars to her eyes and scanned the horizon. "There's nothing out here but ocean. I'm a little disoriented."

The disappointment in her voice struck a chord with him. He'd hoped for more too. He pointed. "The lighthouse ruins are there." He moved his finger to the north. "The lifesaving station where she was taken is there."

"So that's why we're here?"

"I suspect whoever took her brought her out here right away. I suspect they killed her almost as soon as they grabbed her. That's why Bree found her things where she did." When she stiffened, he touched her shoulder. "Whatever happened, her things went overboard out here. The shoes and clothing washed ashore too quickly for them to have let much time elapse."

Her expression grew somber as she stared out at the sea, and he wished he could carry some of her pain. Was she imagining Nicole's last moments here, struggling for survival? No, she was seeing a different scenario. One where Nicole was alive and awaiting rescue.

She let the binoculars hang down from her neck. "Now what?"

He pulled out a currents chart he'd brought. "The only other place where her body might have washed ashore is here." He stabbed a finger to the north of the lighthouse ruins.

"We were there the other day. We walked right past."

"It was flooded then, but the water has gone down now. I'm going to anchor offshore and see if we can find anything." He avoided saying the word *body*.

She swallowed hard. "Okay."

He squeezed her hand. "I won't leave you." He saw Bree turn her back as though to give them more privacy.

Libby stared at him. "Are you for real?"

"What do you mean?"

"I didn't think men like you existed. Strong, steady, spiritual. I think I must have dreamed you."

Her admiring amber eyes brought heat to his cheeks. "I'm just an ordinary guy."

"You're anything but," she said softly. She looked past him to the shore. "Do you think Brent is behind this, Alec?"

He'd hoped she wouldn't ask. Not until he poked around a little more. "It's possible," he admitted. "The money he was promised for the land could corrupt anyone."

"Ten million."

"How'd you know that?"

"Poe offered me the same thing after I arrived."

"What did you tell Poe?" He couldn't keep the dislike from his voice.

"You've met him?"

"Once."

"You don't like him."

He pressed his lips together. "He's out for his own interests."

She sighed. "Isn't everyone?"

"The Bible teaches God first, then others, then self."

"I don't think I've met anyone who followed that."

"Your dad did."

"We're not talking about my dad but about Poe."

He shrugged. "He makes money brokering deals for investors in New York. You could probably get more money if you asked for it."

"Would you sell it?" There was only curiosity in her voice.

"No way. Your dad was adamant about preserving Hope Beach. He owned enough property to keep out most investors. And his influence swayed those who might have sold out. He also snapped up houses for sale, then gave them to deserving families."

Her eyes widened. "You're kidding! He gave away *houses*?"

"Property is cheap here. He wanted to keep the town for the fishermen, the little guy. If he let a market boom start, the only people who could afford to live here would be rich tourists who come for the summer."

She fell silent, her gaze still on the shore. "Poe said I didn't have long to decide. That if I waited too long, his investor would just move on to another property."

"There *is* no other property of its size with beachfront. The state owns much of the shoreline. They'll have your property, or the resort idea is toast."

"That does make it more valuable. How much more do you think I could get?"

She obviously hadn't listened to a thing he'd said. He wasn't sure he had the words or the inclination to dissuade her. If she couldn't see the ramifications of her actions, then she had more of a mercenary heart than he'd thought. "Another five million. Maybe ten."

"You're mad at me," she said. "I'm sorry, but I have to think of my future too. If I keep the inn, how will I even afford the upkeep? There's no money to do the repairs that it needs."

"Some of the men from town would help. I can swing a pretty good hammer." But when he remembered how much needed to be done, he knew his offer wouldn't make much difference.

He motored toward shore. Change was coming to his small island whether he liked it or not.

THIRTY-TWO

A crane swooped low over the water and caught up a wriggling fish. Gulls screeched overhead as Libby waded ashore. "I love this place," she said. "It's so peaceful here."

Bree and Samson had already disappeared from sight. There was no one around but Libby and Alec, and she found herself walking closer than necessary to Alec. If she had the courage, she'd hold his hand. Her gaze went to the lighthouse ruins. The maritime forest beckoned but not as much as the ruins did.

"You're a historian," Alec said, smiling. "If there's a ruin around, you're content."

"Exactly right." She stepped close to the lighthouse foundation. "What secrets are hidden here? Wouldn't you like to know? The men who manned this lighthouse saved lives, but I'm sure they had hidden heartaches too."

She would rather daydream about lives gone by than face why they were here. What if they found Nicole's body in this place? Glancing at Alec, she saw he understood. Words seemed unnecessary between them. She'd never been with anyone who was so in tune with her.

The wind ruffled his hair. "Can't you just imagine Blackbeard coming ashore where we did?"

"I'd like to live out here," she said. "Maybe I could have the inn moved to this spot."

"Way I hear it, this spot is right where Poe's New York investor wants to build his resort."

She frowned. "Here? I thought it was going to be where Tidewater Inn is standing."

"Who knows. Rumors are floating all around. Ask him." He nodded toward the water.

While they'd been talking, another boat had anchored and sent a dinghy ashore. Poe stepped out of the rubber raft. He shook sand from his shoes, then headed toward them with a set smile.

Libby suppressed a sigh. They didn't have time for this.

"I was told you might be out here," Poe said, stopping when he reached them.

His face was pink with sun, but it only enhanced his good looks. Libby was sure he knew it too. "You came all this way to find us?"

His smile never faltered. "It's a lovely day."

"I haven't had a chance to think about your offer," she said. "I do have some questions though. Where exactly will the resort be built?"

"He has plans for this entire stretch of coastline."

"Even here? This is almost sacred ground," she said.

"Oh yes, most certainly here. With all the legends about Blackbeard, he'll want to capitalize on that. Maybe a wedding chapel." He dismissed the topic with a shrug. "That's not our concern though. We simply need to come to an agreement. I realize you're still looking for your friend, but my client is growing quite insistent. I suspect he'll move on to another idea if you don't make up your mind."

"Nicole is dead," Alec said.

Libby opened her mouth, then closed it again. Protesting wasn't going to change anyone's mind.

He blinked. "Y-You're sure? I haven't heard anything about that. Where was her body found?" Tugging at his tie, he shifted his feet in the sand.

Why would he be so agitated? Was his client that eager to get her land?

"Her belongings were found," Alec put in.

The tenseness seemed to go out of Poe in a rush. "I'm so sorry."

The words seemed sincere, so she decided to accept them at face value. "You understand that selling this property has been the last thing on my mind."

"Of course. But as I said, my client is growing impatient."

"There is no other land for him to buy here, so quit harassing the lady," Alec said. "You and I both know this is his only shot."

Poe's lips flattened and his nostrils flared. "Her father was the one opposed to selling. I'm sure others in town would be willing to let their property go for the right price. Her brother was quick to agree."

"This is the only stretch of beach that can be purchased. The rest is state land."

Poe shrugged. "My client has connections. If he wants state land, I suspect he could get it." He turned to Libby. "I'm prepared to make an offer of twelve million. But we must sign the deal this week."

"What's the rush?" she asked. "I told you I need to think about it."

"These things take time, and my client wants to start construction this fall."

"I'm sorry, I'm just not prepared to make a decision." If only he would just leave. They had an unpleasant search to make and he was in their way.

"Very well. I'll check back with you in a few days."

She watched him walk stiffly away, then clamber back into the rubber raft. She turned to study the peaceful setting. "So this place will be gone. That makes me sad."

"You have the power to stop it," he said.

"Not really. That's a lot of money to walk away from. I don't think I can do it. I see it upsets you, but I suspect you've never been poor. I think of all the good I could do with that money. And the pantry will always be full."

"My family wasn't wealthy, Libby," he said. "But I don't believe money solves everything. If you don't have money problems, you have health issues or personal problems. God uses whatever means at his disposal to mold and shape us." He took her arm and turned her back toward the ruins.

She'd never thought of it that way before. But she still couldn't see letting go of such an unbelievable sum of money.

They poked through the ruins for an hour without seeing anything of import. On their way back to the boat, she heard a shout. Bree was jumping up and down and waving. Libby broke into a jog.

"Look at this," Bree said, pointing to the ground. "Have you been down there?"

"What is it?" Libby asked, stooping to lift away some bricks. "It looks like a door to the cellar."

"This area used to have a lot of brick heaped up. The storm surge must have moved enough of the debris to reveal the trapdoor," Alec said.

"You didn't know it was here?" Libby asked. She shoved several bricks out of the way. "We might see things that haven't seen the light of day in decades. Can we take a look?"

He began to help her and Bree move bricks. "Probably nothing important, but if you want to explore, we can."

───

The flashlight in Bree's hand pushed back the shadows and showed water in the bottom of the hole. A rickety ladder descended into the darkness. "Musty," Libby said, wrinkling her nose.

"You can hold the light," Bree said, handing it to her.

Libby peered past her. "Wonder what's down there? When do you suppose the last people were in here?"

Alec flipped on his flashlight. "Late eighteen hundreds maybe. That's when the whole place came down."

Her pulse sped up. No telling what she might find down there.

"There might be rats or spiders," he warned.

She stopped. "I'm not afraid." But her quivering voice told a different story, so she cleared her throat and forced strength into her tone. "They'll run from us."

He gave her a skeptical glance, then shrugged. "I'll go first and make sure it's safe."

He put the handle of the flashlight in his teeth and began to climb down the ladder. Libby heard the ladder groan several times and held her breath, but the rungs held. His feet splashed into the water, and she trained her light on him to see how deep it was. The water came to his calves.

"It's not too bad," he called up. "I'll hold the ladder if you're sure you want to come down."

"I'm sure," she said. She tucked her flashlight into the waistband of her shorts and began to step down.

Even the ladder felt damp. The musty odor filled her head. She climbed down until she was standing in knee-high water that made her shiver. It was colder than she expected. She plucked her flashlight out and flipped it on. With a little more light, she felt more confident.

"Stay," Bree told Samson. She joined them in the cellar.

Alec swept his light around the room. "Looks like it was a root cellar. There are old jars of canned food down here." He moved to a shelf that held Ball jars. "Looks like pickles."

Libby followed him and peered at the contents. "I think they're still good."

"I wouldn't eat them," he said, his voice laced with disgust.

"Me neither." She followed him, sloshing through the water to explore the rest of the cellar. Bree was examining the walls.

Old barrels, tools, and items from yesteryear floated in the water or hung on the walls from rusty hooks. She didn't recognize some of the tools and glanced at Alec.

"One of the keepers was a doctor," he said.

Whale-oil casks bobbed in the water. She paused at an over-turned case of shelves. There was less water here. Her foot struck something and she looked down to see what it was. Horror froze her in place when she realized a human skeleton lay partially sub-merged at her feet. Uttering mewling noises, she grabbed Alec's arm. Her muscles finally obeyed her, and she turned and ran for the ladder. She thought Alec called her name, but she didn't stop until she was crouching in the sand and heaving. Samson whined by her ear as if to commiserate with her distress.

A few moments later Alec's hand was on her shoulder. "It's okay," he said, his voice soothing in her ear.

She shuddered. "That was a person." Details she hadn't noticed at the time came back to her. "A woman. I saw a blue sundress." She sat back and swallowed hard, then allowed Alec to help her to her feet.

"I think I know who it is," he said, his voice grim.

Bree clambered up the ladder and stood beside her. "Are you okay?"

"Did you see the skeleton?"

Bree nodded. "It's not Nicole."

"No, no, of course not." She stared into Alec's face, noting his pallor. This hadn't been easy for him either. "Who was she?"

"I think she was Ray's wife, Tina," Alec said.

Libby stared back at the opening. "Tina? I don't understand. She was murdered? I just heard she died."

223

Alec turned to look at the cellar hole too. "She went out on a boat ride and never came back. Her skiff was found broken up and half submerged, but her body was never found. So it was assumed she hit a rock and drowned."

"What does this mean?" she asked, trying to take it all in. "How do you know it's Tina?"

"She always wore a dress. And there was a picture of this dress all over town."

She looked at the yawning hole in the ground and shuddered. "D-Do you think someone killed her and threw her down there?"

"That was my first thought. I suppose it's possible she went exploring and got trapped."

"But the boat . . ."

He nodded. "Exactly. Someone would have had to deliberately scuttle the boat."

She hugged herself. "I don't like this."

"Neither do I."

She looked away from the dank hole. "When did she die?"

"Three years ago. The news caused Ray's first stroke, a small one. He loved her very much."

Pity stirred for her father. "I'm glad he's not alive to see this. If she was murdered . . ."

"The press is going to have a heyday with this." He took her arm and turned her toward the boat. "One good thing is that it might deflect attention from your friend's death for a while."

She stopped and clutched his arm. "I want attention to stay on her. That's the only chance we have of finding out who killed her."

"You don't suppose there could be any connection between Tina's death and Nicole's, do you?" Bree asked.

He frowned. "I don't see how."

"Nicole came out here," Bree said. "What if she saw something? Something that put her in danger?"

"Maybe. But she didn't get into the cellar. It was covered over until the storm surge." He stared back at the cellar. "I need to let Tom know about this. I saw a passageway when we were down there. It looked like it went toward those rocks." He pointed to a rocky point of land jutting into the sea. "I've seen a cave there, but I always thought it was shallow and not very big."

He took Libby's arm and led them all to the cave. They waded into the water and out to the rocks, where he pointed out a small opening.

Stooping, she peered into it. "It's bigger than it looks."

Bree glanced into the cave, then glanced at Libby. "Any chance Nicole would have gone exploring?"

Libby nodded. "Oh yes. She explores caves every chance she gets. Last summer she went on a spelunking vacation with some friends. She mentioned finding one here on the island."

Alec's lips tightened. "We might have a connection, then."

THIRTY-THREE

The palm tree provided a little shade. Nicole had been out since morning watching for a boat, any boat, but the sea remained empty. Her stomach growled, and she worked on ignoring it as best she could. The bread was soggy, and the thought of plain peanut butter wasn't appealing. Besides, she had no idea if the boy would even come back. Her eyes grew heavy, so she propped up her head with her arms and closed her eyes for a few minutes.

A gull cawed and she sat back up, rubbing her eyes. When she stared back out to sea, she saw the reason for the gull's displeasure. A boat skimmed the tops of the waves as it headed for her tiny beach.

Scrambling to her feet, she dusted the sand from her legs and hands and went down to meet the boy. He was wary as he dropped anchor and splashed ashore. It was going to take all her persuasion to convince him she wasn't crazy.

"Got your supplies," he said, dropping a sack onto the sand. "See ya."

"Wait!" She ran to catch him.

When he held out his hands to shove her back, she stopped. "I won't touch you. Just talk to me for a minute, okay? It's lonely out here by myself." Tears sprang to her eyes and she sniffled.

Concern replaced the wariness on his face. "Hey, don't cry. I can stay a minute. Just don't try anything, okay?"

She nodded. "Okay. I'm sorry about before. I was just scared." She searched his gaze. "Is anyone back on Hope Island looking for me?"

"Why would anyone there be looking for you? You're from Raleigh."

She shook her head and decided to go ahead with her plan. The truth. "I live in Virginia Beach. My partner and I have a restoration business. We were hired to restore some buildings in the downtown. My partner's name is Libby Holladay. I'm Nicole Ingram."

He gasped and took a step back. "How'd you hear about that? Did you talk to the Ingram girl sometime?"

"I *am* the Ingram girl. My birthday is July 4. I'm twenty-five. Libby is Ray Mitchell's daughter, but no one on Hope Island knew about her."

His eyes narrowed. "You're lying."

"I'm not." She reached out toward him, but he flinched and stepped back. "Please, check it out. Ask to see a picture of me. You'll see I'm telling the truth. I don't know what all those men told you, but it wasn't true. I was at the boardwalk by Tidewater Inn, and two men kidnapped me. Is Libby in town?"

She was sure of the answer to that. Libby would leave no stone unturned until she stood on this beach and rescued her.

"You don't know anything," he said. "Nicole Ingram is dead. They found her belongings on the beach."

The revelation made her take a step back and gasp. "I fought them. My pink cover-up came off in the struggle. One of them tossed it. And I lost my flip-flops when I jumped overboard. That's all they found, right?"

"I don't know what they found. Just that Nicole's clothes were on the beach."

"Libby didn't believe it, did she? She's still on the island?"

"She's still there. Poking around to try to find out who kidnapped her partner. But I'm not convinced you're the one she's looking for. Your brother told me you were wily and not to believe any story you concocted."

She managed a smile. Even if she didn't get off the island today, he would go back and investigate. He'd find out she was telling the truth. "So don't believe it. Check it out for yourself. Then tell Libby where I am. I'll make sure the police know you were duped, that you weren't an accomplice."

As soon as she said the word *duped,* she knew she'd made a mistake. No guy liked to look foolish.

"I'm not stupid," he said. "You're the stupid one. Trying to snow me with a crazy story like this."

"Look, I know it sounds crazy. But it's even crazier that someone would kidnap me and stick me here in this place. Think! What would be the motive? Locking up a crazy sister? There are places for that. His story makes no sense, and you'd know it if you had any brains at all!" She was past caring if he was mad. Past worrying about hurting his feelings. "You've got to see the truth."

"I'm out of here," he said, turning on his heel. He stomped off toward the boat.

Nicole ran after him and grabbed his arm. "Check it out," she said desperately. "That's all I ask. My picture has to be in the paper. Or online. You'll see I'm telling the truth."

He brushed her hand off. "I'll check it out, and then I'll let you know how crazy you are."

She tried on a winning smile. "What's your name?"

"Zach," he said.

"You have a nice boat."

"Yeah. My uncle likes to fish."

"He's a commercial fisherman?"

He shook his head. "Works for the Coast Guard mostly. Fishes in his spare time."

"And your parents?"

"Dead."

A common bond. "I'm sorry. My dad has cancer, and I'm afraid he won't make it. It's hard."

"What about your brothers?"

She saw where he was going with that. "No brothers. Only two sisters, and they both live in California."

He stepped into the waves. "I gotta go. I'm going to be late."

She wanted to scream and beg him to take her with him, but she forced herself to smile and wave. "Thanks for the supplies, Zach. Don't forget to look up my picture."

———

Alec held the door to the sheriff's office open for Libby. He knew by her expression that she dreaded being interrogated by his cousin. "I'll do the talking," he whispered, guiding her toward Tom's office with his hand at the small of her back.

She held her head high as several workers glanced at her curiously. Her courage impressed him. Not many women would have gone into that cellar hole with him. Not many women would hold up under the suspicion she'd been under.

They found Tom at his desk scowling at the computer. He straightened when he saw them. "Hey, what's up?"

"We found something out at the old lighthouse ruins." He pointed to the first chair. "Have a seat, honey." He nearly bit his tongue off when he realized he'd called Libby *honey*. She smiled and didn't seem to take offense, though, so that was good. He sank into the chair beside her. "We could both use something to drink. Got any bottled water?"

"Yep." Tom reached into a small refrigerator behind his desk and extracted two bottles. "You both look pretty puny. I don't think I've ever seen you so white."

"Thanks." Alec uncapped his bottle and took a swig of water. "It was a rough day. The storm surge uncovered a cellar out at the ruins."

"A cellar?" Tom frowned. "I didn't know about a cellar."

"It's been there all along. Remember that pile of bricks toward the back? It was under there. The force of the water moved the bricks and uncovered the trapdoor. Libby, Bree, and I went down to explore."

"And?"

In answer, Alec pulled out his smartphone and pulled up the picture he'd taken. "We found this." He handed the phone to his cousin.

Tom studied it in silence. "No telling how long that's been down there."

"I'd say about three years."

Tom looked up sharply. "Three years? Why would you say that?"

"Take another look. Recognize anything?" When Tom's face stayed blank, Alec leaned forward and poked his finger on the blue dress. "That's Tina's dress."

Realization dawned on Tom's face. "Tina Mitchell?"

"Yeah. A picture of her in that dress was plastered all over the state for a month."

"You're right. Holy cow." Tom sat back in his chair. "How did she get there?"

"We've been wondering the same thing." Alec told him about going back into the cellar and finding the other entrance.

"So anyone who knew about that could have gone in there. How did Tina know? And did she get trapped in there by the tide or something?" His face changed. "No, that's impossible. Her boat was clear down the coast. It had to have been deliberate."

"That's what I thought too. Someone put her body there, probably after they killed her, then scuttled her boat to make it look like an accident. Forensics can maybe tell what happened."

"Or maybe not," Tom said. "Doesn't look like there's much left."

"Nicole was an avid cave explorer," Libby put in. "What if she found the cave leading to the cellar? What if she found the body and the murderer saw her?"

Tom stroked his chin. "Maybe." But he glanced at her with a hard expression.

"It makes sense," Alec said. "Whoever took Nicole didn't keep her long. It was like they grabbed her and disposed of her right away. I'm guessing they didn't want her to tell anyone about the cellar and what it contained."

"Seems a little far-fetched to me," Tom said. "She wouldn't know who anyone was, killer or victim."

"But the minute she reported it, you would have known as soon as you saw Tina. I think there's evidence in that cellar that will lead us to the killers."

"I'll call the state detectives. They have more resources than we do. I don't want to muck up this investigation. Holy cow," Tom said again. "Tina Mitchell was murdered. But why?"

"When we know that, we might know who."

"Ray maybe? No relationship is perfect."

Alec bristled. "Don't even go there. Ray was a good man. The best."

"Even good men snap," Tom said. "You know it's usually the person closest to the victim." His gaze slid again to Libby.

"Not this time," Alec said.

"One of the kids?" Tom suggested. "I remember hearing they were having some battles about Brent's lack of a job. He expected his parents to hand out money, and they wanted him to work."

Alec glanced at Libby. She should tell Tom about the attack and how Brent had a wetsuit, but he knew she wouldn't want to get her brother in trouble.

Libby leaned forward with her hands clasped. "Please, Sheriff Bourne, I didn't kill Nicole. Or my mother. I'm not some kind of monster."

Tom tapped his fingers on the desk. "Can we place Nicole at the cellar?"

"I know she'd been out to a nearby cave. She told me in the call."

But then Tom's face hardened and he stood. "Good work, Alec. Staying close to her has paid off, hasn't it?"

Alec went hot, then cold. He leaped to his feet with his fists clenched. "Let's go, Libby." He held out his hand.

She took it, glancing from him to his cousin and back again. "What do you mean 'staying close to her'?"

Tom was white. "You didn't think he was hanging around because he liked you, did you? I asked him to keep an eye on you."

Alec stared at Tom. Why was he doing this? Libby stared at him with eyes filled with pain. "Libby," he began.

Without a word she turned and rushed for the door. He started to go after her, then turned back to Tom. "Why did you do that?"

"I thought if she was shook up, she might reveal something."

"She's a good woman, Tom," Alec said. "I'd better leave before I bust your face in and you have to throw me in jail for attacking an officer."

He stormed from the office. Libby was nowhere in sight.

THIRTY-FOUR

I t was a long hike back to Tidewater Inn, but Libby needed
the time to compose herself. She vacillated between anger and
hurt. So Alec's support had all been a ploy. She should have
known he couldn't be the superstar he seemed. She paused to
sniffle and wipe her eyes.

An old Buick slowed and she saw Pearl behind the wheel. The
window came down, and her aunt beckoned her to get in the car.
Libby went around to the passenger seat.

"What are you doing walking alone?" her aunt scolded.
"Especially after what happened to your friend?" She studied
Libby's face. "You've been crying. Have a spat with Alec?"

"He tricked me," Libby burst out. "He was just pretending to
help me. All the time he was trying to see if I killed Nicole."

"And who told you this?"

"The sheriff." Libby glanced around the car. "You've got a
block on the pedals."

"So I can reach them." Her aunt pressed her shoe against the
block on the accelerator and the car jerked into motion. "Let me
tell you something about our sheriff. Tom idolizes his cousin. But
he's also jealous of Alec. Tom knows he'll never be the man Alec
is. So he tries to bring Alec down to his own level every chance he
gets. I've seen it over and over again."

"But he didn't deny Tom had asked him to find out what he could."

"I'm sure Tom *did* ask him. He likely saw the way Alec looks at you. Tom wouldn't have liked it."

Libby's cheeks heated. "Alec looks at me? What do you mean?"

Pearl laughed. "Oh, honey, a blind woman could see that besotted expression. The guy fell hard right from the start."

"I don't think so." But Libby's heart sped up at the possibility. Could it be true?

"He took vacation to help you. He's been underfoot every moment since you arrived. The man is smitten." Pearl's sideways glance was sly. "I believe he feels as strongly about you as you do about him."

"He's just a friend." Fresh tears blurred her vision. "At least I thought he was a friend."

"Uh-huh. A friend. You can talk to your old aunt. You feel way more for him than friendship."

"We haven't known each other all that long."

"Long enough to recognize the attraction."

"Well, yes. He's unlike anyone I've ever known. I *thought* he was, anyway. Now I don't know."

"You know." Her aunt turned the old car into the drive. "Huh. Looks like we have company."

Libby stared through the windshield. "It's Horace."

The attorney was getting out of his big Cadillac with a folder in his hand. He mopped his brow as he waited for Libby to step from the car.

"Horace. I wasn't expecting you," Libby said, shutting the car door behind her. She smiled at the older man. "I could use some sweet tea. How about you?"

"Sounds mighty fine, Miss Libby, mighty fine." He held up his folder. "I took the liberty of coming out to bring you the first draft of your will."

"I'd forgotten about it." It was the last thing she wanted to worry about right now, but the man had gone out of his way, so she smiled to hide her disinterest.

"A good attorney never forgets a client's needs," Horace said.

They went up the steps to the porch. "If you want to have a seat on the swing, I'll bring out the tea," Pearl said. "That way you can talk in private. We have a lot of visitors at the moment."

Horace settled on the chair with the cushions. Libby took the swing and tucked her feet under her. They ached from walking. Would Alec come after her? Maybe she should have waited around to talk to him. She was still hurt, but maybe Pearl was right, and Tom was trying to wreck their relationship before it had a chance to start.

"Miss Libby?"

With a start, she realized Horace was speaking to her. "Sorry, what was that?"

He tapped the paper he'd slid toward her on the table. "You want to read over this will?"

She took the paper and began to skim it, though the chore was the last thing she wanted to do. When she got to the part about her beneficiaries, she stopped. "I want to leave half the money to Vanessa."

"And the historic preservation foundation?"

"The other half." She glanced at him. "What happens if I die before this is executed?"

"The laws of the state will prevail. In this case, your next of kin would inherit. That would be Brent and Vanessa."

So Brent would have had motive for drowning her the other night. But was it motive enough to believe that he would hurt her? She hated to think her own brother could be so cold and calculating.

She slid the will back to Horace. "How long before this is ready?"

He pursed his lips. "Just a few days. My secretary is on

vacation, and I'm quite hopeless with a computer. As soon as she gets back, I'll have her amend this and draw up the final papers. Is there anything else you'd like to add?"

She toyed with the idea of leaving Alec something. After her near drowning the other day, she'd been thinking about death. No one knew when their time would come. But it was too soon to think that something permanent might develop between her and Alec.

She shook her head. "I think that's it. Thanks for getting to this so quickly. I'd like to wrap it up as soon as possible."

"We'll do that, Miss Libby."

Her aunt bustled through the door with a tray. "Here we go, Horace. I took the liberty of bringing you some cookies as well."

Libby saw Alec's truck kicking up dust behind it on the road. Her pulse jumped, and she rose to excuse herself from Horace.

———

Alec waved to Horace as he drove off. Libby vanished inside the house as he started up the porch steps. Clenching his jaw, he followed.

Pearl saw him and pointed. "She went into the greenhouse."

He thanked her and went down the hall to the back of the house. Ray had built the greenhouse for Tina twenty years ago. When she was alive, she grew orchids. They still bloomed in the large, sunny space, though Delilah didn't have the green thumb that Tina had possessed.

"Hey, Libby," he began.

She was standing in front of a particularly beautiful white orchid. She didn't turn when he spoke.

"Look, don't freeze me out, okay? Turn around and talk to me."

"There's nothing much to say," she said, still bending over the flower.

"Tom was out of line."

"Was he? It seems he asked you to keep an eye on me. Or is that not true?" She finally turned and stared at him, her hands behind her back. "Did you suspect that I killed Nicole?"

He didn't want to answer that, but with her somber gaze on him, he couldn't lie. "I had to consider the possibility."

"Is that the real reason you asked Earl to do an article? So he'd dig and find out what you couldn't ask?"

"I wanted to find Nicole. At the time that's all I was thinking about."

"So you agreed to stay close to me and see if I was a murderer?"

"Yes. But I quickly realized you would never hurt anyone."

"I thought we were friends," she said, her voice soft. "I thought you were my only true ally here in town. Now I find out that you were just helping out your cousin. And that hurts."

"We *are* friends." It was much too soon to tell her that he was developing feelings for her that were stronger than friendship. "Please don't let what Tom said derail our friendship."

The hurt in her eyes didn't lessen, but she nodded. "I'll try. I'd like to talk about Tina. Do you have any idea what might have happened to her? Did she have any enemies?"

He'd been trying not to think about her. "It's a puzzle. She was as well liked as your father. He was devastated when she died. Walked the beach for weeks hoping to find her."

"If we figure out who killed her, it may lead us to who kidnapped Nicole. I think it's very possible she found Tina's remains."

"I agree. The first thing we might do is talk to Pearl. She knows more about the town than anyone. And she knew Tina better than anyone else except Brent and Vanessa. I suppose we'd better tell them too."

"It's going to be a hard day for Vanessa. First she finds out how our father lied to her, then she discovers the woman she thought was her mother was murdered."

"You sound sympathetic."

"Of course I am. She's my sister. I'm going to work hard to build a relationship with her."

Pearl stood in the doorway with a tray in her hands. "Anyone want coffee and cookies?"

Her eyes were bright and curious. She was probably dying to know what was going on. "I'll take some," Alec said. "We need to talk to you anyway."

Pearl set the tray on the table. "Libby, I hope you accepted his apology."

"I did," Libby said.

He should have known that Pearl would sniff out any news. "Did Libby tell you we found Tina's remains?"

Pearl's smile vanished. "Tina Mitchell?"

Alec nodded. "There's a cellar at the lighthouse ruins. The storm surge revealed it. She was there." He explained how they'd found the cellar and the other entrance.

Pearl was pale. "So you're thinking Nicole was killed because she found Tina?"

Libby nodded. "Alec says you knew her better than anyone, except maybe the kids. Did she have any enemies? Did she seem worried in the weeks before she died?"

The chair groaned when Pearl settled into it. She frowned as she took a sip of her beverage, which was more cream than coffee. "I told Tom that something was wrong back when she came up missing. He dismissed me. So I was right."

Alec frowned. "What do you mean? What did you see?"

"She was withdrawn, sad. I thought maybe she was suffering from depression and spoke to Ray about it."

"Had he noticed?" Alec asked.

Pearl shook her head. "He'd been gone on a trip. I called him while he was in California. He said she'd been quiet on the phone, but he assumed it was because she was tired from taking care of things while he was gone. He promised to talk to her about it when he got home. He arrived on an afternoon. She went missing that evening."

"So he didn't talk to her about it?"

"I didn't want to bring it up. I was afraid she . . ."

"Drowned herself?" Libby asked. She clasped her arms around herself as if she were cold.

Pearl shivered. "Exactly. I didn't want Ray to blame himself if that's what happened."

Alec tried to remember that time when they were all searching for Tina. "Did you see her with anyone during that time?"

Pearl looked away. "Some rich investor from New York named Lawrence Rooney. He'd come to see Ray but spoke to Tina. He hung around a few days." Her tone was careful.

"What did he want?" Libby asked.

Pearl pressed her lips together. "Tina never said."

"And that upset you because she usually told you everything?" Libby guessed.

"I didn't want to think she would be interested in another man." Her chin jutted. "I still don't think Tina was interested in him."

"Maybe I'll see what I can find out about the guy. There might be a link." This long after Tina disappeared, he feared there would be little evidence left. "Maybe."

Pearl rose. "You realize we need to tell Brent and Vanessa?"

"I know," Libby said.

Pearl sighed. "What a terrible day. I'll send them down to speak with you." She hurried away as if she couldn't wait to leave them behind.

Alec's gut tightened. From Libby's tight expression, he knew she was dreading it too.

THIRTY-FIVE

Vanessa's eyes were red as though she'd been crying. "What's going on?" she asked when she came into the greenhouse, glancing at Alec, then over to Libby.

Vanessa was wearing her father's necklace. Libby hoped it would help her sister through this. "Have a seat."

Brent slouched in with his hands in his pockets. He sank into a white wicker chair by a large geranium. "More drama?" he asked in a bored tone.

Libby pressed her lips together. "There's something you need to know, and we didn't want you to hear this from anyone else. And your perspectives may help Tom's investigation as well."

Vanessa straightened where she sat on the wicker sofa. "What's wrong? You're all so serious."

"There's news about Tina, Vanessa," Libby said.

Vanessa frowned and glanced at her brother. "I don't understand. She's been gone for three years. Why are we talking about her now?"

Libby wished she didn't have to tell them. "Yes, yes, I know. But her remains were found today."

Vanessa's eyes grew wide. Brent inhaled sharply. Libby tried to put herself in her siblings' shoes. No matter how much they distrusted her, they were bound by blood. She needed to help them through this if she could. They were all grieving something.

"Where was she found?" Brent asked.

Libby reached toward him, then dropped her hand. "Out at the lighthouse ruins. In the cellar."

Brent frowned. "There's no cellar."

"It's been hidden all this time. The storm surge knocked debris out of the way. But there's another way in." Libby glanced at Alec. "Would you explain, Alec?"

Vanessa and Brent listened in silence. Their expressions changed to incredulity, then to shock as they realized their mother had been murdered.

"But maybe she just found that cave," Brent said.

Vanessa shook her head. "The boat, Brent. The boat had to have been deliberately scuttled. Otherwise, it would have been found nearby on the shore. Even if she pulled it ashore and then found the cave and the tide dragged it back to sea, it would have been found closer to the ruins. Not where it was."

Tears slid down her cheeks, and she kept her head down. Libby wished she knew the best way to comfort her.

"Exactly," Alec said. "We also have to wonder about Nicole now."

If only Libby had had more time to talk to Nicole that day. So many regrets. "Nicole loved caves. The last time I talked to her, she said she'd found a new cave with something exciting in it. Before she could tell me what that was, the men appeared."

"Did you happen to hear Mr. Rooney talking to your mother?" Alec asked.

"Mr. Rooney? You mean that investor guy?" Vanessa asked. "He took us to dinner in Duck one night. You should have seen his yacht!"

"He was trying to impress Mom," Brent said. "Kept telling her that she and Dad could travel the world, have a house wherever they wanted."

"You didn't like him?" Libby asked.

He shrugged. "Not so much. Mom didn't either. When he tried to pressure her to talk to Dad, she told him to take her home."

"Why did she agree to go to dinner in the first place?" Alec asked.

"You know how Mom was. She didn't like to hurt anyone's feelings. And he'd come all that way to talk to Dad."

"Why didn't he call first and make sure D-Dad was home?" It still felt strange to say *Dad*.

"He did," Vanessa said, her tone implying that she didn't appreciate any criticism of her father. "But Daddy got called out at the last minute. One of his businesses in California burned, and he went to make sure the employees were taken care of."

"So your mother tried to placate the guy by talking to him herself." Alec put his hands in his pockets and paced. "Did you hear what he wanted?"

Brent shrugged. "What they always want. This strip of land on the ocean. I think this is the guy that Poe represents. He offered ten mil."

Libby bit her lip to keep from telling him the offer had gone up.

"Did your mother seem tempted?" Alec asked.

Vanessa shook her head. "Mom never wanted to leave the island. She didn't care about yachts and travel. It was all Daddy could do to get her to go to Virginia Beach from time to time."

"She was a homebody," Brent agreed.

"And it's not like Daddy was hurting for money," Vanessa added. "He gave her anything she wanted."

"Did they know the state was talking about putting in a ferry system?" Libby asked.

"Oh yes," Vanessa said. "Daddy made several trips to try to talk down the proposal. He was determined not to let them ruin our island."

"How did you feel about that?" Libby asked, glancing at Brent so he would know she wanted to know what he thought as well.

Brent shrugged. "Dad didn't care much for progress, but lots of younger men like me would like to see more jobs. Even tourism would pay a steadier wage than fishing does at times. And what is there here except fishing?"

"Is that why you were going to sell this place?"

"Maybe. If I could have sold it and started a shipbuilding business here, it would have brought in jobs." His grin was cold. "And it was a lot of money."

Just when she thought she could warm up to the guy, he turned everything around again. Libby had no idea how to read Brent.

———

"Come along, Poe," Lawrence said. He glanced at his daughter. That color dress made Katelyn's skin look like a pumpkin. An unfortunate following after fashion.

Poe rose from the Rooneys' dinner table. "I'll join you in the game room in a few minutes," he said to Katelyn. "All right?"

"I'll be waiting." Her flirtatious glance lingered on him.

Lawrence led the boy to his office. Closing the door behind him, he approached the desk. "I can tell something is on your mind. Has something gone wrong?"

Poe sat in the chair across from the desk. "There's a rumor that Nicole Ingram is dead."

"What? Did you do something to her?"

Poe shook his head. "It wasn't me. Her shoes and cover-up were found, and the authorities are presuming her dead."

"That's not catastrophic, then. They can't blame us for something we didn't do." He eyed Poe. "We didn't have anything to do with this, correct?"

Poe shook his head. "Libby doesn't believe it. She's tenacious. She's got a search-and-rescue dog team there."

Lawrence dismissed the concern with a wave of his hand. "The dog can't tie us to something we didn't do."

"True enough." Poe inhaled and leaned forward. "That's not all though. The cellar has been found. And Tina's remains."

Lawrence bolted out of his chair. "You said no one would ever find her. We should have dumped her body in the ocean." His scowl darkened. "This is your fault."

Poe spread out his hands. "I agree I should have just hauled her body from the cellar when I found it there. But at the time, I was afraid the discovery of her body would heat up the investigation and derail our plan. If they thought she drowned, the hunt would die down. And that's what happened."

"Is there anything you aren't telling me? You didn't kill her, did you?"

"Absolutely not. She must have fallen and hit her head. She was dead when I found her."

"You'd better not be lying."

Poe held his gaze. "I'm telling you the truth. If you have doubts about me, now is the time to say so."

Lawrence looked away and shook his head. He didn't want to alienate Poe when things were going so well with Katelyn. "The problem now is what do we do? Investigators will be poring over that cellar."

"They may not find the cache."

"I'd rather not take the chance," Lawrence said.

"What do you propose?"

"I don't know yet. I'll have to think about it."

Poe relaxed in the chair. "I have an idea."

THIRTY-SIX

When Delilah served the Tidewater Inn guests after-dinner coffee, Alec gestured to Zach and they stepped outside. Over the meal, Alec had caught Zach staring at Libby quite often. Did his nephew see the attraction between them?

"School will be starting soon," Alec said, stooping to pick up an unbroken conch.

Zach folded his arms across his chest. "I'm not going back to school, Uncle Alec."

"Now, Zach," Alec began.

"Don't try to talk me into it. You know I just want to be a fisherman. It's an honest profession. I don't need college to catch fish. I already know the ocean like the back of my hand."

"I know you do. But the world is changing. What happens if the fishing falls off? It's a hard life, Zach. I'd like to see you have something else to rely on. There's plenty of time to try different things. You don't have to set your course right now. At least go to two years of college."

Zach's chin jutted out. "I don't want to. And you can't make me."

The boy—no, Zach was a man now—was in charge of his own destiny. Much as Alec wanted to insist on college, how could he know what was best for Zach? How could any man know what was best for another man? There was no denying that Zach was a natural-born waterman. He was in his element when he rode the seas. His dad, Alec's brother, had been the same way. It was probably why he'd been so hard for their father to handle. Zack, like Darrell, just wanted to be back in Hope Beach.

Alec made one final attempt. "What about online classes? Just a couple to keep learning."

Zach hesitated. "I'll think about it."

"That's all I ask."

"I don't know what classes I'd even take though."

"What about something like marine biology? You'd be good at that, and you'd be helping the ecology." A flicker of interest in Zach's eyes encouraged him. "The Banks have some challenges to face. Maybe you could be part of finding help."

Zach had quit listening. His gaze went past Alec, and Alec turned to see Libby heading toward them with a newspaper in her hand. She looked pale and upset.

"Something wrong?" he asked when she reached them.

She held out the newspaper and he saw it was a New York paper. "The story has been picked up. Front page." She opened the paper to reveal a picture of Nicole.

"I'm sorry," Alec said. It had been a total miscalculation to get Earl involved. The reporter was probably rejoicing at all the interest and might even follow up with more damaging articles.

"I should have expected it," Libby said.

"Can I see it?" Zach asked, holding out his hand. Libby handed it over and he studied the article. Zach handed back the paper. "I'm sorry."

"Thanks, Zach." Her eyes narrowed as she stared at him. His Adam's apple was bobbing, and he didn't meet her gaze. "You are on the water a lot. Would you keep an eye out for anyone suspicious? There were two men. One was in his forties with a cap pulled low over his eyes. He had a beard. The other was in his late twenties. He had blond hair and it looked like he hadn't shaved in a couple of days. He might not always look so scruffy though."

"We did a police sketch. That might help," Alec said. He gave a curious glance at his nephew, who seemed unusually still. "Stop by Tom's office and take a look. Keep your eye out for the men."

"You're sure she's dead?" Zach asked.

Alec shot a glance at Libby. She seemed to be holding together all right. "As sure as we can be without a body," Alec said. "I think I know where the men dumped her." He told Zach about the spot offshore from the old ruins.

"I don't want to accept it," Libby said, her voice quiet. "One minute I'm resigned to it and the next I'm sure she's still out there waiting for me to find her."

"I get out there some. I'll keep an eye out," Zach said. "You think the men were local?"

Alec frowned. "I don't, no. I would vouch for every resident male on the island. This isn't the kind of thing our people would do."

Zach put his hands in the pockets of his denim shorts. "I guess people can hide their true natures sometimes."

An uncommonly perceptive comment from his nephew. Alec sometimes despaired at how little progress he felt he was making in shaping Zach. But hadn't he been the same way when he was Zach's age?

"One of my friends is having a party on the beach," Zach said. "I thought I'd go."

"Be careful." Alec wanted to add *don't drink*, but he knew Zach would hear the implied admonition in his voice. Not that it would matter what he said. Zach would do what he wanted to do. All Alec could do was pray.

Zach nodded and jogged to his old pickup.

"Zach is a good boy," Libby said. "You need to trust him a little."

"I *do* trust him."

"Your tone didn't indicate much trust." She turned to stare out to sea. "I keep thinking that there's something I could have done to stop them from taking her."

"It wasn't your fault," he said gently.

She turned back toward him with a pained expression.

"God is in control of life and death and everything in between, Libby. We can drive ourselves crazy by thinking of all the what-ifs in life."

Her eyes were luminous with tears. "I just feel helpless."

Did he make the first move or did she? He wasn't sure, but the next thing he knew, he was holding her with her face buried in his chest. It was the most natural thing in the world to press his lips against her fragrant hair.

———

Libby could feel Alec's heart thudding under her ear. She wanted to preserve this moment and stay in the safe circle of his arms. Right now it felt as though no harm could come to her. She'd stood on her own for so many years that she hardly knew what to make of this desire to be protected and nurtured.

His hand moved in a caressing motion down her hair, and he pressed his lips against her forehead. "You're a special person, Libby," he whispered. "I love how fiercely you treasure family. You even care about Vanessa and Brent when they've been nothing but cold to you."

"Vanessa is warming up."

The scent of man and sea was an intoxicating mix. She burrowed closer to the solid warmth of his chest. If she lifted her head, he might kiss her again. Part of her wanted that, but the fearful side kept her cheek firmly pressed against his shirt. If he kissed her again, she might lose her heart completely. Right now, if she walked away from this place, she might survive. If she gave too much of herself away, it might destroy her. And she didn't know what the future held.

His arms gripped her shoulders and he created a small space between them. His fingers tipped her chin up. She closed her eyes and held her breath. His lips were warm and persuasive, and she dropped any pretense of holding on to her dignity. It was too late to hang on to her heart. She kissed him back with all the depth of feeling she didn't know she possessed. The beat of his heart sped up under her right palm, trapped under her. She exulted that she moved him as much as he moved her. Whatever was developing between them was something they both felt.

He pulled away. "Want to go for a walk along the beach?"

She nodded. That was safer than being pelted by feelings she had to resist. They strolled along the dense sand, hand in hand. The companionable silence lulled her. She didn't feel the need to fill it with chatter.

He stopped by a fallen tree, pulling her down with him to sit. The moon glimmered on the water and the salty breeze from the ocean lifted her hair in a sultry caress. "I haven't kissed a woman in a long time. I didn't want you to think I was some kind of Lothario."

She had to smile at the anxiety in his voice. She hadn't even considered that he might worry about that. "Thanks for telling me. I don't even know the last time I went out with a man. I've been too focused on my career."

A smile tugged at his lips. "Glad to hear it."

"What about Zach?" she asked, hoping he wasn't offended by the question. "I got the impression I interrupted an argument."

His smile faded. "You did."

"I'm sure he's still hurting from his parents' death."

"Dave was a fisherman too. He had a charter boat based in Hatteras. Zach was with him all the time until he died. That's all the kid has wanted to do—be on the water. He wants to be a commercial fisherman. My parents couldn't control him. I think he wants everyone to know how miserable he is."

"So you took him?"

"He landed in jail for vandalizing the school the day before you showed up. So yeah, you could say he's been a handful."

"You were doing your duty," she said.

"It's more than duty. I love the kid. He and I have always been close. Right now, he's pushing me away, but I think that's starting to change."

"He's a good kid."

His glance was warm and tender. "I think so. When he first got here, he was sullen and distant, but he's coming around. He loves the sea. Being a waterman is therapeutic."

"Waterman?" She liked the romantic sound of the word.

"It's what we call men out here who make their living off the water. Fishermen, ferry workers, charter-boat owners."

"So you're a waterman too?"

"We all were. Me, Darrell, even my sister, Beth, works with the sea. She's a marine biologist," he said. "Guess I shouldn't come down too hard on Zach. It's in our blood. He can't help it."

"You don't want him to be a waterman?"

"I want him to have something to fall back on. Fishermen have a hard life fighting weather and tides all the time. They're at the whim of the capricious ocean. When you came out, I was trying to talk him into taking some online classes. He doesn't want to go away to college."

"Maybe he feels safe here. And closer to his parents."

Alec slipped his arm around her waist. "Yeah, I guess so." His lips grazed her forehead. "Why aren't you married? A girl as beautiful as you is usually taken early on."

He thinks I'm beautiful. "I've never been close to marriage. I guess I've been afraid to trust anyone. Dealing with my mom's instability has made me cautious. I've never even had a steady boyfriend. We moved around so much that there was never a chance to develop any kind of relationship."

"You think you can trust me?"

She stared into his face. "Can I?"

"I'm a man of my word, Libby. I'd like for us to see where this relationship might go. Are you game?"

"I think so," she whispered.

His lips found hers again and she turned off the warning in her head.

THIRTY-SEVEN

W e generally don't allow guests in the library," Delilah said, unlocking the glass-paned door. "You're hardly a guest, of course, but I wanted you to be aware that there are many valuable books in here."

Libby stepped into the room and inhaled the aroma of old books. Her aunt, Alec, and Bree were right behind her. Their presence would make the job easier, though she would have gladly spent hours here alone. There was nothing she liked better than to delve into history. She slid her glance to Alec and back again. Their earlier walk on the beach still lingered in her heart.

"Do you need me to show you around?" Delilah asked, her tone indicating she hoped to be released.

"No, I'm sure we'll figure it out."

Libby glanced around the large room. There were floor-to-ceiling oak shelves on two walls, a desk on the wall with the window, and a library table against the other wall. The floors were polished oak. The wood hadn't been stained, and the naturally light color was attractive.

"I haven't been in here in years," Pearl said, walking to the nearest bookshelf. "What do you want to see first?"

"I want to take a look at the history of the lighthouse." Libby's attention was distracted by a picture on the desk of a woman in her fifties with auburn hair and hazel eyes. She was on the bow of a boat with a man and they were both laughing. Her father and Tina looked so happy and carefree.

Libby moved past the picture to study the books. The ones on architecture caught her eye but she forced herself to skim by them. A large book on the Outer Banks looked interesting. She took it to the library table.

"I found it," Pearl said, turning toward her. "This is the oldest one. Ray found it twenty years ago. There aren't many copies in existence, and it's in pretty bad shape."

"What do you hope to find in the book?" Bree asked.

Alec pulled a chair out for Libby. She settled into the chair and gently opened the book. "No one knew about the cellar, but I thought there might be pictures of its history in the book I'd heard about."

"What can I be searching for?" Bree asked, turning back to the shelves. "Any other books we need to study?"

"See if there are any on the history of the island. I know it's unlikely, but what if there are more tunnels that lead to where Nicole might have been taken?" And searching through what had happened in the past might provide a clue to the present.

The paper of the book Libby examined was brittle and yellow. She checked the front of the book. Published in 1923. "When did the lighthouse cease operation? You mentioned the late eighteen hundreds. Can you be more specific?"

"I believe it was in the hurricane of 1899," Pearl said. "It was known as the Great Hurricane, and we lost many lives. I wasn't born yet, of course, but my grandparents used to talk about it."

The pictures Libby thumbed through were faded but legible. She paused to read some of the text, then continued to skim the book. "Hey, wait a minute," she said. She picked up a piece of paper stuck in the middle of the book. "This is a light bill. In Nicole's name. She was reading this book." She stared at the page marked by the paper. "This shows a cellar door. So it wasn't a secret back in its heyday."

"And it proves she knew about the cellar," Bree said.

Alec stepped behind Libby and leaned over her shoulder to look at it more closely. His breath whispered past her cheek, and she fought the attraction his close presence generated.

He flipped the page and began to read aloud. "'The lighthouse was self-contained. The keeper and his family grew vegetables on a small plot of cleared land and stored the harvest in the cellar.'"

"Just like every other family," Libby said. "That doesn't tell us anything."

She couldn't read, couldn't think, with him so close. His neck was close enough that if she leaned over, she could press her lips against his warm skin. She needed to concentrate on figuring this out, so she shifted away.

"There's more," he said. "Listen to this. 'Blackbeard was said to have escaped through one of the secret passageways from the cellar to the rocky cliffs at the water's edge.'"

"So it mentions the passage you found," Libby said. "And Nicole would have seen this. Knowing her, she was sure to have looked for the cave." She leaned over to read the book. "Passageways, plural. So there is more than one."

"There *were*," he corrected. "No telling if they're still there."

Bree was staring at the book. "The name Blackbeard conjures up all kinds of images of treasure."

"People have searched for his treasures in the Outer Banks for years," Pearl said.

"Could Nicole have heard the legends and decided to look herself? Maybe she decided to hunt by herself."

"It sounds like something she would do," Libby said.

"We can go back there and take a look for other tunnels," Alec said. "Though the tide is wrong right now. We can take a look tomorrow afternoon though."

Libby shut the book. "I want to see if we can find any sign of Nicole."

He looked away and nodded. She knew he was thinking that the kidnappers likely killed Nicole. Libby could only pray he was wrong.

———

Libby had an hour before she and Bree were supposed to meet Alec at his boat. Libby stepped over the warped floorboards in the living room of her father's house. "I was afraid they were ruined," she told her sister.

"Insurance will replace them," Vanessa said. She still wore the necklace Libby had given her. "Daddy was adamant about keeping up on the insurance." She started for the stairs. "I'm not sure what you're hoping to find in his bedroom."

"I don't know either." Libby followed her up to the second floor. "But someone harmed Tina. Maybe there's a clue in her things to what happened. I appreciate you allowing me to investigate."

Vanessa shrugged and opened the bedroom door. "Here you go. I'll help if you tell me what to look for."

Libby glanced around the room. "Anything out of the ordinary."

The blue comforter on the king bed was smooth. Assorted pillows were heaped at the head. Libby paused at the dresser and studied the pictures. One showed her father and Tina with Vanessa and Brent. They were dressed in red and stood by a Christmas tree.

"That was our last Christmas together," Vanessa said. "Six months later and Mom was gone."

Libby put the picture back. There was a jewelry box beside it. "May I?"

Vanessa nodded. "I used to love to go through Mom's jewelry box when I was a little girl. There's a secret drawer in the bottom." She reached past Libby and lifted out two trays full of necklaces and earrings. The bottom showed no sign of having any compartment.

"Is this the same jewelry box?"

Vanessa nodded. "There's a switch here." She pressed a spot on the bottom and one edge sprang up. "Mom used to hide notes in it telling me she loved me."

"That's so sweet."

"I still have some." Vanessa lifted the fake bottom from the drawer.

Libby expected to see an empty space, but it contained several folded papers. "Letters or bills?"

Vanessa unfolded one. "This one's a letter."

Libby wanted to read it, but she didn't want to offend her sister. Vanessa had been warming up so dramatically. She could wait until Vanessa offered the information. The letter might be very personal.

Vanessa's frown darkened as she read. She finally handed it to Libby and selected another letter. "This doesn't make any sense. It almost sounds as if . . ."

The paper was stiff in Libby's hand. "As if?"

Vanessa pressed her lips together. "As if Mom had a lover. But that's impossible. She loved Daddy."

Libby held the letter in the light of the window.

Tina,

Seeing you again brought back all the love I thought I'd torn up by the roots. Even now I would leave my family if you would agree to do the same. It's not too late for us. Think about it and give me a call if you want to talk.

Yours, L

"L. Who could that be? First name, last name? Any idea?" Libby asked.

"Not a clue," Vanessa said, still reading another letter.

"Anything in that one?"

"This one sounds angry." Vanessa handed it over.

"Angry? Like in murderous?"

Vanessa's expression was troubled. "Maybe."

Tina,

I can only assume by your actions yesterday that you intend us to be at odds. So be it. You'll find me a cold adversary. I will take what I want and you'll only have yourself to blame for the consequences. Your rejection only strengthens my determination. Your life is about to change.

L

Libby glanced up. "Wow, very ominous."

Vanessa hugged herself. "The tone of the letter gives me the creeps."

"Is that all?" Libby glanced into the jewelry box and saw nothing more.

"Just this." Vanessa held out her hand, palm up. A charm was on her palm.

Libby held it up to the light. "Looks like a stingray or something."

"It's a skate. Mom had a charm bracelet with sea creatures on it. She loved it. The skate was lost a few weeks before she died. She wasn't sure where she lost it."

Libby handed it back. "She obviously found it." Now was the time to ask, but she still hesitated.

Vanessa frowned. "She never mentioned that she'd found it. Mom loved the skates but shuddered when she saw their egg sacks. She couldn't understand why they had a pretty name like mermaid's purse when they were so ugly. Daddy used to take early walks and pick them all up so she didn't have to see them on her morning run."

"Did you put a dead jellyfish under my door?"

Vanessa's hand closed in a fist. Her lips flattened, then she shrugged. "So what if I did?"

"Were you trying to scare me off or what?"

Vanessa leaned against the dresser. "I'm sorry I did that. I was angry. I thought you'd take the warning and leave. Were you frightened?"

Libby opened a drawer. "More mad than anything."

Vanessa opened her fist and fingered the charm. "It's odd this was in her secret drawer and not back on the bracelet." She turned it over and squinted. "I never realized it was engraved." She walked to the window and held it to the light. "*Love, L.* I know the original wasn't engraved."

"The man who wrote the notes gave it to her."

Vanessa turned back toward her. "And she refused to wear it."

"Which might have added to his anger with her. Let's go see the sheriff."

Alec took a gulp of stale coffee and shuddered. "Anything from the coroner on Tina's remains?"

The circles around Tom's eyes were pronounced, and his clothes were rumpled. "He couldn't determine cause of death."

"So no clue to what happened to her."

"Nope. And it being three years ago, I'm having trouble piecing together what happened the day she disappeared. I have the old notes, but we thought her boat hit a rock and she drowned.

We didn't treat it as foul play, so there's very little in the file. A statement from a fisherman who saw her speeding toward the old lighthouse ruins is all we have. And he's dead now."

"What about the cellar itself? Anything there?"

"One interesting detail. There was a rope tied around Tina's left ankle. We have no idea if it was put there before or after death though."

The door opened behind Alec, and he turned to see Libby and Vanessa enter the sheriff's office. Neither was smiling.

Libby shot a quick glance his way, then held out two pieces of paper to Tom. "We found these in Tina's belongings."

Tom took the papers and began to read. Alec looked over his shoulder. "Looks like Tina had a secret admirer," Alec said.

"There's this too." Vanessa held out a charm. "Look on the back."

Alec took it and squinted at the tiny lettering, then handed it to Tom. They listened to Vanessa tell them about a lost charm and how this apparent replacement had been in the secret compartment.

"Who is this L person?" Tom asked. "Any ideas?"

"Not a clue," Vanessa said. "Sheriff, you have to find out who did this to Mom."

"I'm working on it, Vanessa."

Alec studied his cousin's expression. He didn't seem to be staring at Libby with suspicion. Maybe he was finally beginning to look elsewhere.

"Ready?" Alec asked. "Bree and Samson should be at the boat by now."

———

Bree held the clothing Libby had given her under Samson's nose. The breeze on the water ruffled the dog's thick fur. He sniffed the shirt and whined, then lifted his nose above the bow of the boat. "Search, Samson," she said.

Libby watched in awe. "Can he really find a person by sniffing the air? I thought dogs sniffed the ground."

"Samson is an air tracker. A person gives off skin rafts that float in the air. A trained dog can detect them."

"But it's been almost ten days since Nicole was taken," Alec said.

"He may still get a scent." Bree looked away.

Libby stared at Bree. Hadn't she said something about Samson finding someone after two years? Then the memory clicked into place and she remembered that dogs could smell dead bodies for a very long time. A lump formed in her throat, and she prayed the dog would find a live scent. Something to lead them to Nicole.

The boat accelerated across the tops of the waves. It was calm and beautiful today, though humidity hung in the air. Bree's curls were a little frizzy from the moisture. Sea spray struck Libby's bare arms and felt good on her heated skin. She prayed for a sign from God today, anything that would allow her to hope that her friend was still alive.

"How can you tell if he smells something?" she asked Bree.

"He'll bark. I'll be able to tell," Bree assured her. "Alec, run the boat in a crisscross fashion across the bay so he gets more exposure."

It seemed they looped back and forth across the water for ages, but glancing at her watch, Libby realized they'd only been at this for two hours. She was beginning to lose hope that they'd find something today.

The dog continued to sniff the air as Alec guided the boat back and forth across the gleaming water. The village of Hope Beach beckoned in the distance. A few people on the pier waved as they scouted the area. Libby waved back, suddenly feeling part of the community.

Samson's ears pricked. He stiffened and barked, straining toward the harbor. "Go that way!" Bree shouted, pointing toward the pier.

Libby's heart pounded. She stood, then nearly fell when the boat accelerated.

"Hang on!" Alec seated his hat more firmly on his head and the boat surged.

Samson was barking frantically. The next instant, he leaped over the side and swam toward a boat. He reached it and tried to paw his way onto it, but it was too high for him.

"That's my old boat," Alec said, frowning. "I don't use it much, but Zach had it out this morning."

His boat? Libby stared at him. Surely he wouldn't have had anything to do with this?

He cut the engine and the craft slowed, then stopped near the dog. He tossed the anchor overboard, then reached down and helped Samson clamber up the ladder. The dog shook himself, spraying water over everyone. He rushed to Bree's side and whined. He strained toward the old boat, a Chris-Craft.

Libby stared at Alec. "What does this mean? The dog is saying he smells Nicole on your boat. Right, Bree?"

"That's right," Bree said, rubbing Samson's ears. "Let's board the boat and let him sniff around."

Alec took an oar and maneuvered the two boats close enough together that they could step from one deck to the other. Samson leaped onto the boat and began to bark. He ran to the side of the boat and his barking grew more frenzied. Bree stepped aboard the old boat, and Libby followed her.

"What's he trying to tell you?" Libby asked.

"It looks like Nicole was here or something of hers is here. He's indicating that area there," Bree said, pointing to the starboard side.

Alec joined them. "That's impossible. She would have had to swim out here and board it. What would be the point?"

"You never use this?" Bree asked.

He shook his head. "Zach uses it sometimes, but he's never met Nicole."

"That we know of," Libby said. She'd rather believe Zach had a hand in this than the alternative—that Alec was guilty.

"What are you saying?" he asked.

"Is it possible Zach was involved in her kidnapping?" She didn't want to accuse the boy, especially to his own uncle, but the dog's reaction meant something.

"No," Alec said, his voice clipped. "I can't believe you'd even think that."

No one would want to think his nephew would be involved in something so heinous, but Libby couldn't ignore this. "I need to talk to him, Alec. Right away."

"I won't have you accusing him," Alec said. "And based on the reaction of a dog? That's ridiculous."

"Is it? You've admitted that he's been in some trouble."

"Alec, Samson is definitely reacting here," Bree said. "This isn't just some mistake. Nicole was either on this boat, or at the very least, she touched it. He doesn't give false positives."

"Look around," Alec said. "Let's see if there's any other evidence. I can't accuse the boy without tangible evidence."

Her lips tight, Libby opened doors and peered under seats. Under the cushion where Samson stood, her hand touched something soft, and she pulled up a ponytail holder. It still held strands of blond hair. "I have to talk to Zach."

Alec paled. "Don't accuse him of anything," he said. "There has to be some explanation."

"That's all we want," Libby said. "Where is he now?" Zach had left the inn before nine this morning.

"He said he was delivering the supplies for his job and then was going to help do some cleanup around town," Alec said. "There's a group in the square washing the mud off the stores."

He started the engine and guided the boat to the dock. Libby grabbed a post as they neared, then threw the rope around it. She was the first to leap to the boardwalk. Maybe they would find Nicole today.

THIRTY-EIGHT

The townspeople were out in force today. Great strides had been made in the cleanup over the past week. Paint shone clean and free of the mud and mildew. Alec spoke to several neighbors as he searched for his nephew. No one had seen Zach, and Alec began to wonder if the boy had lied about where he was going today.

The business district, such as it was, ended at the juncture of Oyster Road and Bar Harbor Street. A few residents were on Bar Harbor, but Oyster Road just led to the fish house. "Let's check the fish house," he said.

"What's a fish house?" Libby asked, falling into step beside him.

"It's where the fishermen gather and sell their day's catch. Zach likes hanging out there," he said. "I think he feels close to Dave there. I know I do. My brother was always laughing with the other fishermen in there, swapping fishing stories."

The low-slung white building was at the end of a pier where rowboats and water jets docked. He stepped over nets and crab pots on the way to the door of the fish house. The scent of fish was strong.

He nodded to the few men outside the door. "Anyone seen Zach?"

"He's out back helping Rolly unload," one of the men said.

Skirting the building, Alec continued on down the pier, where he found his nephew lifting crab pots off a friend's boat.

When Zach saw him, he frowned. "What's up, Uncle Alec?"

"We need to talk to you. In private." Alec jerked his thumb back toward the street, away from listening ears. Getting a rumor going was all they needed. Zach was getting enough of a reputation as a troublemaker.

Zach wiped his wet hands on his shorts, then slipped on his flip-flops to follow them. He glanced at Libby, who was studying him. "What? Did I suddenly grow horns?" he demanded.

She looked away. "Sorry. We just need to ask you some questions."

They reached the road. There was no one in earshot. Alec put his hands in his pockets. "You know Samson is here to look for Nicole?"

Zach glanced back at the fish house with a longing expression. "Yeah. So?"

"He picked up a scent for her."

That got Zach's attention. "That's good, right?"

Alec nodded. "But the scent is on my old boat. According to the dog, Nicole was on there. So we searched and Libby found something." He glanced at her.

She held out her hand, palm up to expose the ponytail holder. "This is Nicole's."

Zach went white. He took a step back, then whirled to walk away, but Alec grabbed his arm. He had a sick feeling in the pit of his stomach. "Zach, what did you do?" he whispered.

Zach looked at Alec's hand on his arm. "I didn't do anything. You're always willing to think the worst about me, aren't you?"

"Then how did that hair thing get on my boat?"

Zach bit his lip. "I was going to talk to you about it." His face worked. Then his shoulders slumped. "I just take her supplies," he said. "I didn't know who she was until I saw her picture in the paper last night. Then I didn't know what to do about it."

Libby's face lit. "She's alive? Really, Zach?"

He nodded. "I saw her a couple of days ago. Took her some water and food."

"Where?" Alec asked. He'd figure out what to do about punishing Zach later.

"A little island northwest of here. I have the coordinates."

"Who put her there?"

He shrugged. "I was taking the old boat out to fish. Two guys stopped me and asked if I was looking to make some money. The older man told me that he'd had to stash his crazy sister on an island until he could get her into the hospital he wanted. Said she'd tried to knife him and to be careful because she was dangerous. I was only supposed to drop off supplies every couple of days, then leave."

"That sounds like a fishy story," Alec said.

Zach's lids flickered and he made a face. "He made it sound plausible. I know now it was stupid for me to believe him, but he gave me all these details and I swallowed his story. And they were paying well."

"Why didn't you tell us when you figured out who she was?"

Zach looked down at the ground. "It was just last night. I wanted to tell you, but I was afraid you'd think I had something to do with it."

"Have they paid you every time you've gone?"

Zach shook his head. "They gave me a thousand dollars to buy food and to pay for my services. They told me what to take her too. I just did what they said."

"I wish you would have trusted me," Alec said. "Come with us. We have to get her."

⌒

Libby could hardly sit still as the boat skimmed the waves. They were so far out to sea that she couldn't see land. Where was that island? She prayed that Nicole was holding on to life, that she would be well and whole when Libby found her.

"Where is it?" Alec asked Zach.

The boy pointed to the horizon, and Libby saw a faint speck that might have been land. They drew closer, and she realized it was a tiny island barely twenty or thirty feet in diameter. How had Nicole survived the hurricane? Libby strained to catch a glimpse of Nicole, but all she saw was a hovel of a building. The place appeared deserted.

"Where is she?" she demanded.

"Maybe in the shack," Zach said. "Though she's usually out as soon as she hears the motor."

Alec took the boat in as close to shore as he could and shut off the engine. Zach tossed the anchor overboard, but by the time it splashed into the water, Libby was already knee-deep in the waves and barreling toward the tiny beach. Bree and Samson were right behind her.

"Nicole!" she shouted.

She rushed to the door of the building and yanked open the door. It took a moment for her eyes to adjust enough to see that the one room held nothing but a few pieces of broken furniture.

"She's not here!" she told Bree, who came in behind her. "Where could she be?" Zach and Alec entered the building.

Zach glanced around. "Her food and water aren't here," he said.

"What does that mean?" Libby asked.

"I brought her a jug of water, peanut butter, canned stuff. None of it is here."

"Has someone else come after her?" Alec asked.

Zach shrugged. "Beats me."

"Who were the men who hired you?" Alec asked. "Didn't you get their names?"

"I didn't know them. One said his name was Oscar Jacobson. The other never told me his name. All I cared about was that they were paying me cash."

"Sounds like a fake name," Alec said.

Bree took Nicole's clothing out of the paper bag and held it under Samson's nose. "Search, boy!"

The dog nosed around the shack, his tail wagging. He barked at the bed, then ran to the door and around the side of the shack. "He smells her," Bree said.

Libby and Bree followed with the men rushing after them. The dog darted around the island with his nose in the air, then went back to the beach and stood with his tail drooping. He whined when Bree reached him.

"She's not here," Bree said.

"She couldn't have gotten off the island without help," Zach said.

"Look here," Alec said, staring at marks in the sand. "Looks like a raft or something was dragged here."

Bree knelt and touched the indentations. "Could she have built a raft and tried to escape that way?"

"She tried that once before and I found it torn apart on the beach," Zach said. He glanced toward the shack. "Whoa, looks like some of the roof is missing."

"Might she have used the roof for a raft?" Libby asked.

"It would be foolhardy," Alec said. "The ocean is treacherous around here. They don't call it the Graveyard of the Atlantic for no reason. Shoals, rocks—all kinds of things can tear a boat or a raft to pieces in a heartbeat. Would she be foolish enough to try that, Libby?"

She tried not to take offense at his question. "It's not foolhardy to try to escape kidnappers," she said. "Who knows when they might come back?" She turned to Bree. "Could Samson help us find her?"

"Maybe. It's a big ocean out there. He's lost her scent right now, but we could go out and see if he smells anything."

"That's our only option," Libby said. Her voice broke and she swallowed hard. What if Nicole was already capsized and drowning, crying out for help? The thought sent her rushing to the boat. "Come on! We have to find Nicole."

The rest of the crew ran after her, and in moments they were cruising the waves again. Bree gave Samson another refresher sniff, and the dog had his nose in the air. He strained at the bow of the boat. Alec crossed back and forth in front of the area where they'd seen the markings in the sand. Then Samson's tail began to wag. He barked furiously and strained out over the water until Libby thought he might fall in.

"He's got a scent!" Bree called. "Good boy," she crooned. His tail drooped as the boat headed west. "Wrong direction," Bree said. "Try north."

Alec corrected his course, and the dog's countenance perked again. Libby went up to sit by her friend.

Bree saw her and squeezed her hand. "We'll find Nicole."

"I just hope we're not too late."

"I'm praying and I'm sure you are too."

"I am," Libby admitted. "Constantly. But I'm so afraid."

"Put it in God's hands. He loves Nicole. He's out there in the big ocean with her."

The thought comforted Libby. Nicole wasn't alone. No matter what happened, God held her securely.

THIRTY-NINE

The sun beat down on Nicole's head as she sat on her raft. Her skin was tight and hot, and she knew she was going to be hurting from a sunburn later. There was still no land in sight, and she wasn't even sure if she was floating farther out into the Atlantic or nearer to the mainland. All she could do was cling to the boards and hope. How long had she been here? She slanted a glance at the sky. Three hours.

Her food had made the trip past the breakers all right, but though her tummy rumbled, she wanted to save what she had since there was no telling how long she might be adrift. She wiped her forehead and stared at the horizon. Nothing. Her lids grew heavy, and she decided to sleep if she could. On her stomach with her head pillowed in her arms, she listened to the lapping of the waves and felt the gentle rise of the swells under her raft.

Where was Libby now? Her eyes grew heavy and she let them close. Sleep was good.

She wasn't sure what awakened her. Sitting up, she rubbed her eyes. The sun was lower in the sky. It must be nearly four or five. Then she heard it. The sound of an engine. She turned toward the *putt-putt* and saw a boat growing closer in the distance. Leaping to her feet, she screamed and waved her hands.

An answering shout came from the boat. Was that Libby? Nicole strained to see. It was!

"Libby, I'm here, I'm here!" Jumping up and down, she could barely breathe for joy.

Nicole recognized only Zach and Libby in the boat. Another man drove, and a woman with a dog stood in the bow. Zach must have realized she was telling the truth and gotten help. She would have to thank him.

The boat reached her raft. The man's strong grip clasped her arm and helped her climb the ladder to the deck, where she collapsed.

Libby sank down beside her and grabbed her in an almost painful grip. "Nicole, I thought they killed you." Her voice was choked.

Tears poured down Nicole's face, and she clung to Libby. "I knew you'd find me. I just knew it."

The two remained locked in an embrace for several seconds, then Libby pulled away and stared at Nicole. "Who did this to you?"

"I don't know. I can't remember anything. I woke up on the island and I've been there ever since. Alone, except when Zach brought supplies."

Libby hugged her again. "I'm so glad to see you. We found your flip-flops and cover-up. Everyone told me you were dead, but I didn't believe it."

"I knew you'd never give up on me," Nicole whispered. "You've always been a rock."

"Let's get you home," Libby said. "We'll get a doctor and make sure you're all right."

Nicole rubbed her belly. "And real food. I'd love a chicken quesadilla."

"I think we can find one of those," the handsome man said.

Nicole glanced at Libby, who was blushing. She was going to have to question her friend about her relationship with the guy.

After Nicole's checkup at the doctor's office, Tom asked her questions until Libby insisted her friend needed some food and rest. Libby took Nicole to the restaurant while Alec and Bree stayed behind to talk to Tom. Libby was filled with gratitude as she watched Nicole eat. It was a true miracle that they'd found her. Libby filled her in on the events of the nine days.

"Who's the guy?" Nicole asked.

Libby hated the way her cheeks heated at the mention of Alec. "Alec Bourne, Zach's uncle."

"You like him?"

How did she answer that? *Like* wasn't the most accurate word. "Well, he's been a big help. He's been right on the front lines helping to look for you."

"Even though his nephew kept me confined to that island?"

"He didn't know anything about it."

"Are you sure?" Nicole put down her fork. "Wouldn't Zach have been gone? Wouldn't he have taken the boat? Surely Alec would have asked what he was doing with the boat."

How would she make her friend see? "He's a good man, Nicole. I think you'll like him."

Nicole's eyes flashed. "I don't want to know him, that's for sure. I want to get out of this place and back to Virginia Beach now."

Libby opened her mouth to agree, then shut it again. The thought of leaving this island left a pit in her belly. "We have work to do here. I've started work on the lifesaving station. And have you seen those lighthouse ruins? I love it out there."

Nicole rubbed her forehead. "There's something about those ruins. When I think of them, I get a funny feeling in my stomach."

"Fear?"

Nicole shook her head. "Not fear exactly. Excitement maybe. Oh, why can't I remember?"

Libby reached across the table to squeeze Nicole's hand. "The doctor said you might not ever remember. He doesn't know what drug they used on you, but it might have wiped out that time period permanently. So don't stress about it. If you remember, great. But right now all I care about is that you're here and well."

"I'd like to see the lighthouse ruins. Maybe seeing them will help me remember."

Libby released her hand and signaled for the check. "Do you remember talking to me in front of the beach cam?"

"No." Her eyes widened. "Have you been working any of our projects besides the station? And have you heard from Rooney?"

"Your investor?" Libby shook her head. "I've been out of the office looking for you."

"You've been checking in, of course?"

"Of course. But no messages from him have come in."

"How strange. He's been pushing so hard for me to get the deal sewed up here."

"He's been trying to buy that property for years, from what I understand."

"I never had a chance to tell him that you own the property he wants and not your brother."

Something about the reference to Rooney nudged at her. Then it hit her. "His first name is Lawrence, isn't it?"

Nicole nodded. "And don't call him Larry. He hates that. It has to be Lawrence. Why?"

Libby told her about the notes she found in Tina's room. "L could stand for Lawrence."

"Or Laban, Lance, Levi, Lloyd, or any number of other names," Nicole said. "Even Libby! That's a stretch to think that Lawrence might be implicated in Tina's death."

"Maybe not. Vanessa and Brent said he was with Tina not long before she disappeared."

"He's going to want to talk to you. You own that property, Libby! You're rich."

"Only if I sell it."

"Of course you're going to sell it. Think of what it would mean. We could expand the business. Or rather I could. You'd never have to work a lick again."

The two of them were worlds apart now, even though they'd only been separated for a couple of weeks. "I've been learning there are more important things than money," Libby said.

"You've changed. It's that guy, right?"

Libby shook her head. "It's my dad." She began to tell her friend about the kind of man Ray had been and all that she'd learned, but Nicole's expression only grew more incredulous.

Explaining a sea change to someone was impossible. Nicole would just have to learn about it by watching her.

Though she should have been exhausted, Libby couldn't sleep. She finally gave up and went up the steps to her father's third-floor retreat at the Tidewater Inn. The light in the room was already on. Brent was sitting on the sofa with their father's Bible in his hand.

Her first impulse was to demand it back, but she restrained herself and smiled and joined him on the sofa. "Couldn't sleep either?"

He shook his head. "I like to come up here. I feel closer to Dad."

"Me too." Had he been reading Scripture? She hoped so. "I'm sorry I suspected you of hurting Nicole, Brent. I hope you can forgive me."

His brows rose. "It was understandable."

"Will you forgive me?"

"I'm not even sure I know what that means." He rubbed his forehead. "I quit going to church with Dad when I was fifteen. I thought I was too old and wise to swallow all that stuff." He stared at her. "But I've been watching you, Libby. You're different, just like he was. Maybe I'll go back to church."

Her throat closed. If only she could believe she'd had an eternal impact on this brother she longed to love. Her gaze fell on the Bible. *Give it to him.* She resisted the internal nudge. Did she have to give up everything dear to her?

Give it to him.

Her shoulders sagged. How could she resist God? "Would you like to have Dad's Bible?"

His eyes widened. "I know how much you love it. You come up here and read it all the time."

"I know. But there are special passages he's marked that might mean even more to you than they do to me." She leaned toward him and flipped to a highlighted verse in the worn book. "This is my favorite. Psalm 37:25. 'I have been young, and now am old; Yet I have not seen the righteous forsaken, Nor his descendants begging bread.' I know I'm not old yet, but I believe we are blessed because our father was a righteous man."

Brent's Adam's apple bobbed. "I know that's true." He clutched the Bible to his chest. "Thank you, Libby. I'll never forget this."

The sun was just coming up, casting a glorious display over the water. Alec sat on the porch railing and inhaled the scent of the sea. The door opened behind him, and he turned to see Libby stepping out dressed in hot-pink sweats with her hair up in a ponytail.

"Couldn't sleep?" he asked. "It's only six."

She shook her head. "It seems incredible that we found Nicole. Thank you for all you did for us."

"I'm glad it turned out so well." He averted his gaze. She was way too pretty this morning. Her eyes shone with excitement. "What's on the agenda for the day?"

"I'm going to go out to the lighthouse ruins with Nicole if she feels up to it. I'm hoping being out there will jog her memory in some way."

"I'll come with you."

She smiled and nodded. "We won't be gone long. I want to show her what I've gotten done on the lifesaving station too. We have a business to run, and it's been neglected for almost two weeks."

She would be leaving soon. He saw it in her expression. "Have you decided what you're going to do about the inn?"

She settled beside him on the rail. "Not yet. I don't want to sell it, but I don't see that I have a choice."

He wanted to protest again, but it wasn't his call. "Uh, could I take you to dinner tonight at Kill Devil Hills? We could take the boat and go to Port O' Call. They've got great crab legs and she-crab soup."

Her smile came immediately. "I'd like that."

The door opened again. Vanessa and Pearl joined them. "I thought we were the only ones up early," Vanessa said.

"You got in late last night. I heard your door after I'd gone to bed for the second time," Libby said. "I wanted to talk to you, but I was too sleepy to get up again."

"Oh?" Vanessa sat on the top step. Pearl pulled a rocker closer.

Libby leaned against the post. "I wanted to ask you about Tina's meeting with Lawrence Rooney. Did she ever tell our dad what he wanted?"

"You knew about that meeting?" Pearl asked Vanessa. Her voice was high and strained.

Vanessa nodded. "We were there with Mom and Mr. Rooney."

"His first name is Lawrence," Libby said.

Vanessa gasped and straightened. "They talked outside for a minute, and I heard her tell him to leave her alone. I thought it was because he was pestering her about selling the inn. But do you think . . . ?"

Pearl sighed. "He was engaged to Tina when Ray first met her," she said.

Vanessa gasped. "Mom was engaged to another man?"

Pearl nodded. "It was quite the scandal for a while. Tina came to town for a two-week visit with her grandmother and met Ray. It was love at first sight for them both. She broke off her engagement to Lawrence and was married to Ray three months later."

"I imagine Rooney didn't take that very well," Libby said.

"I think Tina was actually a little afraid of him. He threatened to ruin Ray."

Libby leaned forward. "He wrote that note I found in your closet!"

"Who can say for sure, Libby? But yes. It was likely his doing. He's always been powerful, even back then. His family owns a lot of properties. Ray tried to meet with him about Tina, but Lawrence refused. Over the years he's been a thorn in Ray's side on occasion. He's wanted the Tidewater Inn for all this time. I wouldn't be surprised if he thought he could get Tina back too, at some point along the way. He was an annoyance, of course. But I never thought he would harm your mother."

"I bet he wrote those notes we found in Tina's jewelry box," Libby said to her sister.

Alec shifted on his perch. "Tom needs to know about this. I

bet he's going to want to talk to Nicole about Rooney. I'll run into town and talk to him. I'll meet you out at the ruins later, Libby."

———

Libby flopped on the sand beside her friend and drew in a deep breath. The long run to the lighthouse had tuckered her out. She turned her head and smiled at Nicole. Her heart overflowed with thankfulness. Nicole was alive! What a wonderful miracle and blessing from God. Nicole had begun to remember what happened to her too, but the men who kidnapped her weren't familiar.

She sat up and inhaled the clear air. "What happened here?"

Nicole stood, dusting the sand from her palms. "I came here the morning before I was kidnapped. Vanessa was going to bring me to see the ruins, but I was too eager to wait on her. I figured I'd let her show me around like I hadn't seen it. There's more here than you know though."

"The cave?"

Nicole nodded. "You know about it?"

Libby pointed toward the cellar opening. "We found it after we saw the cellar."

"Then you know about the treasure?"

"Treasure? All we found was poor Tina."

Nicole smiled. "Want to see? You're going to be excited."

"You're being very mysterious," Libby said, following her friend. "Where is it?"

"In the caves. Just outside the entrance to the cellar. You're going to love this."

"You know about the cellar?" Libby asked.

Nicole nodded. "I found a map in your dad's Bible."

Libby followed Nicole back into the water. They waded through a shallow pool to the base of the rocks.

278

"You have to dive here to see the opening," Nicole said. She took off her shorts and top to reveal her bikini. "I was snorkeling here and just happened to find it. It's not hard though. Follow me." She held her breath and ducked under the water.

Libby stripped to her one-piece suit and followed. The opening was barely big enough to wiggle through. Nicole disappeared through the hole and Libby went right behind her, determined not to let her friend out of sight. They surfaced in a cave about twenty feet in diameter. The ceiling was ten feet from the surface of the water. Several holes in the rocks illuminated the space, though Libby had to squint to see.

"Bet it gets tight in here during high tide," Libby said.

Nicole nodded. "I wouldn't want to be here then." She swam to the other side and hefted herself onto a flat rock. "This way."

"I can't believe you came in here."

"I had a flashlight with me that day," Nicole said. "Wait until you see this though." She rose and went to the curving wall. "Someone put everything we need right here."

Libby heard a rasp, then light flared from a match. Moments later a light was flickering. "What on earth?" She heaved herself out of the water and went to where Nicole stood. "Someone has put candles and matches in here?"

"Look how old the candlesticks are," Nicole said.

Libby examined it. "It's bronze. Looks late sixteen hundreds maybe."

"It goes with the other things I found. Follow me."

Nicole led her down a long narrow passageway. The sound of dripping became stronger. The floor was damp and slippery under Libby's feet. At one juncture her inclination was to go right, but Nicole led her left.

"Where are we going?"

"The other room is this way. Almost there."

The candle cast flickering shadows onto the wall. Libby wanted to be back in the sunlight instead of this dark, dank place.

Nicole dropped to her knees. "Now we have to crawl."

"How on earth did you find this?"

"I dropped something right here. It rolled under this ledge and I found the opening." Nicole and the light disappeared under the rocky ledge.

Panicked at being left in the dark, Libby hurried after her and emerged into a larger cave. The candle did little to illuminate what felt like a vast space. A moment later another candle flared to life.

"Look around," Nicole said, smiling. She handed Libby another candle.

This candlestick was also old. Libby held it high and turned toward some objects on the wall to her right. Artifacts leaped out at her: a ship's bell, candlesticks, tin plates and cups, several portholes and helm items. Several cannons were in a jumble. There were many objects she didn't recognize.

She stepped closer. "What is this room?"

"I think it was a headquarters for Edward Teach."

"Blackbeard? Come on, Nicole."

"Look." Nicole stepped to the jumble and held her candle close to the ship's bell. The words *Queen Anne's Revenge* were engraved on the brass.

"Blackbeard's pride and joy," Libby said.

"I found a ship's log too. It says it's Teach's. But I don't see it now. Funny—the stash is smaller than I remember. This stuff is probably worth a fortune to museums. There's no gold or jewels but a wealth of information."

This rich history was more exciting to Libby than gold coins. "I bet the government will want to make this a protected area. Either a state park or a federal one."

"Probably. Archaeologists will have to confirm the artifacts' authenticity, but it all looks real to me."

"But the ship sank offshore somewhere around here. Wouldn't the bell have gone down with it?"

Nicole turned. "You're right. I hadn't thought about that. Did someone find the wreck and bring these things up?"

"Maybe. But this place might be more than a storage room. There are wooden bunks and old blankets. What's left of them anyway." Libby turned to stare at her friend. "It's going to take some professionals to figure this out. Did anyone know you found this? Maybe finding this was why someone wanted to shut you up."

"I don't think so. I only told Horace."

"I think we won't tell the professionals," a man said from behind them. "We won't tell anyone."

Both women whirled. Horace stood with a gun held casually in his hand.

"Horace?" Libby's gaze went to the gun in his hand. "What's this all about?"

"I can't let you ruin all my plans," Horace said. "I'm sorry. I didn't want it to come to this, but you leave me no choice."

Libby saw the determination on his face. "Nicole, the lights!" she screamed as she snuffed hers out between her forefinger and thumb. At the same time she threw herself atop her friend, and Nicole's light went out too. The cave was plunged into darkness. Then a bright light flashed from the gun.

FORTY

Alec told his cousin what he'd discovered about Lawrence Rooney. Tom called the state police in New York, and they agreed to pick up Rooney and question him about Tina's death. Alec thanked Tom and returned to the inn. The visit had taken longer than he'd expected, so he thought the women would be back from their outing to the lighthouse ruins.

He found Bree on the beach with Samson. "Is Libby back yet?"

She shook her head. "I haven't seen them. How long have they been gone?"

"A couple of hours."

"I cried just watching their reunion," Bree said. She rubbed Samson's head. "Reminds me of when I found Davy after thinking for a year that he was dead."

Alec had heard the story. "I have to admit, I thought Nicole was dead. Libby never gave up hope though."

Bree's smile held amusement. "It shows, you know."

"What shows?"

"How you feel about Libby."

His face warmed. "She's a friend."

Bree laughed. "She's more than that and you know it."

"Maybe she *could* be. We'll see where our relationship goes."

Kade and the children came to join them on the beach.

Samson rushed to them and licked Hannah's face. The little girl giggled and threw her arms around his neck. The older boy, Davy, ran ahead and splashed into the waves up to his knees. Alec's gaze lingered on the children. He'd always wanted a houseful of kids. What did Libby think about children?

He glanced at his watch. Where were they? Though they could just be lingering at the ruins, he felt a sense of unease. "I think I'll walk toward the lighthouse and intercept them. Lunch will be ready soon, so I'm sure they must be heading this way."

Bree's green eyes crinkled with amusement. "Have fun. I think I'll take the kids to build a sand castle." She put her arm around Kade's waist. "I haven't seen this big guy in days."

He hugged her back. "The twins have been asking for Mommy."

Alec went the other direction. The sand was soft, and he kicked off his sandals. When he still hadn't seen the women after ten minutes, he began to quicken his pace. Some unexplainable anxiety gnawed at his belly.

Someone had put Nicole on that island for a purpose. What if the women had stumbled into more danger? He broke into a run and was breathing heavily by the time he reached the ruins. There was no movement but the rustle of leaves in the maritime forest. The place was deserted, though he saw Libby's and Nicole's clothes on the beach.

He cupped his hands around his mouth. "Libby, Nicole!" His voice rose above the murmur of the waves. He listened, but there was no answering shout.

He walked to the water. The tide was going out, so their footprints were still intact in the sand. The footprints went into the water and didn't come out. What had happened here? Did they swim out to board a boat? If so, why weren't they back at the inn? And why did they leave their clothes? Not for the first time, he wished his cell phone would work on the island.

"Libby!" he shouted again. Where could she be?

He waded a few feet into the water. The waves were gentle today. He glanced at the rocks. The cave. Could the women have gone into it? Libby had said Nicole was an avid spelunker. Maybe she'd coaxed Libby into going in. It would explain the footprints leading back to the water. Could they have gotten trapped in there?

He sloshed through the waves to the mouth of the cave. He peered in but saw nothing. He shouted for Libby. His voice echoed off the stone walls, but he heard nothing. He exited the cave and waded to shore. The cellar door was closed. He opened it and descended as far into the darkness as he could, then shouted again. Still no answer.

Adrenaline gave Alec the energy he needed to make the run back to the inn. He was going to need Samson to help find the women.

———

The sound of water dripping penetrated the woozy feeling in Libby's head. She opened her eyes and blinked. A couple of candles flickered in the darkness. "Nicole?" she called out. Where was her friend?

"I'm here," a small voice said to her right.

Libby turned her head and saw Nicole against the wall. Her hands were tied in front of her. "Are you all right?"

"Yes. How do you feel?"

Libby's wrists were bound together. She raised them and touched her throbbing head. Her fingers came away sticky. "I'm bleeding. I think I hit my head."

"He shot you. Horace shot you." Nicole's voice rose.

Libby touched her head again and discovered a furrow. "The bullet just grazed me. I'm okay. The bleeding is stopping."

Clang. The noise across the room drew her attention, and she focused her bleary eyes as Horace used a sledgehammer on the wall.

He paused to wipe his brow. "Sorry about this, girls. I didn't want to hurt Nicole, and I really liked you, Libby. So I'm going to let the sea have you."

"I don't understand," she said, struggling to think through the roaring in her head.

"When I get this hole through, the tide will fill this cave. All evidence will be drowned. And no one will ever discover this cave full of secrets."

"But why? What harm could it do to let the world know about these artifacts?"

When he shrugged and began to pound again, she tried to think of what might happen if the world knew about this place. It would be an attraction to tourists. Knowing what she did about historical preservation, she was sure the government would take it over and run it as well. The state would want to preserve it, likely as a park. How could that be worth murder?

Kenneth Poe. She thought of what he'd said. *This* would be the spot of the new resort. But not if the state had the land. In fact, there would have to be access to the area. There would be no room for a huge resort complex on this side of the island. Poe's investor would not be allowed to purchase it.

Horace was an attorney. Had he been hired to help make sure the deal went through? Was he a partner with Lawrence Rooney? It made sense.

She waited until he stopped pounding again. "You're helping Poe? There's no crime in helping to close a sale."

"You think that's what he wants me to do?" Horace barked a laugh.

Libby weighed this revelation. And then the truth clicked.

"He knows you're a diver. He's paying you to get this stuff out of the cave before the state learns about it and steps in."

He stepped closer. "I don't expect you to sympathize, but I'm nearly bankrupt. Everything was sliding out of my fingers. The money I can get for this loot will save me. I'll be able to keep my boy at Harvard. I won't lose my house in Saint Croix. If this deal goes south, I'm finished. I'll have nothing left. I can't let that happen."

"And an old ship's bell is worth murdering two people?" Libby couldn't wrap her head around that kind of thinking. "Then why even tell me about the inheritance? You could have destroyed that will and let Brent and Vanessa inherit. They were going to sell to Lawrence."

His eyes narrowed. "That was my intention."

Libby caught her breath. "But Mindy mentioned it to Nicole."

"Stupid woman can't keep her mouth shut. I should have fired her long ago."

Libby struggled to get up and couldn't. "You can always start over somewhere else. Life isn't over just because your money is gone."

He seemed to be listening for a moment, then he shook his head. "It's gone too far now. If you live, you'll turn me in. I'll go to prison. My boy will have to quit college. My wife will have no support. Her family is all gone and I'm all she has. I'm sorry, but it has to be this way."

"We won't say a word, will we, Nicole?" Libby managed a smile. "I like you, Horace. Don't do something you'll never be able to live with."

His eyes filled with confusion, then he stepped back. "We both know you're just trying to save yourself. The minute you got home, you'd be calling Tom. I'm sorry. I really liked your father, you know. I'm glad he's not alive to know about this."

"He's watching from heaven," Libby said. "You think you're

doing this in secret? The Bible says we are surrounded by a great cloud of witnesses. And God sees everything."

Horace swallowed. "Don't you understand? I have no choice."

"There is always a choice to do right."

"Not this time. I'm boxed into a corner." He turned back to his task and began to whack at the wall again.

"Wait! You'll destroy all this treasure!"

He paused and turned back toward her again. "I got out what I could, but what's left is nothing compared to my family. And if you hadn't been snooping, I would have had time to transfer all of it to my basement. All but the cannons. So you have no one to blame but yourself." He lifted the sledgehammer again.

Thwack! Thwack! Two strikes from his sledgehammer and the wall began to crumble. He continued to pound until the hole was about three feet in diameter.

"I made it as large as I could so the end is quicker," he said. He dropped the sledgehammer. "Do you want the candles extinguished, or do you want to watch the water pour in? I want this to be as easy for you both as possible."

"Leave them lit, please," Libby said, trying to keep the panic from her voice.

Nicole began to struggle. "Please don't leave us here!"

Regret showed in Horace's eyes. "I'm so sorry," he said. "If I had any other option, I'd take it. God forgive me." He plunged through the door that led to the lighthouse cellar. Moments later the door shuddered and a deadbolt slammed home.

Though her ankles were bound, Libby began to struggle again and finally managed to get to her feet. "We've got to find a way to cut these ropes!" She jumped her way to the wall of artifacts. Surely there was a knife here somewhere. Or an ax. "Help me, Nicole!"

Nicole was crying, but she got on all fours, then managed to get upright. "We can't die here. I don't want to drown!"

"Stay calm," Libby said. "And pray." With her wrists tied together, all she could manage was an awkward sorting through of the artifacts. Bowls, cups, nothing sharp. "There's nothing here," she said.

She glanced toward the door. But no, she'd heard it lock. "Maybe we can hop out through the cave."

"We won't be able to swim."

"Alec will come looking for us. I know he'll look there."

As they moved toward the passage, water began to rush through the opening, faster and faster until the water was swirling around their ankles.

"Libby!" Nicole screamed.

FORTY-ONE

His lungs burning from his run, Alec stopped to catch his breath. He saw Bree and Kade still down the beach a ways. Brent was with them too. "Bree!" He broke into a run again.

She leaped to her feet when she saw him coming. "What's wrong? Where are the girls?"

"Missing." His breath heaving, Alec told her and Kade what he'd found. "Can we take Samson back to search?"

She snapped her fingers for the dog. "Right away." She glanced at Kade with an appeal on her face.

"Go, hon, I've got the kids. I'll be praying."

Relief flooded Bree's face. "You're the best. I'll grab Samson's vest from the SUV." She rushed up the hill to the drive.

"Bring flashlights," Kade called after her.

Brent's eyes were shadowed. "Libby's all right, isn't she?"

"I hope so."

Brent turned and looked out to sea, then back at Alec. "I need to tell you something. I wasn't sure before, but remember that diver who tried to drown Libby?"

"Yes."

"I saw what looked like a bite on Horace's arm the other day.

I saw him out at the lighthouse yesterday too. He was in his diving gear. I watched him through the binoculars, but I couldn't tell what he was doing. But he disappeared for a while under the rocks. I think there's a cave there."

Alec couldn't imagine that the jolly, absentminded attorney could be dangerous. "Maybe it just looked like a bite. Horace wouldn't hurt Libby or Nicole. I know about the cave, but I looked in there too."

"I suspect there's more there than you know. He was in there a long time and came out carrying a bag of something."

Bree returned with the flashlights and Samson's vest. "Ready?"

Alec took the flashlights. "Let's go. Thanks for the information, Brent. Tell Tom what you know. Come on, Bree. We'll take the boat." He turned and ran for the dinghy bobbing at the dock. He told himself Libby and Nicole were probably fine, but he didn't really believe his own reassurances. Something was wrong. Libby wouldn't worry them intentionally.

When they finally reached the ruins, he pointed to the cave. "There. The entrance to the cave is there." The boat scraped bottom. He leaped over the side and dragged it onto the sand, then handed Bree one of the flashlights. "Will Samson go in a cave?"

"Sure." She snapped her fingers. "He can sniff their clothes." Kneeling, she pointed to the pile of clothing without touching it. His tail wagging, Samson sniffed the clothing. "Search, boy!"

Samson whined, then his nose went up. He crisscrossed the beach, then barked and splashed into the water toward the rocks. "He's got a scent," Bree said.

Alec ran after him. "I had a feeling they were in there. But I called and they didn't answer." His gut clenched. What if someone had killed and dumped them? He pushed away the unspeakable thought.

The dog had reached the cave opening but seemed unsure

about how to enter. Alec ducked down, then clambered onto the ledge. He was dripping wet and realized he'd lost his flip-flops. "Come on, boy. Here, Samson."

Whining, Samson looked back toward Bree. "I'm going too," she told him. She splashed through the opening, then joined Alec on the ledge. "Come on, Samson."

The dog barked, then ducked his head and was inside. Bree helped the dog onto the ledge. Alec switched on the flashlight. The beam pushed back the shadows. "Libby, Nicole!" His shout rebounded off the walls and back at him. The cave floor was cold under his bare feet.

"Search, boy," Bree urged. She flipped on her flashlight as well and joined Alec. After a few minutes of walking, Samson's tail drooped. "Samson seems to have lost the scent," she said.

Alec pointed with his light down the passage. "The cellar is that way, but I checked the cellar."

"Let's check again anyway."

"Okay, this way." He illuminated their path with the light and led her toward the cellar. A few minutes later, they stood at the door. "Nothing," he said.

"I noticed what looked like a narrow passageway deeper into the rock a ways back. Let's check it out," Bree said.

"I didn't see it." He followed her back until she stopped and shone her light.

"There," she said. "It's narrow, but I think we can get through."

The passage seemed more a crack in the rock. He'd be able to get through, but just barely. "Would they have gone down there? They had no light."

"They might have seen it anyway."

He nodded. "I'll go first." He squeezed through the opening and found that the passageway widened to an even bigger space than the path that led to the cellar. "It's okay!"

Bree came through with Samson on her heels. "Search, Samson."

The dog wagged his tail and trotted forward, but it was clear that he hadn't picked up the scent again. Alec was beginning to feel discouraged. "This is leading through the rock to the ocean on the other side. I doubt we can go much farther." He tipped his head. "Hear that?"

Bree listened too. "Sounds like rushing water. You're probably right. We're going to find an opening into the sea up ahead. We might as well go back." She half turned, then Samson barked. He shot forward. "He's got a scent!"

Alec jerked forward into a run. The dog disappeared around the corner. Alec caught up with him in front of a locked door. There was a padlock on it, and water was pouring from under it. He pounded on it. "Libby!"

Samson's barking was frenzied. "She's close," Bree said. "Libby! Nicole!"

The roar of the water that they had heard was beyond this door. He had to get it open. There was nothing to use to bust off the lock. He heard a woman scream and he tensed. "Libby!" He jerked on the lock, but though it was rusty, it held. He didn't even have a shoe to help.

The flashlight! It was metal. "Hold your light on it," he ordered Bree. She shined the light onto the lock. He battered it with the flashlight that was in his hand, but the lock didn't budge. Moments later, his flashlight was in pieces.

Someone pounded on the other side of the door. Libby cried out, "We're here, Alec! The room is flooding. We're going to drown!"

"There's a lock on the door. I can't get it off. Hang on!" He turned around, looking for a rock, angry with himself that he hadn't thought of that before now.

Bree grabbed his hand. "There's no time! Look!" She pointed and he realized water was seeping out the sides of the door.

He clenched his hands. How was he going to save her?

———

Water was pouring through the opening Horace had made. It was now up to Libby's calves. She pounded on the door. "Help us, Alec!" Panic threatened to steal her power to reason. *Breathe.* She took a deep breath, then another. There had to be a way out of here.

Nicole had hopped along the cave floor to join Libby at the door. Her face was grim in the light of the flickering candle. The water was only a few inches from where the candle sat on a chest. When it was gone, Libby wouldn't be able to see Nicole's face.

"Lord, help us," she prayed.

"Are we going to die?" Nicole whispered. "I'm not like you. I never go to church. I haven't given God a thought through most of my life. I'm not ready to die, especially not with all I've done."

Peace seeped into Libby's soul. Whatever happened, God saw them. He held them close in his arms. "All you have to do is ask him to forgive you, Nicole. He's here with us. No matter what happens."

Nicole was sobbing. "I can't. I don't know how." She leaned against Libby.

The weight of her friend's body pressed against her, and Libby lurched to the side. When she did, she heard something splash into the water. Horace's sledgehammer. Had he left it behind? It could knock loose the lock. Would it fit under the door?

She pressed her lips to the crack in the door. "Alec, are you there?"

"I'm here. We're looking for a rock."

"I'm going to try to slide a sledgehammer under the door. Hang on." She knelt and grabbed the tool with her bound hands. The water was to her neck. She tried to slip it under the door. It stuck. "It won't fit!"

"Try turning it the other way," Nicole said. "Or slide it to a different spot. The bottom of the door isn't even."

Libby did as Nicole suggested. The water was rising fast. It was to her lips and the salt burned the cracks in her skin. She had to submerge to get enough leverage to push the tool. The sledgehammer moved under the door's edge. Almost there. She jiggled it and slid it a few inches the other way. She felt a tug, then Alec pulled it away.

Gasping, she surfaced and sucked in air, but she had to float on her back to get it. The water was above her nose if she stayed on her knees. How could she regain her feet?

"Got it!" Alec yelled. "Step away from the door."

Libby tried to struggle back, but she was only able to move a few inches at a time with the water swirling around her bound hands and feet. "Move away, Nicole," she said as the door shuddered and rebounded with pounding on the other side.

The water was to Nicole's chest. She hopped away, managing to stay on her feet. Hanging on to Nicole's leg, Libby tried to get to her feet but couldn't. The candles sputtered and went out. The darkness wasn't quite complete because a little light came in from the hole where the water poured through. She released Nicole's leg and tried to float. The water seemed to be roaring into the cave now. The sound filled her ears, blocking out all thought. It was like floating in eternity, and she suspected she was about to die. She felt no fear though.

She reached her bound arms over her head, and her fingers touched Nicole's arm. Feeling her way to her friend's hand, she realized the water was nearly to Nicole's neck. The end would be soon. "Please make it painless for Nicole, Lord," she whispered. "Receive us into your arms. Pray, Nicole."

She inhaled what she thought would be her last air, then a strong hand grabbed her around the waist. Alec's lips were against her ear.

"I've got you," he said.

"Nicole!"

"Bree has her. Let's get out of here." He propelled her through the water. "Hold your breath," he said. "We have to dive."

The roof of the cave was just above her. She sucked in as much air as she could manage, then nodded. With his arm around her waist, they dived. She opened her eyes, ignoring the stinging saltiness of the water. The dim light from the opening was just ahead. She saw Bree go through it with Nicole. *Thank you, God.*

Her head bumped the side of the opening, then Alec maneuvered them both through. The current caught them as they exited into open water. Her lungs began to burn with the need for oxygen. She cast her gaze upward. The top of the waves seemed so far away. She wasn't sure she could make it. Her panicked glance at Alec caused him to propel them faster.

Just when she thought she would have to inhale water, her head broke the surface. She dragged in air, then choked when a wave splashed her in the face. Alec still had his arm around her, and they floated in the waves.

He cupped her face with his hands as they floated. "I thought I'd lost you." He kissed her.

She clutched him and kissed him back, relishing the heat that swept through her veins, exulting in the fact that she was very much alive. When he lifted his head, she was even more breathless. "Where are Nicole and Bree?"

"On shore. I can see them." He turned her in the water so

she could see her friend waving. Bree and Samson were with her. Libby's limbs went weak.

"Let me see if I can loosen these ropes." He tore at the knots, then shook his head. "They'll have to be cut off. I'll help you." With his arm around her, they began to swim toward the shore.

It was slow going with only one of them able to propel them. She tried to pretend her bound legs were the fin of a mermaid, but it was awkward. Her muscles burned by the time her foot touched sand. Alec lifted her in his arms and staggered to shore with her, where they collapsed in a heap on the beach.

Samson licked her face and barked. "Good boy," she crooned. Nicole dropped to her knees beside her and burst into tears. "It's all right," Libby said. "We're safe."

FORTY-TWO

Tidewater Inn was even more beautiful after Libby's brush with death. It was home already. But what was she going to do about the mansion? She loved it so, but she couldn't afford to keep it up. As Alec guided the boat to the pier, she soaked in the sight of the lovely old Georgian house. She'd never own something so wonderful again.

"Libby!" Vanessa waved from the porch and ran down the curving steps.

Libby nearly fell off the pier when her sister grabbed her and held on as though she'd never let go. "Vanessa?"

"You're okay! I was so afraid when I heard you'd disappeared."

Libby hugged her back. "We're both fine."

Alec hovered at her side as though he feared letting her out of his sight.

"I'll talk to you later," Bree said. "I need to check on the children." Smiling, she went toward the house with Samson at her heels.

Libby followed with Alec close beside her. She wished she dared to reach out and take his hand.

Vanessa was still smiling. "Everyone is inside. The pastor came over to lead us in prayer for your safety."

Libby's gaze went to the necklace around Vanessa's neck. Maybe she'd really begun to think about what it meant. "We needed the prayers more than you know." She told Vanessa what had happened as they walked to the house.

Vanessa stopped at the base of the steps. "I know I've been nasty to you, Libby. I'm ashamed of myself when I remember all the terrible things I said. I'm sorry."

"You were in pain," Libby said. "I understand."

Vanessa shook her head. "I don't deserve for you to let me off the hook so easily. I know we have a long way to go, Libby, but I realized today when I thought you might be dead that I wanted you around. I want to learn what makes you laugh and cry. I want to try to learn to like reggae."

Libby smiled. "I'm not promising anything about oysters, but I'll try."

"It's a deal. You're not leaving, are you? You're staying here?"

Libby's smile faded. "I think I have to sell this place, Vanessa. There's no money for repairs." She gestured to the roof. "Look at the rot going on around the eaves. It's going to take a lot of money to fix it. But I'll split the sale price with you and Brent."

Alec tensed beside her. She wanted to explain her decision, but there was no way to make him understand.

Vanessa shook her head. "I realized today that if this place goes, everything will change. Brent argues that it will be change for the better, but I don't think so. There would be no more long walks on a nearly empty beach. No more pure sound of the waves and wind." Her voice broke. "There has to be another way. How much would it cost to fix it? I have an inheritance. I'll help."

Though the offer touched her, Libby shook her head. "It would be a hundred thousand dollars, I think. I couldn't let you do that. I'll pray about it. Maybe God will show us a way to save it."

Brent opened the door and came toward them. "I brought

Tom up to speed. He left to go arrest Horace. It took some talking to convince him I was telling him the truth. Horace has been part of this village forever. He was born and raised here. One of our own."

"I really liked him," Libby said. "I still can't believe it."

"The state police are going to come out and get a statement this evening. Are you up to that?" Brent asked. "You look wiped out."

"Yes. I just want it over with."

"I'll be inside," Vanessa said. "I want to talk to Brent." She joined her brother and they went inside.

Alec slipped his arm around Libby's waist, and they walked up the stairs together. "It's all over. Hard to believe. Now what?" he asked when they reached the porch.

"I'm going to make the biggest mess of chicken fajitas you ever saw and slather it with guacamole."

He grinned. "I'll even eat the hot sauce with you." His fingers traced the outline of her jaw. "You haven't answered my question."

She couldn't think with his touch igniting feelings she didn't know existed. "I don't know. I have to sell this place, Alec. You know I do."

"Don't decide too quickly. Are you willing to see what door God might open?"

"When you put it that way, how can I refuse?"

Laugh lines crinkled around his eyes. He bent his head and kissed her, then pulled back. "I think I can sweeten the pot a little. I don't want you to go. I want you to live here where I can take you out to dinner and to the movies."

Her heart was full to bursting. "You mean to see year-old movies?"

His breath stirred her hair. "I want to neck with you in the balcony and I don't care how old the movie is."

Her blood warmed at the expression in his eyes. "I'd like that too."

"I think we have something special, Libby. Something that will last. But you have to stay here to find out. You game?"

"I'm game," she said, suddenly breathless.

———

Her family. Libby's gaze lingered on every person around the large dining room table. Mr. McEwan, with his rheumy eyes and sparse hair. Delilah and her no-nonsense love for this place and for Ray. Bree and her family. Old Mr. Carter, who had already grabbed the homemade bread in the middle of the table. Her siblings Brent and Vanessa, already so dear. And Aunt Pearl, whom Libby loved so very much already. Only Nicole was absent. She'd given her statement to the state investigators, then gone back to Virginia Beach to attend to business. At least she wasn't pressuring Libby to sell the property.

Libby locked gazes with Alec, who was sitting across the table from her. Whatever happened, she wanted to live here on Hope Island, even if it wasn't in the beautiful old inn. This was home now.

Horace was sitting in jail awaiting trial, and everything he'd schemed to avoid would happen to him and his family anyway. Though he deserved his punishment, she grieved for his wife and children. He wasn't leaving a legacy of generosity like her father had. The police had checked out his computer and confirmed he had erased the video of the men he'd hired to get Nicole out of the way. With Horace's information, they'd been arrested too.

The police had discovered that Rooney and his goons hadn't actually killed Tina. She'd fallen and drowned in the cellar's standing water. When Poe found her, he'd panicked and left her there, then scuttled her boat to make it appear she'd been lost at sea. He was also in jail.

"I need your advice," Libby said during a lull in the conversation. "I don't want to sell this lovely old house. But I have no idea how to keep it." Libby listened to the hubbub around her as folks argued against selling the property.

She held out her hands. "Nothing would please me more than to keep Tidewater Inn, but I need some suggestions on *how* to make that possible. I got some quotes on restoration. Material alone is going to be seventy-five thousand dollars."

The group fell silent, and the dismay she saw on various faces made her heart plunge. But she could do a lot with the money from the sale of the property. Help her stepbrother and his family. Fix up the lifesaving station and other historic buildings in town. Help people recover from the hurricane. Buy Alec a new boat. There would be compensations for the blow to her soul if she had to give up Tidewater Inn.

Old Mr. Carter in his straw hat pointed a tobacco-stained finger at her. "I'd like to donate the money you need, young lady." He reached down to the old suitcase beside his chair, the same case he'd asked Alec to rescue during the hurricane evacuation, and it opened to reveal stacks of money. "There's plenty in here for materials if the townsfolk will donate the labor."

There was a group gasp around the table. "I couldn't. It might be years before I can pay you back, Mr. Carter," Libby said. She didn't want charity—she wanted a viable solution.

"Oh good grief, Libby," Vanessa said. "I've been looking at Daddy's art. There's our answer. Sell them."

The Allston paintings. Such an easy answer. Why hadn't she thought of it? "You're right," she said. "They are worth more than I need." She glanced at the dear faces around her. "But what about the town? Is selling better for the town, for progress? We need to be realistic."

"The ferry is still coming," Delilah said. "Tourists will need a place to stay. Why not here? The rest of the town needs to think about what kinds of businesses are lacking and fill the need. We could end up with the best of both worlds. Like Ocracoke."

The ideas began to flow quickly. Libby couldn't stop smiling. She took notes in between bites of chicken fajitas, then later, after the table had been cleared, carried the dessert of flan out to the swing with Alec.

"Hey." He put his flan on his knee and slipped his arm around her. "I told you it would work out. You ready to accept the answer?"

"It's more than I'd hoped for." She touched his cheek with her fingers. "*You're* more than I hoped for."

His gaze held her rooted in place. "I look forward to exploring the future with you. Want to go to a movie tonight? I hear *An Officer and a Gentleman* is playing."

"Now that's *really* old," she said. "But I always sigh when Richard Gere sweeps her into his arms and carries her out of the factory."

"Would you settle for a moonlit ride in my fishing boat?" His smile was teasing.

"Will there be kissing involved?"

"Most certainly," he said.

"Then I accept." She didn't wait for the promised kiss, though, and lifted her face toward his in the moonlight.

ACKNOWLEDGMENTS

This book is a little bittersweet for me. It's my twenty-first project with Thomas Nelson, and Erin Healy has edited all but three of those stories. She's a fabulous writer in her own right, and *Tidewater Inn* is her last book to edit before plunging full time into her own wonderful novels. Thank you, Erin, for all the things you've taught me in the nine years we've worked together. We have been partners from that first Rock Harbor novel, *Without a Trace*. I treasure your friendship and your wisdom, and I'm so grateful for all the time you've spent on my novels. Love you, girl! I will be screaming from the sidelines for you louder than anyone else as you soar to the heights!

My Thomas Nelson team is my family and I love them and thank God for them every day. They helped me brainstorm this particular book too, and it was so fun to write because of that! Publisher Allen Arnold is loved by everyone in the industry—including me! He's a rock star! Senior Acquisitions Editor Ami McConnell (my dear friend and cheerleader) has an eye for character and theme like no one I know. I crave her analytical eye and love her heart. She's truly like a daughter to me. Marketing Manager Eric Mullett brings fabulous ideas to the table. Publicist Katie Bond is always willing to listen to my harebrained ideas. Extraordinary cover guru

Kristen Vasgaard (you so rock!) works hard to create the perfect cover—and does it. And, of course, I can't forget my other friends who are all part of my amazing fiction family: Natalie Hanemann, Amanda Bostic, Becky Monds, Ashley Schneider, Ruthie Dean, Jodi Hughes, Heather McCulloch, Dean Arvidson, and Megan Leedle. I wish I could name all the great folks who work on selling my books through different venues at Thomas Nelson. Hearing "well done" from you all is my motivation every day.

My agent, Karen Solem, has helped shape my career in many ways, and that includes kicking an idea to the curb when necessary. Thanks, Karen, you're the best!

Writing can be a lonely business, but God has blessed me with great writing friends and critique partners. Hannah Alexander (Cheryl Hodde), Kristin Billerbeck, Diann Hunt, and Denise Hunter make up the Girls Write Out squad (www.GirlsWriteOut .blogspot.com). I couldn't make it through a day without my peeps! Thanks to all of you for the work you do on my behalf, and for your friendship. I had great brainstorming help for this book from Robin Caroll. Thank you, friends!

I'm so grateful for my husband, Dave, who carts me around from city to city, washes towels, and chases down dinner without complaint. Thanks, honey! I couldn't do anything without you. My kids—Dave and Kara (and now Donna and Mark)—and my grandsons, James and Jorden Packer, love and support me in every way possible. Love you guys! Donna and Dave brought me the delight of my life—our little granddaughter, Alexa! I hope she understands soon what her Mimi does for a living as I'm about to embark on a children's book project for her.

Most importantly, I give my thanks to God, who has opened such amazing doors for me and makes the journey a golden one.

DEAR READER,

I'm so thrilled to share *Tidewater Inn* with you! The theme of the story—greed versus generosity—is one that resonates so much with me personally. If you're like me, you struggle to find the balance. No matter what resources God has blessed us with, he expects us to use them to help other people. Money isn't our only resource. Time, talents, and other gifts are to be given generously.

I also wanted to share the personal background of a character in the novel who is very special to me. Pearl is my grandma in the flesh, though the name Pearl is my first teacher in Sunday School. My grandma helped shape me in so many ways. She's been gone over twenty years, but I still hear her voice in my head. I strive every day to be more like her. I learned about Jesus at her knee. She taught me about generosity and loving other people. I owe her so much, and I wanted to share her with you. I hope you love Pearl as much as I loved my grandma! People say I'm just like her, and it's the highest compliment I could have. ☺

I so love to hear from you! Email me at colleen@colleencoble. com and let me know what you thought of the story.

Love,
Colleen

READING GROUP GUIDE

1. Libby had struggled to survive monetarily for years so the thought of having no worries about money was appealing. Money is not evil in itself. What do you think about wealth's influence on our spiritual lives?

2. It often seems our culture doesn't honor the older generation. Why don't we and what are we missing?

3. Vanessa and Brent didn't welcome Libby's intrusion into their lives. How would you feel if you found out you had a sibling you didn't know about?

4. Pearl is based on my grandma, and I smiled just writing her into the story. Her love for me and others was always unconditional. Do you have a person in your life who loves you that way?

5. Ray's biggest legacy wasn't money but a spiritual heritage. What do you hope to leave behind for your family?

6. Libby's struggle between greed and generosity is basically a struggle between selfishness and selflessness. What are some other common things we struggle with?

RETURN TO
HOPE BEACH IN
Rosemary Cottage

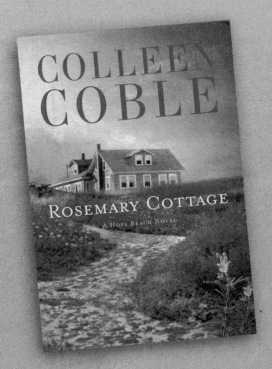

BLUE MOON PROMISE

is a story of hope, romance, and suspense . . . immersing the reader in a rich historical tale set under Texas stars.

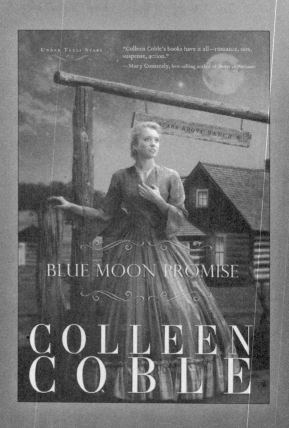

"*The Lightkeeper's Bride* is a wonderful story filled with mystery, intrigue, and romance. I loved every minute of it."

— CINDY WOODSMALL,
New York Times best-selling author of *The Hope of Refuge*

THE BEST-SELLING MERCY FALLS SERIES.

ESCAPE TO BLUEBIRD RANCH

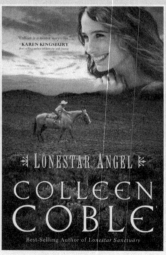

_F_our friends devise a plan to turn Smitten, Vermont, into the country's premier romantic getaway—while each searches for her own true love along the way.

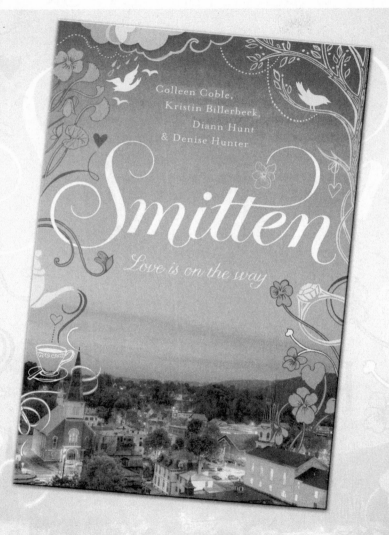

Colleen Coble,
Kristin Billerbeck,
Diann Hunt
& Denise Hunter

Smitten

Love is on the way

ABOUT THE AUTHOR

Photo by Joe Saxton

R ITA finalist Colleen Coble is the author of several best-selling romantic suspense series, including the Mercy Falls series, the Lonestar series, and the Rock Harbor series. She lives with her husband, Dave, in Indiana.